Cold Snap

PRAISE FOR FRANCIS KING

'Up-to-the minute ... beautifully written' **Antonia Fraser**

'Narrative art of a fine order' **Penelope Lively**

'Always accomplished and elegant' **A S Byatt**

'No one writes better prose than Francis King' **Ruth Rendell**

'Will not fail to impress' **Graham Swift**

'Compulsive reading' **Margaret Drabble**

'Brilliantly accomplished' **Paul Bailey**

'A writer's writer, his voice utterly convincing' **Beryl Bainbridge**

'A master novelist' **Melvyn Bragg**

'Francis King, whose writing I love' **Dominick Dunne**

'Francis King is writing novels of a professionalism that few can match'
Allan Massie

'Reveals another magician at the height of his powers' **Hilary Spurling**

'A subtle and fluent writer' **Anthony Thwaite**

'He had me sitting on the edge of my chair and gasping with admiration
even on the second time through' **Auberon Waugh**

'That rare phenomenon, a novel by a gnarled old literary presence that
extends rather than consolidates his position' **D J Taylor**

'Still on top form' **Jessica Mann**

'Defies all expectations in a thoroughly modern and audacious way ...
the author's prose is enriched by a poetic flair equal to his exotic locales'
Richard Zimler

'Accomplished professionalism' **Jonathan Keates**

'Thoroughly engrossing and compulsively readable' **Peter Burton**

'Lit up by poetic and heartfelt tenderness' **Paul Binding**

'Subtle and deeply absorbing' **Kate Saunders**

'His vision is realistic, unflinching and, in its regard for truth, shocking'
Elizabeth Buchan

'Thought-provoking and stylish' **Sebastian Beaumont**

FRANCIS KING is a former International President of PEN and winner of the Katherine Mansfield Short Story Prize and the Somerset Maugham Award. His fiction includes *Act of Darkness*, *Dead Letters* and *The Custom House*. Arcadia published *Prodigies* to great acclaim in 2001, and *The Nick of Time* was longlisted for the Booker Prize in 2003. His most recent works include *The Sunlight on the Garden* and *With My Little Eye*. *Cold Snap* is his fiftieth book.

Cold Snap

A NOVEL

FRANCIS KING

Arcadia Books Ltd
15–16 Nassau Street
London W1W 7AB

www.arcadiabooks.com

First published in the United Kingdom by Arcadia Books 2009

A catalogue record for this book is available from the British Library.

ISBN 978-1-906413-59-0

Typeset in Minion by MacGuru Ltd
Printed in Finland by WS Bookwell

Arcadia Books supports PEN, the fellowship of writers who work together to
promote literature and its understanding. English PEN upholds writers' freedoms in
Britain and around the world, challenging political and cultural limits on free expression.
To find out more, visit www.englishpen.org or contact
English PEN, 6–8 Amwell Street, London EC1R 1UQ

Arcadia Books distributors are as follows:

in the UK and elsewhere in Europe:
Turnaround Publishers Services
Unit 3, Olympia Trading Estate
Coburg Road
London N22 6TZ

in the US and Canada:
Independent Publishers Group
814 N. Franklin Street
Chicago, IL 60610

in Australia:
Tower Books
PO Box 213
Brookvale, NSW 2100

in New Zealand:
Addenda
PO Box 78224
Grey Lynn
Auckland

in South Africa:
Jacana Media (Pty) Ltd
PO Box 291784,
Melville 2109
Johannesburg

Arcadia Books is the *Sunday Times* Small Publisher of the Year

Contents

FOR

All of them –
wherever they are

1947

I

More than thirty years later, while the shrill voices soar upwards to the school chapel roof and then flutter downwards, Christine again hears, as she does more and more frequently now, the precise words spoken by her cousin Michael in the Balliol room overlooking Broad Street. At the time they seemed so trivial, now so momentous.

'Before I introduce you, let me take your coat. I'll hang it here. I'm afraid you must have had to trudge through this ghastly snow. When is it going to end? It's like the war. That too seemed just to go on and on and on forever. Are your feet wet? They look as if they must be. Come and sit here. No, not there. Here. You'll find it much more comfortable.'

Each word is distinct in her recollection. But so far she sees nothing. Then, as he continues: 'Good. Now let me introduce my friends to you,' he and the three Germans miraculously materialise before her.

She realises now, as she did not even suspect at the time, that he deliberately used those words 'my friends' because he could guess, as he could with uncanny certainty almost always guess her feelings, that she did not in the least welcome the presence of the German prisoners in his room.

'Klaus. Ludwig. Thomas.'

As he pointed in turn at the men standing awkwardly in front of their chairs, he might have been exhibiting three geological specimens to his students. On hearing his name, Klaus at once extended a hand in an attempt to shake

Christine's. But deliberately she ignored it. She saw Michael briefly wince, and then no less briefly purse his lips. 'We'll have to speak English now that Miss Holliday is with us. Miss Holliday speaks little German, I'm afraid. That leaves poor Klaus rather out in the cold.' He went on in the near-perfect German that he had acquired with daunting speed during a postgraduate year at Göttingen: 'I hope you won't mind if we speak English now, Klaus. I'm sorry.'

Klaus shook his head, gave an embarrassed giggle, and then gazed down at the shaggy pile of the carpet, the smile gradually fading from his face as if one muscle and then another were relaxing under the taut skin.

Ludwig turned to Christine: 'Miss Holliday.' Typically he had at once filed away her name in his memory. 'I have been learning English ever since I first came to England. That is now two years, five weeks and, yes, four days. You see – I know exactly! Each morning, when I wake, I remind myself. First thing.' He stared across at her for some seconds with large, protuberant, light-blue eyes behind thick lenses. Then he asked, almost coquettishly, head on one side: 'Do you think my English good, Miss Holliday?'

'Very good.' It was the truth.

He was the least attractive of the three men. They all wore shabby clothes, the collars and cuffs shiny with wear. But at least the two others were not merely tidy but had even made an effort to be smart – hair carefully brushed, boots highly polished, battledress trousers, with their regulation patches at the knees, decisively creased. He, in contrast, had not bothered to shave that day, a black stubble already bristling on his narrow, protuberant chin and above thick, red lips that, whenever he flashed one of his frequent smiles, disclosed small, irregular teeth; his hair, worn *en brosse*, was lacklustre; and there was a ridge of dirt under each of his square nails.

'When I came to England, I could speak English hardly at all. But now – I'm an interpreter in the camp.'

'That's good.'

'Yes, it's good. Being an interpreter is far better than working out in the fields. I work in the office – and the office is dry and warm.'

Aware of Michael's gaze on her, she forced herself to prolong a conversation that she would much rather have terminated. 'How did you learn English so quickly?'

'Because I have a special gift.' He laughed. 'No, no, I'm joking! I taught myself. Mostly. That is why I like to talk to English people. But most English people' – he pouted, shrugging his narrow shoulders – 'for them to talk with a German prisoner …' He stared at her and then grimaced, as though, while masticating, he had suddenly bitten on a piece of grit. 'Now I'm beginning to learn Russian too. I always like to be prepared for every possibility.' He cocked his head to one side and, disconcertingly, gave her a wink.

'Ludwig is indefatigable,' Michael put in, sensing her dislike. 'You know they produced a Schiller play – *Fiasco* – at the camp and he was the stage manager. It was far from a fiasco. I went myself. People from outside were allowed to go.'

'Schiller's *Fiasco*! Quite an undertaking.' She was making an effort, not for the Germans but for Michael. She had never heard of the play, much less read it.

Ludwig leaned back in his chair, smiling and clicking the fingers of his right hand. In the weeks ahead Christine was to become used to both that self-congratulatory smile and a clicking, like that of invisible castanets, that seemed to demand 'Look at me, here I am, attend to me!'

'And do you speak English?' Still making an effort for Michael's sake, Christine turned for the first time to one of the other two Germans, who was sitting farther away from the coal fire, his head tilted sideways, so that she could see no more than what the flickering flames intermittently revealed.

'Yes, I speak a little. But not as well as Ludwig, of course.'

'True, true! Not as good as me!' Ludwig laughed, once again clicking his fingers. 'He graduated in English. He taught English at a secondary school. But he doesn't *speak* English properly.' He shook his head. 'That is the truth. You can hear for yourself. His pronunciation is poor.'

From the kitchenette, seldom used except when Michael had his German visitors, Christine suddenly became aware of a faint, flattened whistle. 'Is that your kettle?'

'Oh, God!' Michael jumped to his feet. 'I hope it hasn't boiled dry. What an idiot I am!' He rushed out.

There was an awkward silence, which prolonged itself until his return. 'No harm done. But the water had almost all boiled away. So I had to add a lot more and wait. Sorry about that.'

Soon he was busying himself with pouring out Earl Grey tea from the silver teapot.

'Where shall I put your cup, Thomas? Here?' He turned to Christine, to whom he had already handed a cup. 'It's rather inconvenient for Thomas at present. He was wounded in the right arm and somehow – perhaps they set it badly – it wouldn't function properly and gave him a lot of pain. So recently they decided to operate on it, and then put it into plaster, as you can see.'

Christine stared at the grubby white of the plaster. 'I suppose that means you don't have to work.'

He nodded.

'So you have plenty of time to do what you want to do?'

'Plenty of time.'

'And what do you do with that time?'

'Sleep.'

Was he joking? Although the tone of the clipped mono-syllable suggested boredom, even irritation, he must be joking. After all, Ludwig was laughing and Michael was smiling. She forced herself also to smile.

'Thomas is lazy.' Ludwig lowered his head and gulped noisily from the teacup clasped in both his hands as though to warm them. 'I tell him he must study to improve. Then perhaps he too could work as an interpreter. As I said, his pronunciation isn't good. You can hear for yourself. Like an Englishman speaking German on your Overseas Service. Also his grammar needs improving. English grammar is difficult. Too few rules – or is it too many rules, all contra-dicting each other?'

'Yes, I am lazy.' Thomas muttered. Slowly he put out his left hand, slowly raised his teacup and no less slowly lifted it to his lips, as though to demonstrate that laziness. All at once he looked abject. How old was he? Christine tried to guess. Impossible. There were deep lines on either side of his mouth and muddy shadows under eyes that seemed somehow unfo-cused, as though they were used to glasses. But the skin over his cheeks and forehead had a youthful smoothness. No one could have thought him conventionally handsome, but with his wide lips, straight nose and thick, wavy brown hair, he was, even in his shabby, soiled uniform, an attractive figure. If one saw him in the street, one might well look at him and wonder what were the circumstances that had brought him to a prison camp in Oxford from the war so recently over.

'I tell Thomas that he has so many opportunities,' Ludwig continued. 'I should be very happy to have all my days free. We have so little free time – even in the office where I work – and after work, pouf! One is so tired that it's difficult to study. And the noise, you cannot believe! There are thirty – no, now thirty-one – men in our hut. But during the day Thomas has the hut to himself.' He extended a hand to Christine and all but touched her forearm. 'Don't you agree with me? He should study to improve his life. It's bad for him to be idle.'

'Perhaps he reads.' She swivelled round, a half-eaten sand-wich in one hand, and asked: 'Do you read?'

'Oh, yes, I read.' He gave a perfunctory smile. 'I have read almost every book in the camp library. Many of them are not very good books. Most of them are in German – so they do not help with my English.'

Michael, who had begun to refill Klaus's cup, looked up: 'I can always lend you anything you want. You know that, Thomas.'

'Yes, you are very kind, always very kind.' Biting his lower lip, he stared into the fire. 'I wish I could repay you,' he added almost inaudibly. In the weeks ahead Christine would notice how the burden of gratitude for favours he could not return would make him hostile or sulky.

Yet again Ludwig clicked his fingers, as though to summon an inattentive waiter or a dog. 'If you please, Michael. May I keep that Shakespeare you lent me?' Hastily he added: 'I mean, keep it for another week.'

'For as long as you like.'

'Is it expensive to buy such a complete works?'

'Not really. I suppose you could get one for, oh, about five shillings.'

'Five shillings!' Ludwig's voice squeaked upwards, like

chalk on a blackboard. 'For us prisoners five shillings is *very* expensive.' He turned to Christine: 'We get only six shillings a week. Can you imagine? – a *week*! That's less than one shilling a day. That's not much to buy razor blades, shaving cream, toothpaste – oh, many, many things. It's not much, is it, Thomas?'

Thomas, hands resting one on either knee, gave a small shrug. He did not look at Ludwig.

'It's worse for Thomas. Thomas gets paid nothing – nothing at all!'

'*Nothing*?'

'Nothing. No work, no pay. It's quite simple.' Ludwig glanced round his audience, as if he had just produced a witticism and expected to be applauded for it.

'Then how on earth do you manage, Thomas?' Michael leaned forward in his chair. 'You never told me about this. Why on earth not?'

'Horst – my comrade – lends me money.' He did not look at Michael. His voice was weary.

'Horst makes a lot of money,' Ludwig took up. 'He's very clever. You say "clever with his hands", yes? Horst is clever here' – he tapped on his forehead with a forefinger – 'but also very, very clever with his hands. Give him a spoon and he'll make a bracelet or a brooch for you. He makes beautiful ships in bottles. He makes toys. He's one of our capitalists.'

'And aren't you also one of your capitalists?'

'Me?' Michael's irony was lost on him. He laughed, displaying his crooked, discoloured teeth. 'Yes, I get along okay.' He drew a theatrical sigh. 'Perhaps, if I save, I can afford a Shakespeare Complete Works. I should like one of my own. That more than any other book. But five shillings – five shillings! For a prisoner, that's a lot of money.'

'If you like, you can hang on to mine. Keep it.'

'May I? May I really, Michael?' Ludwig was delighted with what he imagined to have been his finesse in extracting this gift. 'Oh, you're kind, very kind! Michael's always so kind to me, Miss Holliday – to all of us.' Suddenly he jumped up, stooped over Michael and threw an arm round his shoulder. 'Thank you, thank you!'

Michael shifted uneasily and waved a dismissive hand. 'Oh, it's nothing at all.'

'For me it's *everything*!'

Through all this Klaus sat doggedly munching sandwich after sandwich, and thinly cut slice after slice of brown bread and butter. As the others talked, he would from time to time look up to smile or nod, in a pretence of listening and understanding. His appetite was prodigious. So was Ludwig's. Everything that Michael pressed on them they took without demur, filling themselves with fodder as camels fill themselves with water at an oasis in preparation for the dry days ahead. Thomas, on the other hand, merely from time to time took a tiny bite from the sandwich on the plate beside him.

'Sugar?' Michael held out the Georgian silver bowl to him. 'Oh, no, of course you don't take it. Klaus? Take as much as you want,' he added in German. 'I never use it, so don't worry about my ration.' Christine knew that he was lying. He had always liked sweet things. 'Sorry – I seem to have forgotten the tongs.'

In an effort at gentility, Klaus did not help himself from the bowl with his fingers but instead used his teaspoon, rattling it around to gather up lump after lump. Each time there was a plop as the lump fell into the tea, and each time he would give the same embarrassed, apologetic grin. The last lump, the fourth, fell from so great a height that tea splashed on to his hand. Hurriedly he wiped it on his trouser leg.

Ludwig thrust his whole fist into the bowl and drew out at least half-a-dozen lumps. They all went simultaneously into his cup, causing the tea to brim over and slop into the saucer.

'I see you like tea with your sugar.'

Christine had spoken half humorously and half in disapproval of his blatant greed. Surprisingly, he showed himself more vulnerable than she would have expected from his self-confident manner. He blushed, mouth ajar. 'We don't always get sugar with our tea or coffee in the camp.' He looked across at Michael, teaspoon in hand. 'Sorry, Michael. I'm a greedy bastard.'

'Don't worry. Please! I told you – I never take sugar. Have all you want.'

Soon after that another prisoner, remarkable for his towering height and skeletal emaciation, entered the room, cap clasped in bony hands. This was Horst, the 'capitalist' of whom Thomas and Ludwig had spoken. He was several years older than the others, his close-cut hair greying above large, pointed ears and his mouth puckered at the corners. The skin of his forehead was yellow and also puckered. He looked stern, unamiable, ill. He clicked his heels and bowed stiffly from his narrow waist, as if on a hinge, when Michael made the introductions between him and Christine.

In carefully precise English, he explained: 'I am sorry. I came for Thomas. I think that we must go. It is a long walk. And it seems as if it will snow again.' In a low voice he muttered something in German to Thomas, who at once jumped to his feet.

'Yes, yes! I'm very slow in this weather. I'll be glad when

I get rid of *this*.' He raised the arm in plaster. 'It makes me slower. Strange. I don't know the reason. After all, it's not my leg but this arm that's *kaputt*.'

'Couldn't you take a bus?' Christine was prepared to offer the fare.

Horst, not Thomas, answered. 'German prisoners are not allowed on your buses. Didn't you know that? Walking is good enough for us, you understand.'

'I wish I had a car.' Michael turned to Thomas. 'Did you have a coat with you?'

'*Nein*.' That he should answer in German struck Christine as odd.

'But it's bitterly cold outside. Here, take this scarf.' He strode across the room and jerked a scarf off a peg on the door. He picked up some gloves from the table beside it. 'And these gloves.'

'No, no, please! It's not necessary.'

'Of course it's necessary.'

With a mixture of exasperation and tenderness, like a mother with a child, Michael wound the scarf round Thomas's neck and drew it into a knot. Then he held out one of the gloves. 'Give me your hand. You don't want frostbite.' After a moment of hesitation, Thomas held out his left hand. Michael began to ease the glove on to it, screwing up his eyes as though over a difficult task. 'Ah, you have small hands – like mine. I tried to lend these gloves to Klaus the other day, but they wouldn't fit.' He turned to Klaus and translated into German. Klaus nodded vigorously, grinned and held out a huge fist, stretching the fingers to their whole extent. All of them laughed, with the exception of Horst, who turned his head aside with another pursing of the lips.

'Take this too. Wait a minute.' Michael pulled out the top

drawer of a tallboy and scrabbled inside it. Eventually he produced a crumpled brown paper bag. He thrust into it what was left of the chocolate cake.

Thomas raised his right arm in its plaster, as though in an attempt to ward off a blow, as Michael held out the bag to him. 'No. No, Michael! I don't want it.'

'I insist.'

'No! Please!'

Through all this Horst stood stiffly, his arms held to his sides and an expression of mingled disdain and irritation on his face.

Michael began to coax the paper bag into one of the pockets of Thomas's tunic. 'It's greaseproof. Don't worry. It won't leave a mess.'

'I wish … I wish you wouldn't be so kind to me. It's too much, Michael. If I could repay you – if there was anything, anything at all.'

'Repay me? For so little? Don't be so silly. I like having you here. I like seeing you. All of you,' he amended. 'Come whenever you wish. Even when I'm out, you can use my room, you know. It's quiet and warm in here.'

The extraordinary recklessness of the offer worried Christine. Thomas frowned, head lowered, making no response. Then he looked up, left hand extended. 'Thank you, Michael. You're a good friend.' He turned to Christine. ' So – goodbye, Miss … Miss …'

Unlike Ludwig, he had failed to remember her name. Momentarily piqued, she did not remind him. 'Goodbye.' Then, repenting of her abruptness, she wanted to add: 'Good luck. I hope we'll meet again. Tell me if there's anything I can do for you.' She was too late. He had turned away from her.

Clicking his heels, Horst bowed, without a word, first to

Michael and after that to Christine. Then the two were gone, the ring of their iron-heeled boots fading gradually on the stone staircase spiralling down into the quad.

Ludwig, having resumed his seat, leaned forward. 'Shall I continue now?' Horst's arrival had interrupted him in an interminable story about how he had got the better of the camp commandant in an argument about the distribution of prisoners' letters.

He was still talking when, several minutes later, there was a knock at the door and Michael's scout, an elderly man in pinstripe trousers and a white jacket, with a large waxed moustache and a snake of grey hair trained across a shiny area of scalp, made his entry, silver tray in hand.

Seeing the Germans, he recoiled. 'Oh! Sorry, sir.' He raised the tray in one hand and banged it, like a tambourine, with the other. 'Shall I come back later, sir, when the gentlemen have gone?'

'No, that's all right, Warwick. I don't want to delay you. You may take the things now.'

'Very good, sir.'

Warwick began to pile the tea things on to the tray; and since, in some mysterious way, he had made them all feel as though they were children caught out in some misdemeanour by an adult, none of them, not even Ludwig, said anything. There was no doubt of his disapproval; but it was conveyed by signs so subtle – a slight bunching of the lips, an over-deliberation of movement, a refusal to look directly at any of them – that it seeped out of him like an invisible odour.

When he had finally left the room with a precisely inflected 'Thank you, sir', Michael voiced the uncomfortable thought of all of them: 'He doesn't like our little party.'

'He certainly doesn't,' Christine concurred.

'I suppose one can hardly blame him. He spent three years in the trenches in the Great War and his son was killed in this one. Did I tell you, Christine, that he's standing for Labour councillor?' Michael laughed. 'What's the world coming to? A scout standing in a local election!'

Eventually Klaus and Ludwig got to their feet. 'Would you like to change now?' Michael asked Klaus in German. Then, turning to Christine, he explained: 'I've promised to lend him some of my clothes for this evening – if he can get into them. He wants to go to a wrestling match.'

'Oh, is that allowed?'

'Good lord, no. But they constantly break the rules. And usually they get away with it. The camp is so understaffed and the guards chiefly concern themselves with getting themselves demobbed as quickly as possible.'

Michael, hand to Klaus's shoulder, shepherded him into the bedroom.

'Klaus will be caught.' Christine was shocked by Ludwig's gleeful tone. 'He can speak only a few words of English – hello, please, thank you, such things. He's not clever. And – have you noticed? – he always walks like a German soldier. Like this.' He jumped up and marched across the room, swinging his long arms vigorously and puffing out his chest. He burst into laughter. 'Also he looks German. He'll be caught.'

'And if he's caught – what happens?'

'Fourteen days in the calaboose.' He grinned at her. He enjoyed having to explain such things.

'Solitary confinement?'

'Maybe. Every prisoner will tell you it's worth taking such a risk from time to time. But in Klaus's case it's not a risk – it's certain.'

'Then why is he doing it?'

'Excitement. Life's so boring, boring, boring for a prisoner. If for one moment on can escape out of *this* – with a downward sweep of the hand he indicated his uniform – 'and pretend that one's a civilian again, then a week in the calaboose seems nothing. We have so much time, too much time. What is a week?'

Eventually Michael and Klaus returned.

'Witness the transformation! Klaus the German prisoner becomes Klaus the man about town!' Michael patted the German's back. Klaus, blushing with pleasure, lowered his eyes as the other two scrutinised him, Ludwig with amusement, Christine with a feeling of dread for what might happen. His eyelashes caught the light of the lamp beside him and made a fringe of shadow on his prominent cheekbones. He and Michael were of about the same height, but so different in build that the pale grey suit, tailored in Rome before the war, made him look like a huge, carelessly wrapped parcel. Since it had not been possible to fasten the collar of the shirt, a strip of throat could be glimpsed behind the knot of the tie, as the two ends of the collar perpetually edged away from each other. With a repeated gesture he attempted to pull first one sleeve of the jacket and then the other down over his wrists.

Ludwig frowned, drew in his lips and said something in German. Klaus shook his head vigorously: '*Nein! Nein!*' 'Ludwig says he'll be caught,' Michael translated for Christine. Again Klaus shook his head. Then he inserted a finger into the collar in an attempt to ease it. 'Hey, don't do that! It'll come totally adrift if you do that.' Michael raised his hands and tweaked the edges together again.

When the two prisoners had left, Christine followed

Michael over to the long window overlooking the Broad. They both gazed out, waiting for Klaus and Ludwig to pass through the gate. The pair must have decided to separate, since Ludwig emerged first, with Klaus following a few seconds later. Christine and Michael both laughed at the sight of Klaus striding out in the ill-fitting clothes. Then they each felt apprehensive.

'Do you think he'll be caught?'

'Fortunately these days Oxford is full of foreigners – many of them in clothes that don't fit them properly.'

'But it's very risky?'

'Well, yes – particularly for someone as slow-witted as he is. He might well get a spell in what they call the calaboose.'

'I meant risky for you as well as him.'

'For me?'

'Couldn't you get into trouble for lending him the clothes?'

He laughed. 'Yes, I suppose I could.'

'Serious trouble?'

'Perhaps. If I did, I suppose you'd take the view that I'd only got what I deserved.'

'Oh, don't be so stupid! Why on earth would I think that?'

'Well, one would hardly expect a former SOE girl like you to approve of any kind of fraternisation with the beastly Germans.'

Christine considered that for a few seconds. Then she said: 'As you know, I don't often change my mind. Didn't you once tell me, with that charming frankness of yours, that I was the most obstinate person you had ever met? But, well, this afternoon …'

'Yes?'

'I've seen so many German prisoners since I got back here. One can't escape them, they seem to be everywhere.

Don't they? Slouching about the streets. Herded together like cattle in the back of lorries. Even staring at a stuffed ape or fossilised fish in the Pitt-Rivers. I've never felt anything as active as hate for them – hate requires a lot of emotional effort and I'm too lazy for that – but I have felt that, well, they've now got what was coming to them. So, when people – people like you – start to agitate to give them more freedom, to allow them to marry, to send them home quickly, I've found all that rather sickening.' She broke off. 'Am I being too frank?'

'I like it when you're frank.'

'Oh, Michael, Michael! You have such a way of making me feel ashamed of myself.'

'You were saying?'

'Well, when I came into this room and saw those three wretches, I was cross, really cross. In fact, I was furious. Oh, of course, I didn't show it –'

'But I knew, Christine, I knew.'

'Of course you knew. You always know. And I believe you did it all on purpose. You *wanted* me to be furious. You thought it would be good for me. Didn't you?'

He turned away from the window with a shrug and a smile.

'I'm such a sentimentalist. That's my trouble. These people have done such things to us, to all of us, to the whole world, that we should never forget. Never! Never! But set up any personal contact between me and one of those Huns – yes, I like to use that ugly word because it expresses ugly things – and my sentimentality gets the better of me. Just as long as I can think of them as Huns and not as Klaus, Ludwig, Horst and Thomas, I can treat them as they ought to be treated. But having once crossed that line … You've been rather unfair to me! You know me so well. And now I feel ashamed – yes, ashamed of my weakness. When I saw that trio, I ought to have made my excuses and stalked out at once. Instead of which – I sat down and tried to be charming to them.'

'And you were charming to them. I don't think you have any reason to be ashamed of that.'

'No, because to be charming is so important to you. But charm is useless against concentration camps, submarines, machine guns, bombs, V1s and V2s – utterly, utterly useless. Ben had charm and what bloody use ...?' She leaned forward in the chair, hand clasped, knees together and head bowed.

Michael jumped up, knelt beside her chair and put an arm around her shoulder. 'Oh, Christine!'

She straightened, looked up at him and eventually managed a brief smile. Physically reserved herself, she always shrank from his demonstrativeness. 'I keep thinking I'm over it. But somehow ...'

'You will get over it. Eventually. You'll see. After all, it's only – what? – less than three years. I'm afraid that meeting those poor chaps ... It was stupid of me to spring them on you. I didn't think.'

'Oh, don't blame yourself. I'm glad I met them. Truly. Ever since the war ended, I've just concentrated on my classics and put everything else out of my mind. But that can't go on forever.'

'How about a drink?'

She shook her head.

'Why not? Good for you.'

Again she shook her head. 'Tell me about those three.'

'Well – what do you want to know? Let's see ... I met Thomas first – in the Ashmolean. After they said that we could invite them back to our homes, I often wanted to do something, but I felt, well, embarrassed and that I hadn't much to offer. I thought they'd find it – me – rather a bore. And anyway I was busy.' He paused, gazing into the fire. 'That afternoon it was snowing – rather as it's snowing now – and the temperature was several degrees below freezing. I'd just returned from town, pleased as punch that I'd got a new Cotman at Sotheby's at a bargain price – that one over there. So I ambled over to the Ashmolean to show it to Ian Robertson. We talked for a while – he didn't think as much of the Cotman as I had hoped – and he gave me some cigars, beautiful, fat Romeo and Julietas, that he'd been sent in a food parcel by some American chum at the Metropolitan. He doesn't smoke cigars, only Balkan Sobranies. Typically effete, as I often tell him. Well, I was smoking one of his cigars as I emerged from his office, and there was Thomas standing before a picture I've always loved. You may know it, a Richard Wilson, a harp-shaped sheet of water, restful and consoling. Then he moved on. Should I speak to him? His face looked so morose as he passed me that I almost didn't. But then – thank God – courage came to me. Did he like that picture he'd been looking at, I asked him in German? He started at my voice, he probably thought I was going to tick him off for something or other. But when he saw I wanted to be friendly – well, his pleasure was pathetic.'

'How brave you are in starting conversations with total strangers! As you know, I just can't do it.'

'Sometimes the bravery merely results in being landed with a bore. But with Thomas it brought me luck.'

'I can believe that. For all his remoteness, he struck me as a decent sort of chap.'

'When he came to see me a few days later – at first he

was nervous, I had had a job to persuade him – he asked if he could bring a friend. That was Klaus – who, as you must have noticed, is the sweetest of simpletons. Then Ludwig somehow turned up. I don't think that Thomas asked if he could bring him. In fact I've never been sure how he *did* come. One day, suddenly, he was just *there!*' He laughed. 'Ludwig's like that. Always in on a good thing.'

'Tell me about Thomas. He was a schoolmaster, was he?'

'Yes, at first – teaching English at their equivalent of a grammar school. But – as Ludwig intimated with his usual tact – his accent is so poor that it's hard to believe that. Then he became a music student after he had saved enough money. In Düsseldorf, I think. He doesn't talk much about himself. Klaus worked on the family farm – really only a smallholding, I imagine – in East Prussia. He, too, is what I call a "good" German.'

Christine laughed. 'How can you call anyone a good – or for the matter of that a bad – German? You can't possibly know the truth about their pasts.'

'Well, some fifth sense seems to tell me … But – perhaps you're right.'

'Funny that Thomas and Klaus should be friends.'

'Oh, it's a classless society up at the camp. Anyway they were wounded together. When you've lain wounded for seventeen hours in a ditch with someone else, it must make some kind of bond. It's an interesting story, how it all happened, which you can choose to believe or not to believe according to your trust in the two of them.'

'Try me with it.'

'Their lorry broke down and, while they were struggling to repair it, they saw a British tank coming for them down the road. By then everything was pretty hopeless for the Jerries, we had broken through right, left and centre, and in any case their little party had long since run out of ammunition. So – there was nothing for it but to put up their hands and come out into the open. Which they did. The tank passed, and of those twelve men only Klaus, Thomas and one other remained alive …'

'Oh, rubbish! I don't believe that for one moment.'

'That sort of thing often happens in a war. The mistake is to think that the only culprits are Jerries and Japs.'

'And then they lay out by the roadside until they were picked up?' She had vehemently rejected the story only a moment before. Suddenly she believed it.

'Seventeen hours. The third man had a stomach wound. He was quiet at first but ended screaming his head off and finally dying. Klaus was wounded in the chest – one lung perforated. If he weren't as strong as an ox, he wouldn't be living now. He tells one gleefully of how much blood he vomited. Until then, he says, he never knew how much blood a human body contained.'

'What awful things have happened these last years!'

'Poor Klaus! I often wonder what will become of him. They say he'll never be able to do heavy manual work again, but what else is there for him? He's one of a family of seven brothers, you know. Two of them are prisoners here in England, two have been killed, one is a prisoner in Russia, and one is still a schoolboy at home.' He paused. 'Those are the people for whom war is really hell.'

'And life is still hell – and, most likely, will go on being hell. Poor Klaus! I took to him, I took to him at once – although we couldn't talk.'

'I'm glad I've met that crowd – yes, even Ludwig. I don't regret it. Not in the least. But at the same time I sometimes

– just sometimes – find myself wishing I hadn't spoken to Thomas on that bleak evening seven or eight weeks ago.'

'Why on earth should you wish that?'

'Well …' He seemed reluctant to continue. 'I've come to feel responsible for them. As I used to feel responsible for my crew. I find myself worrying about them – what's to become of them, what sort of future can they eventually have in the ruins of Germany? Ludwig's all right, of course, he'll always be all right, he's that sort of chap. But all the others …'

'You mean in addition to Thomas and Klaus?'

He nodded. 'Oh, yes. A least a dozen more of them.'

'They must appreciate your kindness.'

'Some of them. But to the majority – to Ludwig, for example – to them I think I'm just a sentimental ass, good for a meal, the loan of civilian clothes, a bar of chocolate, a packet of fags, a ten-shilling note.'

'Isn't that rather cynical?'

'Perhaps. Well, at all events, I like to think that at least Thomas and Klaus have some kind of affection – and maybe even respect – for me.'

'Of course they do. One can see it at a glance. Of course they do,' she repeated, since he seemed reluctant to believe her. 'But the others. If you think they just use you, why do you bother with them?'

He thought for a while. Then, tossing his half-smoked cigarette into the fire, he said: 'I can't help having a certain admiration for a man like Ludwig. He's never for a moment given in, despaired, relaxed his grip on life. He's got courage – and I've always admired courage. After all, what was he? A chemist's assistant, who was forced to become a private in an infantry regiment. Yet alone of all those privates he had the willpower and energy to teach himself English and so qualify for a privileged job in the camp. He's got grit and guts and all those bold, male qualities that I myself lack.'

'What on earth do you mean? Without grit and guts you couldn't have taken that bomber up for months and months on end.'

'That's easy to explain. I've no imagination. You know that, of course you do. I just couldn't imagine myself being shot down. That was something that only happened to other unlucky bastards. Guts had nothing to do with it.'

'Anyway – what about Klaus and those clothes? That needed guts.'

He laughed. 'Oh, that! That was hardly heroic.'

'I wish you hadn't. Suppose he's caught and they find out that the clothes came from you. I bet your name and address are in the inner breast pocket of that suit. Yes? If the police found it … I don't think they or the college would take a very good view.'

'Oh, to hell with them!'

'But it's such a big risk for such a small thing. What does it matter if Klaus can't see a wrestling match?'

He leaned forward. 'Christine – don't you understand? – I *wanted* to take that risk. I *made* myself take it. The whole trouble with me is that I've always been so soft. Not like you, not at all. All my life I've been desperately careful not to offend people, tread on their corns, challenge the more idiotic of their prejudices, do anything that might seem the least odd or immoral. That's really why I never became a conscientious objector, as I'd often thought of doing. Life has been smooth for me, always smooth. I just glide through things, on and on, with no effort at all. I'm "easy to get on with" – you must often have heard people say that.'

The revelation of so much self-disgust and self-hatred

shocked her. She tried to argue with him. But he kept shaking his head, between deep drags on the cigarette that he had lit off a previous one smoked almost to its filter.

Then, even as she was talking, he abruptly jumped up and went over to the Boulle cabinet in one corner of the room. 'You haven't seen this.' From the bric-a-brac crowding the cabinet he extracted a scale model of a red double-decker London bus. He handed it to her.

'Where did you get it?'

'From Klaus.'

'You bought it from him?'

'No, he made it as a present for me. He was very hurt when I offered to pay him for it. I was terribly touched. Just think – he could get three or four pounds for a thing like that. Look at the workmanship. I'm not at all sentimental, as you know by now, but I think I'd really rather have it than the Cotman, if I had to make the choice.'

Christine turned the model over and over, examining every detail. She was thinking of Klaus's huge hands and his apparent clumsiness. How had he managed to create something so small and so perfect? 'Where did he get the materials?'

'Where indeed! I thought it more tactful not to ask. I suppose he scrounged and pinched them.' He took the bus from her, replaced it in the cabinet and turned the key. As he did so, he asked, without looking round: 'When they've taken Thomas's arm out of its plaster – tomorrow, I think – would you perhaps allow him to practise on your piano?'

She hesitated. 'Well … yes. Why not?' But she could think of many reasons why not.

'I want to get him interested in his music again. Just at present he's so apathetic – as you must have noticed. He doesn't really care about anything at all. When he said he spent the whole day sleeping, it was probably nearer the truth than you can have realised. If he could use the piano, if you could lend him some music …'

'I'd be delighted.'

'You don't sound all that delighted. I hope you mean that. I hope you're not just trying to please me.'

Christine slowly got to her feet and, with a sigh, picked up her things. 'Now I must go, I'm afraid.'

'Unfortunately I can't press you to stay – much though I'd like to do so. I have a wine committee meeting in' – he looked at his watch – 'seven minutes.'

Having run down the stairs so fast that she all but collided with a portly youth puffing up them, Christine emerged into the white vastness of the quad. Opposite, the roof of the Victorian Gothic chapel glimmered iridescent through the clammy mist. Icicles hung from the gaping mouth of the bronze Triton that usually spouted water before the Hall. She set off briskly for her rooms in Wellington Square, her feet sinking deeper and deeper into the freshly fallen snow. When she had first left Michael, racing down the stairs, she had been full of elation, but now that mood had ebbed. Inexplicably it had come and no less inexplicably it had gone, its place taken by a vague unease for which she could not trace the cause. She thought of the work that awaited her – the ochre cone of lamplight, the books open under it on what had once been her landlady's kitchen table, the dipping of her pen into the inkwell and its scratching on a coarse sheet of ruled paper – but these images, usually so satisfying, were now empty of all pleasure. They even intensified the sombreness of her mood.

'Is that you, Chrissie?' Only one person called Christine that.

'Yes, it's me.'

Hoping that Margaret would not hear her footsteps on the stairs, Christine had crept up as silently as possible; but when she had reached the last step but one, the door before her own had opened and the plain, peering face was above her on the landing.

Margaret rubbed fingers, blue with cold, against each other. 'Isn't it bitter?' She shuddered involuntarily as she said the words. 'What a winter! It must be the worst for yonks.' She was barring Christine's way, so that there was no way of not stopping and speaking to her, even though on this evening her usually welcome presence produced only irritation.

'What have you been doing?'

'Oh, working – as per usual in this stinking weather.' Margaret pulled off her glasses and wiped them on the edge of her jumper. She was not attractive, but her face was from time to time transfigured by her love and sympathy for someone like Christine. It was so transfigured now.

Christine edged towards her door.

'Nice party?' To her chagrin, Michael had never invited her with Christine to his rooms.

'Oh, all right. Not really a party.'

Christine gave an indeterminate shrug of her shoulders and disappeared into her room, closing the door decisively behind her. It was impossible to tell Margaret about the Germans because, if she did so, she would only provoke her indignation. 'Oh, Chrissie, how *could* you?' Christine could hear Margaret's shocked voice, could see her blinking eyes. Margaret was fanatical in both her loves and her hates. She hated the Germans so much that, although she had a vast collection of classical records, she had refused to accompany Christine to a concert in the Sheldonian because the *Siegfried Idyll* was to be played. She would always refer to that work as *The Siegfried Nightmare*.

Having taken off her coat and hat, changed her shoes and stockings and then turned up the grudging flames of the gas fire, Christine tried to settle to her work. When she had gone out that afternoon, she had been reluctant to leave the task of putting Tennyson's 'Break, break, break …' into elegiacs before her next tutorial; but now she found that she was incapable of concentrating on it. She leaned across the table and tweaked back one of the shabby beige rep curtains so that she could look out on to the premature dark. Nothing could be seen but a rectangle of falling snowflakes, transformed into a dazzle by the beam of her lamp. All at once, without her volition, her mind was following a train of thought of its own, as she began to imagine the Germans trudging out through the muffled city, past the bars, the shops, the cinemas and the station, and so on up Harcourt Hill, malignantly slippery in that weather, and past the guards into the chilly, noisy camp.

Her reverie was shattered by a knock at the door. Bending once more over the copy of Tennyson's poem, she called, 'Come in!'

'Sorry to disturb you, Chrissie.' The first name constantly seemed to emerge from Margaret as an endearment 'But we never talked about supper.'

'Oh, I really can't think about supper now. I'm working. As you can see.'

'Yes. I'm sorry. I just didn't know whether you wanted to go out or eat in.'

'Getting a meal is such a waste of time and bother …'

'Oh, I don't mind doing it by myself. You can leave it all to me. I've got a tin of baked beans – oh, but you don't like baked beans, they give you the collywobbles. Well, never mind. I could boil you that one egg.'

'Wouldn't it be easier to go to the Kemp?'

'But you're tired. I can see you're tired. You don't want to trek out again in this snow.'

'Oh, for heaven's sake! I don't mind where we eat. But just don't bother me for the next half-hour.'

'Chrissie – you *are* tired! Just leave it to me. I'll get a really nice supper together. There are all sorts of odds and ends in the meat safe. And you can eat at whatever time you want. Just give me a shout when you're ready.'

After Margaret had left the room, Christine stared for a while at the closed door. Then, having carefully placed her dipper pen on to the blotting pad, she got up with a sigh. She crossed the landing and knocked at Margaret's door.

Margaret looked up from her crochet. The whole room was jangling with the sound of Wanda Landowska playing a Bach prelude on the harpsichord.

'I'm sorry I spoke to you like that.' Christine was obliged almost to shout to be heard above the din from the vast horn of the EMI gramophone.

Margaret threw down her crochet and gazed up, mouth open and eyes radiant. 'Well, of course I didn't take offence. No hard feelings, I knew you didn't mean it. You never do.'

II

As Peter Kemball-Smith took the stairs two or three at a time, Margaret, ever vigilant, appeared at her sitting-room door. 'Oh, it's you! Hello, Peter.'

'Hello,' he returned with considerably less warmth. He could not understand Christine's friendship with Margaret, whom he would often describe as 'dim', 'dreary' or 'pathetic'.

'Chrissie isn't quite ready yet. She's upstairs in her bedroom – dressing. She asked me to ask you to wait in her sitting room. I've lit the gas fire. It's ghastly how they gobble up one's money. When is this weather going to change?'

Peter said nothing, merely pulling open the door to Christine's sitting room and going in. Margaret hesitated, wondering whether to follow him or not; but something in his behaviour to her – no more definite than the weary tone of his voice and his refusal to look at her for longer than was absolutely unavoidable – made her turn and retreat back into her own sitting room instead. Kneeling before the gas fire, she gazed at the radiants, her eyes itching from the glare and heat and her mind busy with the question that his presence so often prompted: What could she have done to make him dislike her? Then her mind wandered off on the dream that had so often consoled her during the war years and continued to do so during this interminable winter. She was bicycling alone down a Cornish lane, during one of the family holidays in a rented bungalow in Port Isaac before the war, and the sun was shining, as it had seemed to shine all that summer, day after day, and its warmth was on her forehead and bare arms.

A sports car raced towards her and the driver, a young man with scarf streaming behind him, jammed on his brakes with a screech of tyres. As he swerved up on to the verge he smiled at her and then, left hand on wheel, blew her a kiss with his right. A few seconds later the car had roared round a bend. He had all but killed her, but he had also suddenly made her feel alive, as never before. For the rest of that holiday she had yearned to see him again. But she never did. The rocket-like blaze of his passing was only the first of many others, thrilling but cruelly transient, in the years that followed.

Across the corridor from her, Peter gazed in distaste at the mess that Christine always managed to create around her. Yet it was that disorderliness that, paradoxically, exerted such an attraction on his finicky and fussy nature. He stooped for a book that lay, face downwards, on one of the chairs, smoothed its rumpled pages and then replaced it on the desk. Touching it, he briefly had the erotic sensation that he was touching her. Then, staring at his reflection on the glass of a John Piper watercolour of Windsor Castle under a lowering sky – hadn't that rich, pansy cousin of hers given it to her? – he fingered his already perfectly symmetrical black tie and ran the back of his hand down the left cheek that he had so recently shaved with a cutthroat razor.

When, at that moment a knock sounded, his expectation of Margaret – no doubt with the offer to make some tea or coffee or to pour out a drink – made him call out testily: 'Yes! Oh, come in, come in!'

The door opened. A male, foreign voice said: 'I am sorry. I have come to the wrong room,' and the door closed again.

Peter strode over to it, opened it and shouted after the retreating figure: 'Who were you looking for? You, there! Who were you looking for?'

Thomas halted and turned his head. 'Excuse me, sir. The lady downstairs told me that Miss Holliday lives in that room. Maybe ...'

'Well, yes she does. What do you want her for?'

'It's not important. I'll come back another time.'

'What's your name? If you wait here' – he indicated the landing – 'I'll go up and tell her.'

'No, please! If she's busy now –'

'No harm in telling her. Then she can see you or not see you, as she wishes. What's your name?'

He hesitated, clearly reluctant to give it. Then he muttered: 'Thomas. Thomas Bartsch.'

'Bartsch.' Peter repeated it in a tone of incredulity, as though he could not believe that it was this creature's real name. 'Wait here.'

The sight of Christine seated at her dressing table put Thomas momentarily out of Peter's mind. 'You look terrific, darling.'

'Sorry to have kept you waiting. Somebody must have had a very full bath and I had to wait an age for the water to heat up again. I couldn't face a tepid bath in this weather. Mrs Albert really ought to get a new boiler.'

'There's someone waiting to see you. Downstairs. A POW.'

'A POW? Oh, I expect it's the one who wants to use my piano. I won't keep him a moment. I must just fix a day and time with him.'

Thomas had eventually seated himself on the bottom step of the flight up to Christine's bedroom. At her appearance, he at once scrambled to his feet. Blocking her way, he stared at her. Christine was forced to halt and Peter halted behind her, until, at long last coming to his senses, he stepped down.

Outside the sitting-room door he waited for them to enter first, then followed.

'I came …' He gave an abrupt little cough, and then repeated: 'I came …'

'About the piano?' She smiled, touched by his obvious nervousness. 'Oh, do sit down. Please.' She pointed to a chair and reluctantly Thomas placed himself on its edge, his soiled cap clasped between his hands. 'Michael told me you were a music student. Is that right?' He nodded, twisting the cap in his hands. She took the chair opposite to him, with Peter glowering behind her. 'Would you like a drink of some kind?'

'No, no. No, thank you. You're busy. And I must hurry back to the camp. I only came to ask when it is convenient. That's to say – if you don't mind.'

'Of course I don't mind. I told Michael that. The only thing is – we must pick a time when I'm not working here. Otherwise it would be too distracting for me. And probably also for you. What sort of time would suit you?'

'Any afternoon this week is fine for me. Next week I begin to work again, I think. Tomorrow the doctor takes off my plaster.'

'Well, then – why don't you come tomorrow afternoon? If I'm not here for some reason, I'll ask Mrs Albert – my landlady – to let you in.'

'You're very kind.'

Christine jumped up from her chair and turned to Peter. 'We ought to get cracking. We're going to be awfully late.'

Stricken, Thomas cried out: 'Forgive me! I've delayed you, I've delayed you!'

'Of course you haven't. I took far too long getting ready.'

In a cross voice Peter asked: 'Have you got everything?'

'Yes, I think so … No, my rose.' She hurried over to the vase on the mantelpiece. 'I bought it for my hair. You've no idea what it cost.' She held out the single rose. 'Be a dear and pin it for me. Here's a clip.'

As Peter fumbled with the rose and clip, she looked up through his raised arms and her eyes met Thomas's. Then both of them looked away. 'We're going to a dance. That's why I'm dressed up like this.'

'It's two, three years since I last saw girls in evening clothes.' He gave the words what seemed to be an accusatory emphasis. Peter, having by now finished with the rose, swung round and stared at him.

'I'll go now.' Thomas hurried to the door.

'Oh, why not wait for us?' Christine protested. 'We're almost ready. We might even be able to give you a lift.'

He opened the door and turned. He shook his head. 'Thank you.' He gave a small bow first to her and then to Peter. 'I'm happy that you have let me see you – and will let me play.'

They listened to him, boots thunderous, racing down the stairs.

Peter looked at Christine, his eyebrows raised. 'Well! I didn't much like the tone in which he spoke to you. Are you really sure it's wise –?'

'Oh, don't be silly!"

'Well, I suppose you know your own business. But do be careful!'

'Where did you meet him?' Noisily Peter changed into top gear as the MG lurched round a corner and then began to race up the Banbury Road.

'Aren't you going too fast? This isn't the sort of weather for speeding.'

'Where did you meet him?'

'Meet who?'

'That POW.'

'I've told you. Michael knows him.'

'Oh, yes, of course. He's always been something of a Nazi-lover, hasn't he?'

'Michael? Certainly not. What on earth made you think that?'

'Didn't he help Hogg in the election against Lindsay?'

'So what? A lot of people then believed that the war could be averted. That doesn't mean that they were pro-German.'

'I wonder how he's been graded? Your POW.'

'Graded?'

'Well, they all have to be graded – A, B or C. Didn't you know that? A for the 'good' ones, if such people really exist. B for the indeterminates. C for the confirmed Nazis. Surely you knew that?'

'No. I'm afraid not.' After a moment she added: 'I doubt if Thomas is a confirmed Nazi.'

'That dreadful German self-pity! No pity for others of course but so much for themselves. I kept coming across it when I was posted to Hamburg. Don't you remember?' He produced a crude parody of Thomas's accent as he quoted: 'It is two, three years since I last saw a girl in evening clothes.'

'What's wrong with that?'

He did not answer, smiling to himself as he peered through the windshield into the darkness. 'Are you really going to let him use your piano?'

'You heard me say he could. Any objections?'

'None at all. But I just hope he doesn't start making himself a nuisance. Some of them do, you know. You ask them in once and they start turning up every evening. You do one favour for them and they expect a dozen.'

'Let's stop talking about these Germans. It's becoming a bore.'

'That's fine by me.' There was a long silence. 'Tell me what exactly is the relationship between you and our hostess.'

'My mother was her cousin.'

'Then old Lord St Nesbitt must have been your mother's uncle?'

'No. Her father. My grandfather.'

'Your grandfather! Oh, I hadn't realised that. I met Dulcie St Nesbitt at the Crowboroughs last weekend. I wish I'd mentioned you to her.' He pondered for a moment. 'Then where do the Maxdales come in?'

'They don't. As far as I know. You really ought to buy yourself a copy of *Debrett's*. Why all this interest in genealogy?'

'Oh, I – I just wanted to get it all straight.'

'You mean you just wanted to get me all straight. We do seem to have picked on the most tedious topics during this drive.'

'Sorry.'

There was another long silence. Then, having turned his head to glance at her, he put a hand over hers. 'You're shivering. Aren't you? The trouble with this car is that the wind gets into it as soon as one picks up any speed.'

'I don't *feel* all that cold.'

'Not far to go now. Let me put my coat around you.' With his left hand he reached back into the car for his overcoat. Tenderly, he then helped to wrap it around her, even though she had cried out 'Oh, do keep your eyes on the road!'

'You look marvellous, you know. No wonder that German stared and stared at you, his mouth agape.'

'Rubbish!'

Of the ball, her first since the war had ended, Christine
could afterwards remember little. Hands clasped her hand,
cheeks were pressed against her cheek; voices shrieked or
bellowed their welcomes or whispered their brief confi-
dences; the room swung in a wide, glittering arc as Peter,
an ostentatiously accomplished dancer, swept her around it.
She was buoyant on no more than a single glass of champagne and her own excitement. 'Oh, Peter, you dance beautifully! Wonderful! Wonderful! Oh, if only I could match
you!' The chandeliers bobbed and swayed, skirts swished
and billowed out, and a passing earring caught the light
and became a momentary spark of fire. 'Wonderful, wonderful,' Christine repeated, as though to herself. The lights
dimmed, the music from the little band changed, and innumerable couples glided and rustled over the vast octagonal
floor, pausing, hesitating, melding and separating, while the
music of the tango drifted out into the frosty night. 'When
I'm dancing with you, I can do things I can do with no one
else.'

Eventually they were eating cold chicken and an old
woman who had long ago been Lady Lavrington's governess
was saying to Christine: 'It's just as it all used to be in the
days before the war. Miraculous.' From a reticule made of jet
beads that made it look as if it was encrusted with ants, she
pulled out a handkerchief and held it to the tip of her nose.
She sniffed and sniffed again. Was she about to cry or did
she have a cold? 'Things always seem to right themselves in
the end,' she continued. 'I'm no longer the dreadful pessimist I was. I remember how after the Great War – "our war"
as I like to call it – I thought that things at Branksome would

never be the same again. But they were! And now look at this. And lovely Mark is engaged and ...' Her voice trailed off. Perhaps she had suddenly realised that it might be in bad taste to mention the tall, stiff Texan heiress with the wide mouth and suddenly dazzling smile, who had made possible the whole lavish occasion. 'Isn't Lady Lavrington the most wonderful person?' she substituted.

'Yes. Wonderful.' But Christine had always found her cousin bossy and self-centred.

Back in the ballroom, she realised that, for some unaccountable reason, the enchantment of that first hour had all at once dissipated for her. Involuntarily she yawned, a gloved hand to her mouth.

'Tired already?'

She almost said, 'No – bored.' But instead she replied: 'Just a little. I've been slaving away all day at some ...' She broke off. It would be pointless to tell Peter about the Latin elegiacs for Mrs Dunne.

'We'll sit out the next one.'

'I wonder what time it is.'

He looked at his watch. 'Ten past twelve. One should never ask the time at a ball. Even if one's Cinderella.'

When the music stopped, they walked in silence to the empty drawing room. Peter chose a dilapidated sofa, one of its arms heavily darned, in the shadow of a corner. But almost as soon as they had seated themselves he leapt up to examine a Reynolds portrait of a former Lady Lavrington.

'I thought they'd sold her.'

'That was the idea. Death duties.'

'But now she's had her reprieve? Trust Mark to make a good match. Or his mother to push him into one. They're shrewd, those two.'

'I think Mark's very much in love with Karen. What man wouldn't be?'

'Oh, of course! That goes without saying!' He gave a braying laugh.

'Why do people so often judge other people's motives by their own?'

Christine turned away from him, picking with a forenail at the darn on the sofa cover. All the things that had first attracted her to him – his sleek hair, his engaging smile, his well-shaped, well-fed body in its expensively tailored clothes, his air of relaxed self-confidence – now repelled her.

'Something's worrying you.'

'Nothing's worrying me.'

'Tell me.' He slipped an arm round her waist and placed his cheek, smelling faintly of Caron Pour Un Homme, against hers.

At the contact, she jumped up. 'I've told you. Nothing's worrying me. But I must go and powder my nose. I'll only be a moment.'

In the heavily pocked glass in the bathroom, Christine saw that her rose had already begun to droop and threw it into a corner. Then for many seconds she stared at her own reflection, her hands resting on the marble sides of the huge, shallow basin. 'Is that me? Is that really me?' she silently asked herself, as so often when inspecting her face in a glass. She seemed to be staring at a stranger casually passed in a crowded street. Suddenly she could hear Thomas's voice giving that dragging emphasis to his words: 'It is two, three years since I last saw girls in evening clothes.' She shuddered, but whether at the recollection or at the cold in the vast, high-ceilinged room, heated by no more than a rusty oil-stove in a distant corner, she could not have said.

'Oh, Christine darling, I'm so glad to find you here! I wonder if you would be an angel and help me pin this shoulder-strap.'

It was one of Christine's cousins, a girl of sixteen, in a pale pink dress with a blue sash, her coarse, fair hair held on either side with ribbons of a darker blue. Her eyes were brilliant; she could not stop laughing. 'Oh, what a wonderful, wonderful dance! It's like a celebration for having been lucky enough to be still alive after that ghastly war. There can't have been anything like it since it started. Christine, have you ever seen such frocks? And such food! One would think rationing had ended. Not that I've been able to touch a scrap, I've felt far too excited for eating … Oh, hurry, hurry, hurry!' She began to shift impatiently under Christine's hands. 'Do you know Marcus Philipson?'

'I don't think so.'

'Oh, I thought every undergrad knew him. He's *celebrated* – or is it notorious? He's President of the Bullingdon or one of those clubs. He dances like a dream. I wish I could dance as well. Lessons don't seem to help much when I get on the floor.'

'You were managing very well when last I saw you. '

'Was I? Was I really? Marcus is such a perfectionist.'

'There! I think that's all right.'

'Bless you!' She hugged Christine, pressing her immature, trembling body against hers. Then she stood back for a moment, to gaze at her. 'Oh, you are beautiful! That's what Marcus said. He said there were lots and lots of pretty girls around but you were one of the few really beautiful ones.' She laughed. 'He didn't say I was a beautiful one too. The beast! For a while I was horribly jealous.' She grabbed Christine's hand, held it to her lips and kissed it. Then she was gone.

When Christine began to make her way back to the drawing room, a young man with a round, red, perspiring face and the kind of luxuriant moustache, looking as though it had been stuck on with glue, worn by RAF men during the war, emerged out of the shadows. 'I wonder if you remember me?'

She smiled uncertainly.

'No, you don't. Why should you? I was in the same squadron as Ben Carey. The three of us once had a drink together in an Andover pub when you visited him.'

'Oh, yes, of course! Of course I remember you! It's confusing to see you out of uniform.' But she had totally forgotten him, just as she had totally forgotten so much else of the flotsam and jetsam of those few last weeks before Ben's death. 'Your name is …?'

'Bill. Maxwell.'

'Yes, of course, of course! Hello, Bill.'

Laughing, he held out his hand, and she took it briefly in hers.

'How about giving me a dance?'

The abrupt, breathless manner in which he put the invitation touched her. She thought of Peter, no doubt still awaiting her, and then impulsively put him out of her mind. 'I'd love that.'

'I'm afraid I can't dance all that well. One problem is my tin leg. But the other, greater problem is that I have no sense of rhythm. That's what my teachers have always told me. And my partners too! I'm best in a slow foxtrot.'

'And I think that we're – you're – lucky. It *is* a slow foxtrot, isn't it?'

He held her stiffly, at some distance from himself, as if concerned to have as little physical contact as possible. After they had shuffled back and forth for a while, he sighed: 'This isn't really my sport, I'm afraid. I'm far better at bridge or billiards.'

'I think you're doing really rather well.' She smiled up at him, deciding that she liked his plain, irregular face bisected by that ludicrous moustache. 'What became of you after those Andover days?'

'Oh, I was shot down in the same show that poor old Ben got his chips.' His body became even more stiff and awkward and then he trod on her foot. 'Sorry! This must be absolute hell for you.' He went on: 'And then I was a prisoner for two years. And now I'm up at Wadham.' He laughed. 'An absolute ramp! I managed to wangle a grant out of the government to sit pretty for two years, pretending to read Eng Lit. So far I haven't done a bally stroke. The truth is, I find it almost impossible to settle to anything. Having been a gentleman of leisure for all that time in Germany ... Oh, sorry, sorry!' Once again he had stepped on her foot.

'Would you rather give this up and sit down?'

'I'm sure *you* would. Yes, please.' Releasing her, he pulled a handkerchief out of his trouser pocket and dabbed vigorously at his face, as though he were staunching blood. 'Phew! I feel as if I'd run a mile.'

'Let's get away from all this noise and crush. It'll be easier to talk.'

'How about the terrace? It's such a wonderful night. Yes?'

'*Wonderful?* Are you crazy? We'll freeze to death.'

'I thought that if we got your wrap and my coat as well ...'

'Oh, all right then. But just for a short time.'

'Are you sure?'

'I think so. Yes, I am. '

Once they were outside the French windows, he fumbled

in a pocket and produced a packet of Woodbines. 'How about a fag?'

'I rarely smoke. And certainly not Woodbines.'

'Mind if I do?'

'Of course not. Someone once wrote a little poem – don't ask me who. "Come into the garden, Maud, The black bat night is flown, And the scent of the woodbine is wafted abroad – But you'll damn well smoke your own!"'

He gave a momentary, snorting laugh, clearly puzzled.

'A take on Tennyson.'

'Yes. Yes, of course.' Clearly, he remained puzzled.

Christine slipped an arm through his. It seemed a perfectly natural thing to do, an act of comradeship, no more. The sky was clear, the stars hard and bright. The snow gave off an extravagant gleam in the forks of trees, in neat piles along the newly swept paths, and on the hooped rose-trellises.

'What a change from in there. You know, I must confess, I wasn't much enjoying things until I met you. I don't really belong here, that's the problem. Mark and I were in the same POW camp – otherwise he'd never have asked someone like me. There's not a soul here I know. Except two other men from the camp – as much out of things as I am. When I tried out this DJ I thought it fitted me pretty well. Well, I know better now. It belongs to my scout.'

'It looks fine.' But she had already noticed that the sleeves and trouser legs were too long and the lapels dog-eared.

They continued their desultory chatter as they wandered about the neatly intersecting paths of the formal garden. Then suddenly he blurted out, apropos of nothing: 'I'm sorry about Ben. I can't get him out of my mind.'

'Well, neither can I.'

'Of all that gang – he was the best for me. Oh, Christ, what a stupid, stupid business it was!'

All at once a leaden weight descended on them. They became silent. Then, as though by unspoken agreement, they began to hurry back to the house.

He helped her off with her wrap. 'I'm afraid you've been chilled to the bone.' Her teeth were chattering.

'Oh, but I loved it. It was so beautiful – that whiteness everywhere, the glitter, the emptiness. But I've been very naughty. I had someone waiting for me.'

She looked around her. 'Oh, there he is!' She pointed.

With a hard, set face, Peter was dancing with one of Lady Lavrington's many sisters, a gaunt spinster of over sixty, whose presence, even in a black lace evening dress, suggested a life of dogs, horses, Girl Guides and the Women's Institute. Peter made it his business to dance well with even the most unwelcome of partners, so much surprising the old woman with the unaccustomed ease with which she was being waltzed round the floor that there was an expression of girlishly naïve pleasure on her weather-beaten face.

As the couple whirled past, Christine waved to him, but pique made him respond with a brief, blank stare followed by a turning away of his head. However, the dance over, he relented enough to come over and enquire: 'What on earth became of you? I waited and waited …'

'Sorry, sorry. I ran into one of Ben's old chums. They were at Andover together – the same squadron. Let me introduce …'

'You might at least have come to tell me. You knew I'd be waiting and looking.'

'I'm afraid it was my fault,' Bill interrupted. 'I'm sorry.'

'Oh, it doesn't matter.' But the tone made it clear that it did. He turned to Christine. 'Shall we dance?'

'Yes, but first let me just introduce –'

But Bill was already moving off, with an embarrassed smile and a brief raising of his left hand in farewell.

Not a word passed between Peter and Christine during the dance. She felt slack and heavy as automatically she followed him. At the end they faced each other on the emptying dance floor. 'Well, that's that,' he said.

'Shall we go now?'

'Already?'

'What time is it?'

'Not yet three o'clock.'

'That seems late enough to me. Unless you were planning to stay for breakfast. A number of people have gone already.'

'Only the oldsters.'

'Well, I'm beginning to feel like an oldster myself. It's almost an hour's drive, remember.'

'Oh, all right then! Come on! Let's get going!'

As they moved through the draughty hall, Christine saw Bill talking animatedly to one of the footmen. She paused, caught his eye and called: 'Do look me up!'

He hurried over, fumbling in a pocket of the shiny, over-large dinner jacket. 'Then you must give me your telephone number.' He pulled out the crushed packet of Woodbines and a fountain pen and began to scrawl at her dictation on the back of it.

'First time that poor chap's looked at ease all evening – talking to that footman,' Peter said when they were scarcely out of earshot.

The drive began in silence. Then he demanded: 'What went wrong this evening?'

'Did anything go wrong?'

'Of course it did. You know it did. Have I upset you in some way?'

'Don't be silly! I'm tired, that's all. I felt – enough is enough. Sorry.'

'I don't mean just leaving early. You've been, well, *odd* all evening.'

'I certainly haven't. What on earth are you talking about?' But she knew that he was right. She had at once, seemingly for no reason, become disenchanted with him from the first moment of his stepping into her bedroom.

'Oh, well. Let's forget it. If I've done anything wrong, then I'm sorry. I'm sorry, darling.'

His right hand on the wheel, he placed his left one, at once exploratory and proprietary, high up on her thigh.

At once she jerked away.

'What did I tell you? There *is* something wrong.'

'Nothing is wrong. Nothing at all is wrong. I tell you, I'm tired. Tired. That's all. Can't you get it? Tired.'

'I'm damned if I know what I've done.'

III

At ten o'clock the next morning Margaret, flushed from her bath, entered Christine's bedroom with a tray piled with breakfast things. She jerked back the curtains, marched over to the bed, and began to shake Christine's shoulder. 'Wakey, wakey! Rise and shine! It's gone ten.'

'Oh, God!' Christine sat up, rubbed her eyes and collapsed back on to the pillow. 'I thought it was much later.'

'You asked me to wake you at ten, because of your work for your tutorial. Remember?'

'My tutorial!' Christine jerked up again, the back of her right hand pressed to her forehead.

Margaret knelt to light the gas fire. 'You'll feel much better when you've had a cup of tea. I've fixed you that last rasher of bacon and some fried potato.'

'What about you?'

'Oh, I don't feel all that hungry this morning. I'll just have my usual All Bran and some toast and a smidgen of butter. I always feel liverish if I eat bacon in the morning, I don't know why.'

Apart from the lateness, this morning had begun like all their mornings. Margaret had spent at least half-an-hour in a bath continually renewed, to the fury of their landlady, with more and more scalding water, had prepared the breakfast in their shared kitchenette and then, humming to herself, had come in to wake Christine. Christine, somnolent and unamiable, had begun to gulp tea.

'Better?' Teapot in hand, Margaret leaned forward, preparatory to pouring out a second cup.

Christine nodded.

'How was the ball?'

'All right.'

'Tell me all about it. Who was there? Were the eats good? And did you drink bubbly?'

'Yes, the food was good. And, yes, we drank champagne. Gallons and gallons of the Widow,' she added to heighten Margaret's vicarious delight.

'You arrived home earlier than I expected. Usually it's dawn – or later. I couldn't sleep, so I heard the door and called out. But you can't have heard me.' Christine had heard and had then hurried past Margaret's door. 'I thought Peter was looking terribly distinguished. It must have been that look that got him into the Foreign Office. He's not really all that bright, is he?'

Christine raised her cup with both hands and gulped from it.

'Oh, come on, Christine! You seem to be still asleep.' Then another thought came to her. 'There was a POW wandering around yesterday evening – just before you and Peter left. He passed me on the stairs – coming up as I was going down. What on earth do you think he was doing? Not at all the sort of person Mrs Albert would want around her house.'

'Oh, he came to see me.'

'*You!*' Margaret was aghast.

'His name is Thomas. Thomas Bartsch. I met him through Michael the other day – Michael's been kind to him, in fact he's been kind to a number of them. He used to be a music student and he needs a piano on which to practise. So I said that he was welcome to use mine – provided, of course, that he didn't interfere with my work. In fact, he's coming over this afternoon.'

'Chrissie! No, Chrissie! What's got into you? Are you completely mad?'

'What's all the fuss?'

'Well, you've so often said …' Margaret jumped off the bed, her doughy face suddenly blotched with pink. 'When they first allowed our men to fraternise in Germany, I can remember so well your saying it was all a ghastly mistake. And I agreed with you – a hundred per cent! So how can you now yourself start to fraternise …?'

'Because I see I was wrong. That's all.'

'That's all, that's all! I'd have thought you owed it to Ben, if not to all the other men … Do you really mean to say you're going to allow that, that Jerry to come in here and, and bang away on your piano, when for all any of us know he may well have killed friends – or, or relatives – of ours? I can't, I just *cannot*, believe it!'

'Oh, do stop all this nonsense! I must get dressed.' Christine clambered out of the bed. 'I wish you'd learn to mind your own business.'

'But don't you get it? We simply can't behave as though all those horrendous things never took place – the concentration camps and mass-killings and doodlebugs and, oh, everything. Our dear little house was bombed – you know that – utterly destroyed, thank God that none of us was in it. And Daddy's business has never been the same since, and my older brother was away for almost three years. When I think of all that all of us went through and then of those German frauleins palling up with our men just to get things out of them, and of these Germans over here being asked to English homes, well, it makes me sick, physically sick!'

'Oh, for God's sake! Why on earth are you working yourself into such a state? It's not your room, it's not your piano. And I'm not asking you to meet him, let alone be nice to him.'

'You know I've always stuck up for you through thick and thin. No one can say I haven't been a good friend to you.'

'Well, what has that got to do with it?'

'I'd give my right hand for you. There is nothing I wouldn't do for you. But this is – quite simply – a matter of principle. I'd be false to all my beliefs if I didn't tell you what I felt. We can't let those wretches think that they can once again get away with it. Otherwise the whole awful thing will repeat itself in another twenty or thirty years. Can't you see that?'

'All I can see is that you're going to make me late.'

'Oh, very well!'

Margaret rushed out of the room, slamming the door behind her.

'Must you slam the door?' Christine shouted after her. Then she heard Margaret's feet thumping down the stairs.

IV

As Christine struggled to complete her latest assignment for her tutor Mrs Dunne, she found herself returning over and over again to Margaret's protest, until she came to see it not as the transient outburst of an emotionally unstable nature but as, yes, a warning. A warning? She looked again at the half-finished verses, then flicked over the pages of her *Gradus ad Parnassum* in search of a word. A warning. But of what?

Once again she made an effort to concentrate, but the disquiet nonetheless remained, no longer acute but still there, a thorn lodged somewhere in the recesses of her being, so that every thought, every sensation was attended by a vague throb. Again she flicked over the pages, tattered and soiled from the use of many years; and as she did so she suddenly felt that she was being snatched at by an invisible current, with the panic-stricken certainty that she no longer had the strength or, worse, even the will to struggle back to land. She put a hand over her eyes. She was tired, she decided, after that late night. She had drunk too much.

After lunch, eaten in solitude at the British Restaurant in the High – 'cheap and nasty' had been Michael's verdict when she had persuaded him to go there with her – the verses went no better. Eight lines had now been completed, but she was self-critical enough to know that they were bad. For minutes on end she doodled on her notepad, gazed out of the window as she sucked on her pen, or wearily searched the *Gradus* for a word that she all too often forgot as soon as she had found it. She glanced at the small travelling clock on the mantelpiece – its blatant tick-tock had been maddening her, as never before – and wondered when Thomas would arrive. Obviously his practising would be too much of a distraction for her. She would have to move over to the Ashmolean Library, as she had often done in the course of this unrelenting winter in search of more warmth than her niggardly gas fire could provide.

Eventually she heard the deliberate tread of his boots on the stairs. She waited, head cocked and tongue against upper lip, with a mixture of apprehension and excitement.

'Come in!'

'Oh! You're working. I'm sorry. I disturb you.'

'It's quite all right. I was expecting you. I'm just going out to the library. I often work there – with all the books I need to hand.' With flustered movements, she began to gather up her books and papers and to stuff them into a battered briefcase, a survival of her schooldays.

'You're not going because of me? It's easy for me to come another afternoon.'

'And have that long walk for nothing?'

He smiled: 'I can spare the time.' He hesitated, unsure whether to make the confidence or not, and then went on: 'Before I became a prisoner, I used to think the most wonderful thing in the world would be to have time, endless time for myself – to think, to read, to play music, to listen to music. And now – I have all that time and what do I do with it? As I told you before – I sleep!' He laughed.

'You also come to use my piano.'

'Yes. That's good.'

'You'll find all sorts of music here. There's some Poulenc – rather fun, I've only just discovered him – and some of the eighteenth-century people. They're my favourites.' She picked up one of the scores from the top of the baby grand. 'Ravel. Too difficult for me but perhaps for you …' She tossed the score back.

'What's this?' He picked up a score and stared at it.

'Oh, that!' She laughed. 'Carl Müller. An arrangement of the *Eroica* for piano duet. Margaret – my friend – and I have been having a lot of fun trying to play it.' On an impulse, she picked up the score and turned to him. 'Why don't we give it a try? How good is your sight-reading?'

'Us?'

'Why not?'

'The *Eroica* is very long. You must go to your work.'

'Don't be silly! I don't mean the whole thing. We can just start on it.' She looked at her watch. 'Anyway I don't really feel in the right mood for Latin verses. To hell with them!' She opened the score. 'Come on. Let's give it a try!'

After a brief hesitation, he nodded, crossed the room to fetch an upright chair for himself and sat down beside her. She adjusted the height of her stool. They began to play, peering at the score as they did so, repeatedly stopping, getting their hands entangled, and going back when one or other had made a mistake. He was so close to her that she could smell the odour of toil, communal living, unwashed clothes and sweaty bodies that emanated from all but a few privileged prisoners like Ludwig. But so far from it repelling her as at their first meeting, it merely intensified her excitement.

Suddenly the door was flung open. It was Margaret. 'I'll thank you for my score!' She raced over, snatched it off the stand, her elbow jabbing Christine's head, and then ran out, slamming the door behind her. Thomas stared at Christine, aghast.

She did not know how to explain. She jumped up and strode to the door, with the intention of going after Margaret. Then she thought better of that. She shrugged and forced a smile. It was something to be laughed at, she tried to indicate. But neither her shrug nor the smile that followed it rid his face of its expression of shock and humiliation. 'It means nothing. She's like that. Does she really think I should get her permission each time before I pick up something of hers? She constantly uses even my toothpaste and my vanishing cream with not a word … Oh, well, never mind, never mind.'

'I think I must go. She's your friend. Maybe best friend? I've made you quarrel.' He got up from the chair and edged away from the piano. 'That's not good.'

'She'll get over it. She always does. You'd better get on with your practising.'

He shook his head. 'I have no – no more feeling for it.' Again he shook his head. 'No. Sorry.'

'Well, sit down then and I'll make us a cup of tea or coffee.'

Instead of sitting down, he moved over to the built-in bookcase that covered the farthest wall. 'There are more books here than in the whole of the camp.'

'Books are my great extravagance.'

He pulled out a volume and turned over the pages.

'What are you looking at?'

'Burkhardt's *Renaissance Italy*.'

'You can borrow it, if you like. As you see, it's not in the original German but in English. Good practice for you. I'm sure Ludwig would agree.'

'It is not for myself. It is for my friend – Horst. You met him at Michael's. He has wanted to read this book for a long, long time.'

'Well, take it to him.'

He was about to obey, but then had second thoughts and thrust it back on to the shelf. 'Maybe better not. It's so new, so clean.'

'That's only because I've never got round to reading it. But don't tell Michael that. He gave it to me as a birthday present.'

'In the camp it is impossible to keep a book clean.'

'Oh, that doesn't matter a bit. A lot of my books have coffee or cocoa stains on them. Go on! Take it!'

Reluctantly he did so. Then he frowned, head lowered: 'Perhaps I really should go?'

'No, no, stay a little! I'll make that tea. Or do you prefer coffee?'

He hesitated, 'Maybe coffee? Is that possible?'

'Why not? And I won't make it as the English like it. I'll make it strong!'

The coffee made, they sat opposite each other, she on the sofa and he, as though deliberately as far away from her as possible, on the stool, his arm in its plaster resting along the lid of the piano.

'Michael told me you write music.'

'No longer.'

'Why not?'

He stared down into his coffee cup. 'When I was first captured and taken to a hospital, I tried. No good. When one is seventeen, eighteen, one writes poetry, one writes music. It means nothing.'

'It could mean something. I think you should make another try.'

He shook his head, tapping gently with his teaspoon against the side of his cup. 'I have no – what do you call it? – *Werdenenergie*. Power of will. I surrender, like I surrendered as a soldier. Not good. Horst is not like that. He makes himself do things, reads, studies. For him nothing is impossible. For me – most things!'

'Tell me about Horst.'

He frowned, clearly reluctant to do so. Then: 'He is … a good comrade. Good.'

'He looks intelligent.'

'Yes. Very intelligent. Much more intelligent than I am!'

'How old is he?'

'Forty-seven. Maybe forty-eight. I forget.'

Suddenly he sounded impatient and she felt that she had probed enough. They began to talk about other, less personal things – music, books, the life of the university and the life of the camp – with flagging animation.

Eventually he looked at his watch and jumped to his feet. 'I must go. I mustn't be late.'

'But it's been so short.'

Again he looked at his watch. 'Almost two hours. And I've kept you from your work.'

'Oh, to hell with my work.'

He went to the chair over which he had draped his cumbrous greatcoat and began to struggle into it. 'Your work is important, I am sure.'

'I'm not sure myself. I sometimes think it is a total waste of time.'

'Don't say that!'

'I'll walk a little way with you. I need some fresh air – to clear my mind.'

'No, no! Not necessary! It's too cold now.'

'I'd like to come. I mean that. I'd really like to come.'

He shrugged his acquiescence.

They walked side by side through slushy streets almost entirely devoid of people. The icy wind made Christine's teeth ache and her eyes water. He quickened his pace, so that she had to hurry to keep up with him.

Suddenly he swung round, gripping her forearm with his good hand. 'Go home now! Please! You must! It's too cold.'

Such was his urgency that reluctantly she nodded. 'Okay.' She turned her face up to his, almost as though she were inviting a kiss. 'When shall I see you again?'

'Tomorrow I'm going to Michael.'

'Saturday?'

'Saturday I keep for my friend.'

'Horst?'

'Yes, for Horst. He works all week, so on Saturday I go out with him. Always.'

'Well, Sunday then.'

'Thank you.' He nodded. 'But is it – are you sure?'

'Of course I'm sure.'

'So – I say goodbye.' He extended his left hand.

She took it in her right. 'Goodbye, Thomas.'

'Goodbye, madam.'

The sudden formality took her aback. 'Oh, please – Christine.'

'Goodbye, Christine.'

He broke away and hurried off, head lowered before the icy bluster of the wind.

V

Early in the afternoon on the Sunday when she was expecting Thomas, Ludwig and Klaus for tea, Christine was striding down the Cornmarket. Suddenly she glimpsed Thomas with Horst – whom she had deliberately not invited – on the other side of the street. With no regard for her safety, cars braking, swerving and hooting, she raced across.

In her fur cap and coat, her face glowing from the cold and the exertion of her walk, she looked unusually healthy and attractive, in contrast to the two prisoners, whose features were blue and pinched. Thomas was even shivering slightly, his jaw rigid, so that as he spoke the words emerged, with a curious impression of stoicism, through clenched teeth. All around, scraped into hard, uneven mounds, the snow glittered, merciless to the eyes, in the slanting afternoon sunlight.

'How do you like this weather?' Herself so exhilarated, she did not at first notice their despondency. 'Isn't it a wonderful day? I was skating all yesterday morning on Port Meadow. You've no idea how beautiful it looks. Stunning. A real wonderland. One just glides on and on – forever. You can see the grass through the ice – as though it were covered in the clearest of clear sheets of glass.'

Thomas smiled wanly and shook his head. Suddenly she noticed the two tears that the cold had forced into his eyes. One trembled and trickled down his cheek; the other remained seemingly embedded in the corner of the eye like a tiny, opalescent bead. Then she felt ashamed of her delight in the glaring snow and of her feeling of triumphant well-being.

Towering behind Thomas, Horst was staring at her in a manner wary, even hostile, that sharpened her discomfort. He had returned her greeting with no more than a jerky bow. He held his hands, in their rough khaki gloves, stiffly to his sides.

'Were you on the way to my place?'

Thomas looked in submissive questioning at Horst. Then, getting no answer, he said: 'It's too early, no?'

'Earlier than we said. But that doesn't matter. It must be rather miserable wandering the streets in this biting cold. My room should be warm. I keep feeding that blasted meter. Its appetite for shillings is as bad as Ludwig's for sugar.'

Horst stooped and muttered something in German to Thomas, who then, clumsy in his embarrassment, stammered: 'Horst and I must do something first. But thank you. I'll come at three. That's when you said?'

'Oh, come any time!' She forced herself to turn to Horst. 'Why don't you come too?'

'I am sorry. It is very kind of you. But I am busy all this afternoon.' There was no effort to make the excuse sound convincing,

'Did Thomas give you the Burkhardt?' Perversely, she still wanted somehow to win him over.

'Thank you. I will take much care of it. Maybe next Sunday I will bring it back. Yes?'

'Oh, don't hurry. Any time.' She turned to Thomas. 'Which way are you walking?'

Horst indicated Ship Street. 'This way.'

'Not my way then. I won't keep you hanging around in this cold.' She turned back to Thomas, her face relaxing and her voice losing its edge. 'I'll see you later.' Then she felt impelled to make another, no doubt fruitless overture to Horst. 'You must come to tea another time – when you can spare an afternoon.'

He merely gave another of his small, jerky bows.

'Well, I'll say goodbye then. À bientôt, Thomas.'

Afterwards, she wondered what made her stop in her swift passage down Beaumont Street, to pause and look back over the long, glittering vista just traversed. Had she not done so, she would have been spared the humiliating revelation that, so far from turning up Ship Street, Thomas and Horst were walking no more than a hundred yards behind her. She stopped and waited, determined, in her resentment, to inflict on them the embarrassment of knowing that she had seen them. But they were so deep in conversation that they did not look in her direction. Soon they had turned up an alley and disappeared from view.

That was Horst, she told herself as she walked on. It had nothing to do with Thomas. But in that case why had the trivial incident so much upset her? All at once she felt exhausted by the trudge through the snow. The unrelenting glitter had given her a vague throb behind the eyes.

'You look done in!' Margaret's solicitude filled her, as so often, not with gratitude but with irritation. 'Come into my room and put your feet up. It's warmer than yours.' Margaret had been baking a cake for Christine's tea party. 'I persuaded Mrs Albert to let me use her oven. It's so much easier to regulate.' She showed Christine the cake. 'I don't know how it's going to taste. It's a recipe I found in the *Sketch*, with peanut butter in it.'

'Sounds interesting.' In fact, Christine thought it sounded dreadful. 'It looks lovely. You are kind!'

That morning Margaret had suggested that the two of them should bicycle up Boar's Hill to have tea with an elderly woman friend of her parents. Christine had then had to explain that she had already invited the Germans to tea. 'I won't ask you to come because I know you wouldn't want to.'

Margaret flushed and bit her lower lip. Then, after a protracted silence, she crossed over to perch herself on an arm of Christine's chair. 'You know, Chrissie, I've been thinking a lot about this … this German business. And yesterday,' – she had locked her stubby fingers so tightly together that the nails had gone white – 'yesterday I spoke to Father Quinterly about it. I hadn't realised but apparently he does a lot for them – many of them are RCs, you know. Well, we talked, and I told him what I thought, and he told me what he thought. And suddenly, just like that, I felt that … that I'd been wrong all the time. After all, when all's said and done, they're humans – God's creatures – like the rest of us. Aren't they? And we're told to forgive our enemies and do good to those who hurt us – as Father Quinterly reminded me. So …'

'I'm glad that you've come round to my way of thinking. It worried me that you so obviously disapproved.'

'So I'd like to come to your tea party,' Margaret got out in a rush. 'That is, if you don't mind having me.'

'Of course I don't mind. I'm delighted.' But as Christine later acknowledged to herself, she did mind; so that it was with the thought that, if Margaret had already butted in, one more guest would make no difference that she rang Michael to ask him to come too.

'I'd love to come.' Surprisingly, Michael was enthusiastic. As a rule, he preferred to entertain rather than to be entertained. "The only thing is, I've got June Bryson – you know, of Ballet Rambert – on my hands this weekend. Would you mind awfully if I brought her along?'

'Of course not. But I ought to warn you, Thomas is supposed to be playing for us.'

'Oh, June will adore that. She's the most accommodating young woman – prepared to find anything fun, provided it doesn't go on for too long. What time do you want us?'

So now Christine was faced with tea for seven. 'I'm glad you baked that cake, because I haven't a notion what else to give them. I suppose I'll have to set about cutting some sandwiches.' She began to heave herself out of the battered and scarred armchair, but Margaret at once pushed her back.

'I'll do it. I can make some cucumber sandwiches. Michael always loves them.'

'Well, in that case use my marge. It's in the fridge.'

'I have lots and lots.'

'You're not going to use your own stuff on my tea party.'

'Oh, don't be so silly. We always share and share alike, so what does it matter anyway?'

But Christine insisted. She was touched, as so often, by Margaret's generosity and now also by her eagerness to make a success of a party not her own, and yet she was also irritated. She wanted to say: 'It's my show, mind your own business!' She was almost tempted to tell Margaret that, after all, it might be better if she did not come.

At three o'clock, not a minute later or sooner, Thomas knocked at Christine's door.

After they had exchanged greetings, he blurted out: 'I must tell you something. I forgot to tell you when we just met. Klaus and Ludwig can't come.'

'Oh, dear! Why is that?' She did not mind about Ludwig's

absence, in fact was delighted. But she felt disappointed over Klaus.

'Klaus has a cold. Ludwig has' – he raised his eyebrows – 'some other business.'

'Poor Margaret has prepared so much food.'

'I'm sorry, sorry.'

His hands were too stiff from the cold for him to practise without first warming them, so that for a time he knelt before the fire, his fingers outstretched to the flames and his melancholy gaze fixed on them.

Christine lowered the book that she had just taken up again. 'What have you been doing since last you were here?'

He continued to gaze at the fire, not turning. 'On Friday I sang in a concert at the camp. Not solo, in the choir. Otherwise – nothing! There's not much to do in this weather. Oh, but yes! You remember, when last you saw me, you asked me why I did not try to write some music. Well,' – he laughed with sudden, momentary joy – 'all the time that I was walking back to the camp that same evening, music keeps coming to me.' The palms of his hands were beginning to tingle from the heat of the fire. He rubbed them against each other. 'But,' – he sighed and pulled a face – 'I am lazy, so lazy. Instead of sitting down and trying to put this music on paper, I played skat until the lights are put out. To do so was so much easier.'

'What are we to do about your laziness?'

He laughed. 'We can do nothing.'

She looked at him and gave a slow smile. Then, on an impulse, she added: 'Perhaps Horst can.'

'Horst?' He frowned, shook his head. 'Why Horst? What can Horst do?'

Clearly she had upset him with the deliberately needling suggestion.

'Then you must make the effort.'

'Yes, I must do so.' He sighed. 'It's not good to be idle. If one is idle, one becomes bored. And in the camp boredom is the most terrible thing of all. Truly. Every prisoner says so.'

'Yes, I can well believe that.'

'I'll tell you how it is. Yes? One begins to hate those same, same faces of the others, their jokes, their stories, their way of saying things, doing things, their little habits. Everything is so – so *known*.' Once again he gazed ruminatively into the fire. 'But sometimes, sometimes, one meets a comrade like Horst. Not like the rest of us. Always fresh – you understand? – *fresh*. Always interesting, surprising. That's why I like him for my friend. I have no other friend – true friend – in the camp.

'I'd like to get to know him.' And, yes, she meant that, if only because of the relentless curiosity from which she had suffered all her life. 'But I have this feeling that he dislikes me. Or at any rate distrusts me for some reason.'

'Maybe he is bitter. He has had a hard time.'

'He hates us English – doesn't he?'

He rose from his squat before the fire and crossed to a chair. 'Maybe. I don't know.'

'I think he hates us.'

'In England you have many people who hate the Germans very much. Yes? I am right? Your own friend for example.'

'Oh, Margaret?' Christine laughed. 'No, she's changed her mind. In fact she's going to join us for tea. She asked me to explain to you – and to apologise for her behaviour. The poor dear is too embarrassed to do so herself. She hopes you'll forgive her.'

'You English!' He smiled across at her. 'You're wonderful!'

Then, realising from her expression that she had thought that he was being ironic, he added: 'I mean that. Truly. You *are* wonderful.'

'What a pity that Horst doesn't think so.'

'Perhaps he is not what you call a good German but he is – truly – a good man.' There was a brief silence, then he went on: 'Horst's wife was killed in an air raid – the hospital where she was expecting a baby was bombed. Horst's little girl was sent to live with her grandmother in Prussia – far in the east. The war ended but still he has no news of them. If she is alive, the old woman is now eighty, maybe more. I am not saying, of course not, that all this – or any of this – is the fault of the English. But if Horst hates the English, then maybe he has some reason.'

'Of course.'

He had now jumped up and hurried over to the piano. She noticed with what clumsy movements he had begun to select and then arrange a score on the stand.

No doubt on which sides they now stood. For all their friendship, each smarted under the other's unspoken accusations: Cologne, Coventry; Berlin, London; the Ruhr, Docklands … They were suddenly far distant from each other.

But for a short time only. Ten minutes later, as they played side by side at the piano, it seemed impossible that they had come so close to an estrangement. Their faltering performance of another stretch of the *Eroica* had soon erased all memory of the words that had suddenly left them confronting each other across an invisible abyss.

Margaret interrupted them, a plate of thick-cut sandwiches in one hand. 'Hello.' She gave Thomas a brief nod and a nervous smile and then at once put the plate down on a table, her gaze averted from him. She turned to Christine. 'These are the sandwich spread. I'm just going to do the rhubarb jam. I'm afraid I look a sight. My hair doesn't seem to take a perm.' She peered into the glass above the elaborate Victorian mantelpiece, fidgeting unhappily with the tortoiseshell slide that held a bunch of her coarse, sandy hair away from her bulging forehead. She sighed. 'Your hair looks so lovely. Doesn't it look lovely?' she appealed to Thomas.

'Yes. It's very nice,' he agreed in an almost inaudible voice.

'And it never needs a perm or setting. That wave is natural. Some people have all the luck. And you've got a wave too,' she continued to him. 'I don't think that's fair. It's wasted on a man.' She gave a little giggle. 'Ah, well … Back to my labours!'

Thomas and Christine looked at each other as the door closed behind her. Then they burst into laughter.

'She's really rather a darling when you get to know her. Michael calls her my lady-in-waiting. But she's a lot more than that. Do you know what a lady-in-waiting is?'

He shook his head. 'No. But I guess. Maybe *Dame bei der Aufwartung*?'

They were still struggling with the *Eroica* when Michael, dressed in a double-breasted suit and a stiff collar, as for some formal university occasion, arrived with June Bryson.

'Do you know, you're the first German prisoner I've ever spoken to,' June greeted Thomas, a hand on his arm. She wore extremely high, crocodile-skin court shoes, which paradoxically served only to exaggerate her minuteness, a silver-fox fur coat reaching almost to her ankles, and a pillbox hat of the same fur jauntily tilted to one side of her head. 'You speak English?'

Thomas nodded.

'Oh, what fun!'

She pulled off first the coat and then the hat and threw them on to the sofa, before flopping down in the nearest armchair.

'Michael's been giving me a truly super time. He really *is* the world's best host, there's no doubt about that. I always knew that, even in these days of austerity, dons wined and dined like nobody's business but, well, it's been a revelation to me. One wouldn't have thought that rationing existed.'

'I have a lot of friends in America,' Michael put in. 'That helps.'

'Well, I have a lot of friends in America too – or thought I had. But it's not often they think of sending me a food parcel. And dancing makes one so hungry. Worse than a five-mile walk. In the good old days before the war I used to eat a beefsteak every evening after a performance. Now one has to be satisfied with God knows what! Pigeon, horsemeat, whale meat, rabbit. Rat and cat, I shouldn't be surprised, in some of the restaurants to which one resorts in desperation. Even the smart ones.' She wrinkled her small, uptilted nose. '*Quelle horreur*! Oh, you'd laugh if you could see me late at night, sitting up in bed and devouring great hunks of bread with a scrape of marge on them. I'm an awful pig, I'm afraid. I sometimes think I love food more than anything else in life – even sex.' She turned to Thomas. 'What's the food like at your camp?'

'Not good.' He shook his head. 'I think you would often be hungry,' he added with a smile.

'You don't look all that undernourished. In fact, you're quite well upholstered. What sort of things do they give you?'

When he had finished telling her, she gazed at him in horrified incredulity. 'But that's awful! Only bread and potatoes for lunch – and after you've done all that back-breaking work.' She jumped to her feet and snatched one of the plates of sandwiches off the table. 'Here – quick – eat something!'

Thomas shook his head and all of them, except June, then burst into laughter.

'What's the joke? The poor man must be starving. And starving's no laughing matter.'

At that moment Margaret returned with some more sandwiches and the tea. She was wearing, for the first time, a voluminous dress inspired by one of the gypsy figures in a Russell Flint reproduction hanging in her bedroom. She herself had run it up on Mrs Albert's treadle sewing machine. Her face was coated in white powder.

'Yes, we have met before – after a fashion,' she told June as they shook hands. 'You wouldn't know me from Adam – or Eve – but I feel I know you so well. I've always been a huge fan of yours. Do you remember when Sadler's Wells reopened? Of course you do – what a silly question. Anyway – to cut a long story short – I was one of the people who went round to the stage door to tell you how fabulous you were. You were, you know – absolutely fabulous. A dream.'

'Bless you, darling! That's the nicest thing that I've had said to me the whole of this weekend. Michael doesn't exactly go in for saying nice things.'

At this moment Michael jumped up to seize the opportunity of sitting next to Thomas.

'I don't think you two boys should be allowed to sit together!' June cried out.

'I took this chair merely because it's the least comfortable in the room.'

'All the more reason why you should change with me,' Christine said.

'Certainly not. I'll do nothing so unchivalrous. Besides, I have something to discuss with Thomas.'

June turned to Christine. 'You're frightfully brainy, aren't you?' Before Christine could say anything, she ran on: 'Don't even think of denying it, I've heard all about your accomplishments from Michael, so it wouldn't be the teeniest bit of good. And you're frightfully brainy too, I gather.' She turned to Margaret, who blushed and peered down the vee of her homemade dress, while her stubby fingers pinched cake-crumbs together on the plate on her lap. 'Of course you are! What's your subject?'

'English.'

'Oh, how fascinating! Of course I'm an utter, utter nitwit. I left school, believe it or not, when I was barely fifteen. I can only just read and write.' She omitted to tell them what Christine had already learned from Michael: that she spoke French fluently and had already managed to make a sizeable sum of money out of cannily, if recklessly, buying up abandoned London property during the war and then, the war over, selling or letting it at vastly inflated prices.

During this conversation Christine realised that Michael and Thomas were talking to each other in German. She stared across at them, exasperated both by a feeling of exclusion and by what struck her as bad manners. Having eventually become aware of her scrutiny, Michael leaned across: 'You must forgive us for talking German. I'm trying to explain a philosophical point to Thomas, and it's so much easier if I use his own language. German *is* the language of philosophy after all.'

'This is the first time that I've been at a party where

philosophy was discussed!' June cried out. 'And in German too!'

Michael's apology did not appease Christine; and some hint of her displeasure must have conveyed itself to Thomas, since more than once his eyes sought out hers in what seemed to her to be an unspoken plea for forgiveness. At one point he even gave a barely perceptible shrug of the shoulders, accompanied by a fleeting grimace, as if to say: 'What am I to do? It's not my fault.'

Soon Christine was only half listening to June, her attention perpetually straying across to the two men in an attempt to discover, from a rudimentary knowledge of German, derived chiefly from her passion for *Liede*, what they were discussing. Michael was speaking with the unnaturally high-pitched, jerky rapidity that always betrayed his excitement. From time to time, Thomas would nod, frown in deliberation or interject a few words. She was not a naturally jealous or possessive character. Later she was to ask herself, bewildered and uneasy, why she had reacted as she had.

At last their discussion ended, with Michael saying in English: 'Well, at least on that point we're in total agreement.' He smiled at the others. 'Sorry about all that. It was something Ryle raised at a dinner I attended last night at All Souls. What exactly do we mean when we say to people "You really must come over to dinner soon"? I thought it might interest Thomas.'

'Sounds fascinating. I wish you'd shared it with all of us.' Once again it was impossible to tell whether June was being ironic or not. She threw a cushion down on the hearth and sprawled across it. From this position, she began to direct the talk, turning now to one and now to another of them.

Then, as though on an impulse, she jumped to her feet and executed a brief pirouette. The dancer's legs revealed were lean and muscular. She must leave, oh gosh, she was terribly, terribly late. These undergrads, three boys who were mad about ballet, were expecting her to drinks at White's.

'But Thomas was going to play for us,' Christine protested.

'Oh, lawks! I hate to miss that. Sorry, sorry!' She turned to Thomas. 'Sorry, Thomas. Another time, I hope.'

He nodded, unsmiling. In the event, the promised playing never took place. Christine, to her consternation, forgot about it; and he, with his usual diffidence, never reminded her.

'Christine, pet – I must make myself respectable if I may. Even though those three boys are madly *un*respectable.'

'Let me take you up to my bedroom.'

June placed herself on the stool before Christine's dressing table, one leg tucked under her, peered into the glass, and then asked: 'Do I really look a fearful hag – or am I imagining it?'

'You're imagining it,' Christine laughed.

Precisely and quickly, June began to make up her face. 'I like your friend,' she announced, outlining her mouth.

'Yes, Margaret's a dear.'

'Oh, I meant the Jerry. Though of course I like Margaret too. She's the sort of person that people describe as a brick. Brick-like qualities are not to be despised – though admittedly they can make their owners rather heavy going.' She pressed her lips together. 'One can't help feeling sorry for the poor wretches, can one? But of course when one looks at the horrific mess everywhere around us …' She sighed, picked up Christine's hairbrush and, having plucked two hairs out from its bristles, began to brush her hair with strong, sweeping strokes. 'Michael's rather a poppet, isn't he? So *kind*.' The black hair glowed under the punishing silver-backed hairbrush. 'You and he are related in some way, aren't you? Cousins, is it?' Christine nodded. 'You must know him frightfully well.'

'Yes, I suppose I do.'

June threw the hairbrush down and swung round on the stool on which she was perched. 'Tell me about him. Spill the beans. Give me the dope.'

'What do you want to know?'

'Everything! If that isn't asking too much. I don't understand him, not one little bit. We've known each other for, oh, five years now, he writes to me almost every week, wherever I am. Long, long letters that take hours to read. I so often wish that they were shorter. And yet, yet … I sometimes wonder if he would care, really care if he never saw me again.'

'Oh, of course, he'd care.'

'You're just saying that to be kind – or polite.' She swivelled back to the glass and once again took up the brush. She frowned as she patted it against the palm of her hand. 'I think he likes to have me about – just as he likes to have his rooms crammed with all those valuable pictures. He also likes me to look smart. Before I got known – when I was in the Rambert *corps de ballet* – he was so terribly generous with his presents that I began to think I was in danger of becoming a kept woman. He's still very generous to me, even though I now earn quite a whack. He gave me this brooch yesterday.' She touched it, on the vee of her dress. 'A gen-u-ine' – she pronounced the word in deliberate parody of how an American might pronounce it – 'Roman intalgio. Worth a lot, I'd guess. But, oh, I wish, wish, wish … I'm absolutely besotted with him, you know, head over bum.' She gazed at her small, triangular face reflected in the mirror. Then she turned to Christine. 'It's quite crazy, because I'm sure nothing, nothing really serious, will ever come of it. What do you think?'

Christine was at a loss for an answer. How could this woman, who had spent at least half her life in the world of ballet, have failed to grasp the truth of Michael's sexuality? In momentary exasperation she almost blurted out: 'But haven't you realised? Oh, you must have realised. He's what the obituaries call a "confirmed bachelor" – or "a man's man". He's queer. Queer as the proverbial coot.' But all she got out was 'I do sometimes wonder if he's ever been really in love.'

'Exactly! You've conked the nail on the head. I don't think he knows what it means. Being terribly, terribly kind and being terribly, terribly generous are not the same thing. You won't believe this – none of my friends do. He and I have never, never once slept together.' She crossed to the still unmade bed and flopped down on it. 'Now isn't that the funniest thing you ever heard? And, as I said, our relationship has been going on for five – no six – years. It started when he asked me if I could direct him to the loo at a party given by Bobby Helpmann after a charity performance. It turned out later that he thought I was Bobby's sister.'

Christine sought for an answer. 'That doesn't seem fair on you.'

'You can say that again. And the weird thing is that he never minds about anything I get up to with other people. There was this Swiss diplomat, quite a handsome old thing, lots of money. I thought it would make him jealous. Not a chance! Sometimes he even seemed to be encouraging me. Oh, I'm a fool, an absolute idiot. I ought to put him right out of my mind. But somehow … Well, I'm hooked.'

'Then you must get yourself unhooked.'

'If only! Have you ever been hooked like that?'

Christine shook her head. 'Thankfully, no.' Then she thought of Thomas.

June jumped up, slinging her crocodile-skin bag – was that also a present from Michael, Christine wondered? – over her shoulder. 'Ah, well! I suppose we'd better go back and join them and then I must rush off to my two lads. Thank you for being so patient.'

'I only wish I could have been of more help.'

After June and Michael had left, Thomas said that he must go too.

'Must you? We've hardly talked at all. Michael monopolised all your attention,' Christine could not restrain herself from adding. She had forgotten the hour with him at the piano before the others had arrived.

'I've stayed too long already. You have other things to do.'

'I've nothing to do. A complete blank. Even the wireless has broken down, so that I can't hear Eileen Joyce play the Grieg concerto, as I was planning. Please stay. Why not?'

'Okay. Why not?' Suddenly, he surprised her with the brisk cheerfulness of his response.

By now Margaret had piled a tray with most of the tea things and stooped to hoist it up.

'Leave those, Margaret. I'll help you with them later.'

'I can carry them for you,' Thomas intervened.

'Oh, no, I can easily carry them on my own. Please. Why not have a little chat together?' She picked up the tray with a grunt followed by a sigh.

As soon as she had staggered out, Thomas announced: 'Oh, I have something to tell you – tomorrow I must go back to work.'

'So soon! How do you feel about that?'

'Oh, good, I think. I'll earn some money. But in this weather …' He gave an artificial shudder, then laughed. 'I'm not tough – as a prisoner must be. I hate cold, and I become tired too quickly. I'm no longer used to working eight, nine hours each day. I've forgotten how to do so.'

'What job will you be doing?'

'Tomorrow we pick Brussels sprouts. Do you like Brussels sprouts?'

Christine pulled a face. 'On her last visit here Mrs Roosevelt said that Brussels sprouts were the only thing that she disliked about England. She even had to eat them at dinner with Winston Churchill.'

'I also hate them. To have to eat them is bad enough. To pick them – even worse! Where we are working, there are some landgirls and I often see them cry with cold. The sprouts are frozen, the ground is frozen, our hands are frozen, everything is frozen. We have no break, no change of what we must do. Only pick, pick, pick.'

'When are you likely to be sent home?'

He shrugged. 'There is now no home for me. So why think of going home? Perhaps it's better for me here. For many others – mother, father, wife, children waiting – of course it's different. But otherwise …?'

'Things will get better. I'm sure of it. It's only since Christmas that you've been allowed to walk around the town and make visits, isn't it? There'll soon be other concessions. Just wait and see.'

'Yes. You are right. Slowly, slowly things get better.' But he said it listlessly, without any confidence. No doubt the prisoners constantly gave the same tenuous reassurances to each other.

'It's utterly wrong that we should keep you here now the war is over.'

'We must pay.'

Although he said it in a soft, forlorn voice, at first she thought that he was being ironical. The she realised that, no, he was being serious.

'Perhaps you cannot understand this. It's difficult to explain. But I must try. Sometimes I'm glad, yes glad, that I'm a prisoner. I hate my prisoner's life – noise, dirt, bad food, hard work, and bored, bored, *bored*. But – but … I am glad that I *pay*. Yes, that's good, that's right. Perhaps you can't understand that?'

She nodded. 'Yes. Yes, I think I do.' She pondered for a moment. 'Do many of the others feel as you feel?'

'I don't know. It's not a thing that we speak about. Horst cannot understand what I feel. But yes, in their hearts, I think that many prisoners feel like I do. I think so. Yes.'

'What will you do when all this is over and you're free again?'

'I cannot answer that question. I don't know. But for the others … You will laugh if they tell you. For example, Klaus. He will have a ranch in Argentina, because there a German is as good – or as bad – as any other man. If you ask him, he will tell you all about the ranch – how big, how many cattle, everything. He has a wife too in Argentina – no, not a German *fraulein* but an Argentine girl he meets when he arrives. Klaus will be rich, very, very rich, and his lung will be good again.'

'And Horst?' Something that she should have resisted had impelled her to put the question.

'Now Horst – Horst does not want so much. He will go back to the country he loves and first, first of all he will find his little girl. Then he will find work, government work, so he will have – what is the word? – *Einfluss*, yes, *influence*. He will make true his dream of a new Germany – for himself, yes, but also for all others. He wants nothing for himself. He will work only for his country and for his daughter.' He broke off and stared at her with an intensity that she found strangely unnerving. 'It is funny, all this? Comic? But, it is also sad.'

They both gazed into the fire. Then she took up: 'Don't you think that Klaus and Horst and all those others are happier because they have their dream of some sort of wonderful future. Whereas you …?'

'Of course.' He sighed. 'I wish that I also … But. Impossible. I try, try. No good. I'm not a dreamer.'

As he sat there, slumped despondently in the chair before the fire in his begrimed and shabby uniform, she felt an overwhelming desire to jump up, hurry over to him, put her arms around him and hold him to her. She wanted to rest her cheek against his and whisper: 'Dream Dream. Dream.' But how would that restore the faith of which he was destitute? Of what was she thinking? Angry as much with herself as with the whole situation, she searched in her pockets for her packet of Craven A. 'Keep them,' she said when she had helped herself and he, with reluctance, had also taken one. She held out the packet to him.

'No, no!' He shook his head vigorously, almost angrily, as he had done when Michael had offered him the cake.

'You told me you get only six shillings a week.' She tossed the packet into his lap with a casual gesture, realising that only this oblique act of devotion had saved her from saying any of the things that had passed through her mind.

He undid his tunic to place the packet in an inside

pocket; and afterwards, when he had gone and she, alone now, mused with a vague, ashamed pleasure on the events of that evening, the memory of this trivial event – the hand undoing the tunic, then pushing the crumpled packet into the breast-pocket of his khaki shirt – returned over and over again. She had watched the movement of the muscles under the soiled khaki; had stared at the flesh of his throat; had seen the short, golden hairs where his chest was revealed through a gap caused by a missing button.

With a sudden access of energy, she pulled down books from the shelves and began to dust them with a teacloth left behind by Margaret. Then, wearying of this, she went through the letters that had accumulated, unread, on her desk. But, having read them one by one, she realised afterwards that she could remember maddeningly little of their contents.

She lit another cigarette. Then before it was half-smoked, she threw it, still alight, into the empty gate behind the gas fire. Once again she remembered the undoing of the tunic. Then, at last, she forced herself to acknowledge the sudden, strange truth: she had fallen in love with him.

From the desk a photograph of a young man, little more than a schoolboy, with an eagerly grinning face seemed to be impelling her to look at it. She gave it a glance, shook her head as though to dislodge a memory, and then stared more closely. All at once, she was once again pressing herself against Michael, his arms clumsily holding her to him and her body shuddering with grief. 'I'll never get over this! Never, never!'

When in a calm, almost severe voice he had countered; 'Of course you will. One can get over anything in the end,' she had stiffened and pushed him away from her at what had seemed a treacherous failure of sympathy from someone on whom she had always relied. How right he had been! What an irony!

Margaret came back into the room while Christine was still staring across at the photograph. Christine's cry of protest made her switch off the standard lamp as soon as she had switched it on. 'What's the matter?'

'Nothing. I was – thinking. That's all.'

'Oh, Chrissie! It's no good.' She held out her arms as though to a child.

There was no need to tell Margaret. She knew already.

VI

From that evening until the following Sunday, when she was next to meet Thomas, Christine found it impossible to concentrate on her work, her music or any other of her interests. Naturally sociable, she had many friends both in and outside the university, but she had lost all desire to see them, so that when any of them telephoned to suggest a meeting, she made some excuse, no matter how implausible. So extreme was her restlessness that many hours of her day were spent in merely wandering the streets. She would enter bookshops and buy nothing, play over records in gramophone shops only to leave empty-handed, and drink tea or coffee alone in one after another of the innumerable cafés where she would once sit talking the afternoon away with what she called her 'gang'. Her life had become one of dragging impatience for her next meeting with this man whom – and of whom – she knew so little. But what after that? She was not even sure that he cared for her. And if he did? From such questions her mind would swerve away, retreating once more into the world of obsessive fantasy and unassuaged longing in which she now spent so much of her time. Her love for Ben had been no less powerful; but, serene, patient and level-headed, it had produced none of the same disorientating frenzy.

Once, on one of her long, aimless journeyings, she was surprised to see Horst leaning forward, hands in pockets, to gaze into one of Blackwell's windows. She almost veered across the road away from him; but then the hope of hearing some news of Thomas made her halt in her tracks and say hello.

He turned, stared at her, and then merely uttered, 'You?'

'Yes. Me. Aren't you working today?'

He shook his head. 'I have had flu.' His bony face was drained of all colour. He was not wearing gloves and, as he took his hands out of his pockets, she noticed the chilblains that had made them swollen and raw.

Involuntarily she exclaimed, 'Your hands!' pointing at them.

'Yes.' He looked down, as though he too were seeing them for the first time. He frowned. 'Unfortunately one of my comrades must have borrowed my gloves. For German prisoners the word "borrow" has a different meaning than for you. Their "borrow" means "steal". Your Michael often gives Thomas gloves. Very generous. Always they are soon borrowed.'

'If you'd like to come back with me, I can give you a pair.'

'You are a very kind lady. But I am afraid that someone might *borrow* them too. Then – you never see them again!'

'Oh, that doesn't matter. Do please let me give them to you.'

But he said nothing more. He might not have heard her. He turned back to gaze into the shop window in the same rigid stance and with the same intensity of concentration as at her first sighting of him.

She persisted: 'Oughtn't you to be in bed?'

'Tomorrow I start work again. That is what the doctor has decided. I have not been seriously ill. He has said that. And of course an English doctor must be right,' he added with obvious sarcasm, turning once again to face her.

'And how is Thomas doing?'

'He too has chilblains. But he has gloves. For the moment – until some comrade borrows them. Then I think that

Michael must give him another pair. On Saturday he will receive six shillings for his work.'

'That's awfully little.'

'Yes. Awfully little.' He seemed to be imitating her, but she could not be sure.

Yet again surprising herself, she persisted: 'Is he very tired in the evenings?'

'Yes. And in the mornings too. He is not used to getting up at five o'clock.'

As he looked at her in the dimming afternoon – occasional passers-by no doubt wondering what two people so different could have to discuss – Christine at last grasped the extent of his contempt and dislike. But why? What had she done to earn it?

'Thomas tells me he will see you on Sunday. I will send the book with him – the *Renaissance Italy*.' Now that her one desire was to hurry off, he seemed to be determined to prolong their conversation. 'I am glad that Thomas can now play on a good piano. That is very useful for him. He is lucky to have found some English friends.'

'He's a good musician. One realises that at once.'

'Yes, he is one of the lucky ones,' Horst continued, ignoring her interruption. One of his chilblains had begun to ooze blood and, head lowered, he had started to bind it round with a khaki handkerchief pulled from his trouser pocket. 'Those that have something to offer – it is okay for them.'

The insidiously hostile tone all at once made her lose her temper. 'That's not really fair. My cousin often entertains German prisoners who have little or nothing to offer. What about Klaus?'

'Klaus?' He smiled slowly. 'I think that your cousin thinks that Klaus has much to offer.' He gazed into her eyes. 'May I say this? I am not impolite? You have beautiful eyes. Large. Dark. Mysterious. *Eager.*' He gave the last word a vicious emphasis. She thought later that it was if someone had stooped to pet a cat and had then suddenly kicked it.

She took a step away from him. 'I must go.'

He shrugged. 'So – it is goodbye, Miss Holliday.'

She made no reply.

As she walked away an impulse, similar to the one when last she had seen him with Thomas, made her glance back. Erect, rigid and motionless beside the Blackwell's window, he was staring fixedly in her direction.

VII

The next afternoon Christine had her tutorial. All that week she had been battling with some Housman verses, as though to smash open a door locked and bolted against her. She brooded over them late into the night, laboriously substituting one phrase for another that then struck her as even less felicitous. Eventually this joyless chivvying filled her with rage. She had mysteriously lost that capacity for total absorption that had once marked her out as a certain first.

She was prepared for Mrs Dunne's verdict. 'Well, this is a perfectly acceptable beta plus. But it's nothing like your usual work. No distinction. It's marginally better than last week – that's about all that can be said in favour of it.' Leaning across her desk, hands clasped, she scrutinised Christine, much as a doctor might in attempting the diagnosis of a sufferer from a bizarre and puzzling syndrome. 'What's come over you?'

Christine, her gaze fixed on the photograph of the amiably sheep-like face of a former principal of the college that stood in a silver frame on the desk, did not answer.

'What's come over you?' The repetition of the question now had an exasperated edge.

'Nothing.'

'What about your health?'

'That's fine, thank you.' Still she did not meet her interlocutor's gaze.

'Something worrying you?'

'No, Mrs Dunne. Nothing at all. Thank you.'

Mrs Dunne shook her head and sighed. 'Well ... I suppose even the best of us have our off days. But I'm not going to pretend I'm not disappointed. I never expected you to fail me two times running.'

It was then that Christine realised that she no longer cared whether she failed this bulky, dowdy woman with a shiny face and fox-coloured hair or not: something had released her from that bondage of almost two years. Mrs Dunne, a shrewd woman, at once sensed this radical change of attitude, so that, as Christine was about to leave the room, she called out: 'Don't lose interest, Christine! It might be fatal just at this moment – so soon before your Schools.' She opened the silver cigarette box before her and took out a Gitane. With stubby, nicotine-stained fingers she lit it and expelled the smoke through distended nostrils. 'I know one gets restless. I certainly did when I was your age. I even sometimes get restless now and wonder what the hell I'm doing wasting my life! Still ... It's a pity for you to kick over the traces at this precise moment, when a little patience may make all the difference between a distinguished academic career and drudgery as a mistress in some second-rate girls' school.' She nodded briskly in dismissal. 'All right. That'll do for now.'

As she walked home Christine wished that she had had the courage to reply: 'I'm afraid you've got it all wrong, Mrs Dunne. I have absolutely no desire for an academic career, distinguished or undistinguished. I can think of nothing more tedious.' That was now the truth. But, instead of saying that, she had merely murmured, 'Thank you, Mrs Dunne,' and left the room.

VIII

Just before Thomas was due, Christine mounted to her bedroom and changed her dress, sat before the mirror examining her face, ran a comb over and over again through her hair, touched up her lips, and fingered the three strands of pearls, a twenty-first birthday present from her father, that she had just fastened round her neck. How cheap and silly all this was – as if he were to be coaxed into loving her by the artifice of clothes, make-up and jewellery! Suddenly she felt disgusted with herself. She hurried back to her sitting room, sat down at the piano, and began to practise a Chopin prelude. The notes blurred as she held down the *sostenuto* pedal for seconds on end; then, no less impulsively, she broke off, jumped up and slammed down the lid.

'I have brought you this.' He held out a garden pot from which bristled a small cactus. 'I wished to bring you some flowers but at this time of year that's difficult.'

By 'difficult' she knew that he meant expensive. Even that rose bought for the ball had cost as much as a glass of sherry at White's. 'Oh, a cactus is much more interesting – and lasts much longer. You shouldn't have bothered, really you shouldn't.'

'I must tell you the truth. Someone had thrown it away. I found it outside a café with the rubbish. Sorry.'

'A lucky find. And a beautiful one. Thank you so much.' In fact the cactus, looking like a half-blown green balloon covered with vicious, white-tipped spikes, struck her as peculiarly unattractive.

It was clear that he was excited about something but – typically, she was later to realise – he did not at once reveal what it was. In the midst of a desultory conversation, he scrabbled in the breast pocket of his tunic and eventually drew out a soiled and crumpled sheet of paper. He held it out to her. 'I wish to show you this. You told me to write some music. I've obeyed you. See!'

'Oh, that's wonderful!'

As he deliberately unfolded the sheet, from time to time putting it on his knee and then ironing it with a hand, she jumped up to peer over his shoulder at the confusion of notes stabbed in on lines obviously drawn without a ruler. She was now very close to him. She had only to lower her face or move a hand for another six inches or so for them to be touching each other, as they had already so often touched each other in her imagination.

'Difficult for you to read.' He spoke in his normal voice, with no hint of arousal at their close proximity. 'I didn't have time to make a good copy. Today is the day I wash my clothes and I must do that first.'

'Try it on the piano.'

'I must explain. It's a setting for four singers of verses from the psalms. The Bible – you know?' He began to prop the sheet on the piano stand. It slipped off and both of them stooped to retrieve it. It was Christine who reached it first.

'Which psalm?'

'Ah – let me remember! Yes. 337.' He began to quote the verses in German, until she interrupted him.

'You forget. I don't know any German – or hardly any. I have a Bible somewhere over here. I'm afraid I don't often look at it.' She crossed to a bookshelf. 'Yes, here it is.' She began to turn the flimsy pages, tongue between teeth. Then she read out: '"By the rivers of Babylon, there we sat down, yes, we wept, when we remembered Sion." Is that it?'

'Yes. Only the first four first verses.'

'As far as "How shall we sing the Lord's song in a strange land?"'

He nodded.

'Play it for me.'

'So far I've only tried it on the camp piano. Terrible piano, always lots of noise in that room – "recreation room" they call it. And little time. You really wish me to try?'

'Yes, please.'

At the end he swung round on the stool. 'Well?'

She was silent. He turned away from her, head bowed, as though expecting an adverse verdict.

'It's good.'

Swinging round on the stool, legs extended, he gave a radiant smile. 'Truly?'

'Truly. I was moved. Those verses always move me. But they've never moved me so much as now.'

'Now I must try to find a quartet at the camp to sing it for me.' He closed the piano lid, folded the sheet of music and put it back in the breast pocket of his tunic.

'Don't you want to practise?'

'What about you? I don't want to disturb you.'

'Don't worry about me. I have some knitting I must finish. But perhaps it worries you to have someone in the room? I can always go and sit with Margaret or go up to my bedroom.'

'No, no.' He crossed over to her chair and fingered the half-completed sock that she had just produced from her knitting bag. 'You're an expert! So even.' He smiled. 'For your young man?'

'No. For my father. He doesn't like bought socks. My mother used to knit his socks for him, now I have to do that. I have no young man.' On an impulse she then added: 'He's dead. Shot down over Dresden.'

'Ah!' Then he muttered 'I'm sorry, very sorry.'

As she returned to the knitting, the ball of wool fell off her lap and rolled across the floor to his feet. 'Damn!' she exclaimed. He stooped, picked it up and handed it to her. In silence he returned to the piano, drew out the stool and began to practise some of the tediously repetitive exercises that had deterred her from becoming the outstanding player that she might otherwise have been. As he played, totally absorbed in his task, her eyes constantly strayed from her knitting to his hunched back and half-averted face. Although both the windows were closed and the fire had spluttered into life at ten o'clock that morning, she unaccountably felt one shiver and then another shake her body. Soon she had dropped a stitch. Abandoning all pretence of working on the sock, she put it down on her lap and gazed now at the flickering radiants, now at the back of his head, and now at the reflection of his hands in the piano lid.

Eventually, overcome by restlessness, she got up and crossed to the nearer window. From there, leaning against its ledge, she could see three-quarters of his face: the high cheekbones, their pristine gleam betraying that they had been shaved just before he had set out on his visit; the slightly too prominent chin; and the brown hair dipping in an untidy lock across his forehead. Would he become conscious of her scrutiny? Would he look round?' She had always believed that people looked round if one stared hard enough and long enough at the backs of their heads. For many minutes, one hand clutching the dusty rep curtain and her spine pressed against the unyielding ledge of the window, she stood there, willing him to do so. But there was no response. His lips were moving as he counted to himself: '*One*, two, three, four. *One*, two, three, four.' His forehead was tensed in self-exacting concentration. She looked down and watched the cumbrous army boot pressing on the pedal. All at once she was noticing trivial details that would remain extraordinarily vivid in her memory for many days to come: the way his long-sleeved khaki pullover was frayed at the wrists; the grease stain on the collar of his battledress blouse; perceptible lines of stubble below his chin and one ear, which, in contrast to the shiny smoothness of his cheeks, must have escaped his razor.

Outside, huge flakes of snow were whirling down like confetti in the boisterous wind. Prematurely it was growing dark. Christine noticed how Thomas had to screw up his eyes to read the music set out before him. She crossed over to the standard lamp and switched it on. At her touch, the green parchment shade tilted sideways, as it now so often did. She made no attempt to right it.

'Thank you.' He did not look up.

She meant nothing to him. She felt certain of it now. Being kind and sentimental – as she had read those verses from the psalms, had she not felt a sudden ache in her throat, as though something pebble-like were lodged there? – she had felt sorry for him, and for that he had been grateful. Among so much indifference and even hostility, her interest and sympathy must have been welcome to him. Besides, he could use her piano and, as he had told her during his last visit, music was now all that he had to care about. Yes, yes, he was grateful to her – as one would be grateful to someone who pulled one out of an icy river in which one was slowly drowning; but it was not hard to buy the gratitude of those poor wretches: a cup of tea, a slice of cake, the loan of a book, even a friendly word would do the trick. She had his gratitude and the friendship that followed it, of course she did. But love? No. Certainly no.

Once she had reached that bitter conclusion, she went back to her knitting. Finding that she had failed to follow the elaborate Shetland Island pattern correctly, she began, with exasperated perseverance, to unravel it. Now that, in her own mind, there could be no doubt, she accepted the situation with a pain that was not merely a relief but almost a pleasure. Perhaps it was better that he did not reciprocate her love since, if he did, what possible hope could there be for them? But having accepted this consolation, she then at once thrust it away from her. Better to make the descent with him over the cliff's edge than to turn back to the cosy world that offered her a place next to Mrs Dunne on the Somerville staff, an increasingly 'distinguished' career, and marriage to one of the undergraduates who might even now be asking himself why he had not seen Christine for such an age.

She crossed over to the mantelpiece for a cigarette and remained leaning against it. Having blown out a smoke-ring, she extended a hand and ran a forefinger up and down the cactus. The contact with its resilient green flesh was faintly nauseating. 'Damn!' One of the spikes had lodged itself in her forefinger. At the exclamation Thomas looked round; then, seeing what had happened, he rushed over.

'Silly of me.' She tried to squeeze out the spike. 'I just can't get hold of the end.'

'Have you some – what do you call them … *Pinzette*?' He made a gesture of plucking an eyebrow.

'Tweezers? Yes, I'll get them.'

Since it was in the forefinger of her right hand that the spike was embedded, it was difficult to remove it with her left one. Thomas volunteered to do it for her. They both bent over the palm. His fingers were cold against her warm flesh as, anxious not to break the spike or cause her any pain or discomfort, he slowly eased it out. 'There!' He held it up between the tweezers to the light of the standard lamp for her to see. 'You have some iodine?'

She brought some and he began to dab cotton wool soggy with it on to the place. 'I think that's enough.' Having released her hand, he tossed the cotton wool into the waste-paper basket.

It had all been done so casually and yet so expertly – without any of the clumsiness and embarrassment that would have betrayed the thing that she looked for and now despaired of finding. He might have been a male nurse performing a routine task in a hospital. He had held her hand; his face had almost touched hers; their bodies had been separated by only a few inches. And it had meant nothing to him.

She looked at her watch. 'Oh, gosh, it's nearly five. I'll get some coffee, shall I?'

'Please don't worry.'

'But of course you must have some coffee. It's one of the few things not rationed. And I'd also like some.'

He continued to play until she brought in the tray and called to him: 'It's all ready.' Then he left the piano and seated himself, not on the sofa beside her, but in one of the armchairs. 'I think I'm very lucky to know you and Michael.'

At once she recalled the veiled and suggestive hostility of

Horst's remark: 'Yes, he is one of the lucky ones. Those who have something to offer – it is all right for them.' Was there really such a thing as wholly disinterested kindness? She had fallen in love with a prisoner, and so there had been a complete reversal in her attitude to all prisoners. For weeks before she had met him she had seen the glum, heavy figures in soiled battledress trailing through the streets and never once had she felt the slightest impulse to make their lives more tolerable. Yes, for her Thomas had had 'something to offer' – the looks, intelligence and talent with which he had now enslaved her. She had seen him, unconsciously she had wanted him, and so, in the name of charity, she had taken him for her own. Oh, how despicable it was!

'You know, to visit you and Michael makes a big change in my life,' Thomas was saying. He peered into his empty cup, holding it up to the light, with what was almost an expression of guilt. 'I feel – it is not right that I have all this when others ...' Strange how their minds had travelled along parallel grooves. 'For those who cannot speak English it's worse, much worse. Horst thinks ...' He broke off, putting down the cup with a clatter.

'What does he think?'

'I forget. It doesn't matter.'

'He thinks you shouldn't accept our hospitality?' He made no answer. 'Doesn't he?'

He was silent for a while. 'He says that we must not help the English to make their consciences okay. Some of you are ashamed to keep us here so long – Michael, for example. But if they can invite us into their homes and do something for us, then they do not feel so bad.' He broke off for a moment, searching her face for her reaction. 'Also he says we must keep our pride.'

'Pride?'

He nodded. 'I hope I've used the correct word. Pride. *Stolz.* We are like dogs, he says. We let you punish us. And then when you give us a little bit of food or speak kindly to us, we lie down, legs up in air, happy to be your friends.'

'Then does that mean that Horst thinks you should refuse all contact with us?'

'Maybe – yes.'

'But he accepted the loan of my book.'

He stared down at his boots for several seconds in silence. He waggled a foot. 'He did so for me,' he said at last. 'He was angry when I brought it to him, he wanted me to take it back to you at once. But I persuaded him. Difficult but I persuaded him. I didn't wish to hurt your feelings.'

'That was kind of you.' Her tone was bitter.

'No, you mustn't be angry with him. I tell you all this because I wish you to understand how he feels. I wish you both to be friends – Horst and you.'

'There doesn't seem to be much chance of that. I can see he dislikes me.'

'It is not you. It is *things,* not persons. Persons are small. But things are often big, big. No, he's not like the other men in the camp, not like me, because he's so much stronger. He is …'

As he sought for a word, Christine put in: '*Ein Übermensch?*'

He stared at her for a moment, his face assuming the resentful and humiliated expression of someone who has been struck a blow without any hope of retaliation. Then: 'Are we going to quarrel?' he asked in a low voice.

'Perhaps we had better decide not to mention Horst.'

'Perhaps.'

Now, as if released from a long bondage, they began to

talk freely once again. He told her how interested he was in architecture but, despite having now spent more than three years in England, he had so far seen nothing but Oxford. He so much wanted to see Blenheim. He had read about it in an old guidebook at the camp.

'Let's go next weekend,' she at once suggested, delighted with the idea.

He shook his head. 'How do we go?'

'By bus. It's only eight miles.'

'Prisoners are not allowed on buses.'

'Oh, no, of course not. I'd forgotten.' She frowned, and then her face cleared. 'You could wear civilian clothes. I'm sure Michael would lend you some.'

'I don't like to ask him. He's already done much, too much for me.'

'I can ask him.'

'No. Please.'

'Michael won't mind. You're about the same height. You want to see Blenheim, don't you?'

'Yes, but –'

'That's settled then. I'll ask Michael when I see him tomorrow. We can go on Saturday afternoon. How about that?'

'Sunday is better. Michael expects me on Saturday.'

'Oh, dear, I've been asked to a sherry party in one of the colleges on Sunday. I might not get back in time, the buses are so irregular on Sunday. Do you really think that Michael would mind all that much …?'

'I think that I must go to him on Saturday.'

'But he'll have all the others there. He can't possibly mind if for once you don't turn up.' Saturday or Sunday, it did not matter all that much to her, since she was not even sure that she wanted to go to the Sunday sherry party. Her real aim

– yes, she had to admit it to herself – was to prevent him from putting the demands of Michael before her own.

'I must go to Michael. I'm sorry. He expects me.'

'Oh, its ridiculous! Well, never mind. Let's say Sunday then.'

He smiled in relief. 'Good. Thank you, Christine.'

She made an effort to conceal her annoyance that Michael's slender claim had taken precedence over her far more imperative one. She forced a smile. 'So that's settled then. I'll look forward to it.'

But he obviously saw through her pretence. 'I'm sorry, Christine. Don't be angry.'

'I'm not angry, not in the least. Saturday, Sunday – what does it matter?'

IX

Christine had never planned to gatecrash Michael's Saturday tea party. But when the afternoon came and she wondered how she was to pass the long, futile hours that still separated her from the next day and so from Thomas, she decided that it was absurd to endure fretfully his absence when a ten-minute walk would take her to him. After all, she and Michael had never stood on any kind of ceremony with each other. But, nonetheless, as the walked up Broad Street and turned into the Balliol gates, she suspected that he would not be altogether pleased.

'Oh, Christine, how lovely to see you!' No, he was not pleased. But it was only because she knew him so well that she detected the falsity of his reception – beaming, head tilted to one side, arms widely outstretched as though to enfold her in a passionate embrace. 'You're just in time for a lovely cuppa, sweetie. 'Ow's me favourite daughter?' Sometimes his camp assumption, cockney accent and all, of the role of a working-class mum amused her, sometimes it irritated her. It irritated her now.

'Oh, I didn't come for that.' She had already prepared her excuse on the walk over. 'You promised me that Forrest Reid novel and as I had some time on my hands ...' She looked across at the Germans, who had all jumped to their feet at her entrance, and then became aware that there was also a girl seated on the sofa beyond them.

'Yes, of course, love. Which was the one you wanted then?

Was it that *Brian Westby*?' The working-class mum was still in charge.

'That's the one you recommend, isn't it?'

'Ooh, I don't know reely! But *Brian Westby* – that's the one the gentleman I do for gets all excited over.' Oh, if only he would stop this silliness! She wanted to tell him: 'Don't you see how snobbish and boring this turn of yours is?' He pulled the book down from its shelf. He always seemed to know the exact place of every book in his huge collection.

'Thank you. I'll take great care of it.' Tucking the book under an arm, she turned to the Germans, all of whom still remained standing. 'Oh, do sit down. Please.'

'Won't you really stay for a moment? Come on!' Thank God, he was now himself again.

'Well, perhaps for a moment.'

'Good. I'll get another cup.'

'Oh, no! Please don't bother!'

'No bother.' Only a slight pursing of the lips as he said this betrayed his real feelings. 'Now let me make a disgracefully belated introduction … This is Miss Bollinger – who is Ludwig's friend. This is Miss Holliday, Miss Bollinger.'

The girl on the sofa shook the amber bangle on her thin, bare arm, smiled across and said: 'Pleased to meet you, Miss Holliday.'

Having remained still standing despite Christine's urging them to sit, the Germans now advanced, one behind the other, to shake her hand. Ludwig came first, in the clothes that Michael had lent to Klaus two weeks before, his almost white eyelashes blinking rapidly behind his thick lenses. Then Klaus was beaming at her. The grip of his hand was strong but she noticed the pasty grey of his face and, as he turned away from her, she heard his hollow cough and saw how he had raised an arm to cover his mouth with the sleeve of his jacket. Finally Thomas was taking her hand. He pressed it, saying nothing, and smiled.

'Do you work in Oxford, Miss Holliday?' Ludwig's friend asked, as Christine lowered herself into the sofa beside her.

'Well, yes – if you can call it work. I'm up at Somerville.'

'Oh, so you're an undergrad then! I know quite a lot of the varsity boys but' – she laughed – 'you're the first varsity girl.' She began to fiddle with the heart-shaped locket that hung on a gold chain round her neck. 'Do you know Marcus Philipson? He's up at New. A grand family, I'm told. A member of that posh club, the Bullingham or something. President, I think.' Christine shook her head, not revealing that he was her cousin's latest boyfriend. 'Or Steve Canellopoulos? He's Greek. His family are all said to be tremendously rich.' Again Christine shook her head, although she had once been out in a punt with him and several others. 'Steve's an absolute scream and a scamp. Always playing some practical joke or other. But they do say that during the Occupation he did all sorts of absolutely heroic things. It's amazing – and lucky for me – that he didn't get himself killed.' She raised her teacup and daintily sipped from it. 'I meet a lot of the varsity crowd. You see, my business brings me into contact with them – quite literally in fact.' A brief giggle followed. 'That's how I met both Marcus and Steve.'

'What exactly do you do, Miss Bollinger?' Michael asked, having returned with a teacup for Christine.

'Oh, I teach ballroom dancing – at the Carfax School. Yes, I'm an LRCD – for my sins. I like the work because there's never any shortage of new faces. And one's always seeing life. Marcus is a terrific dancer, you know. There's little I can teach him but still he comes round, three o'clock on the dot every Thursday. He's a real perfectionist …' She ran on and on, but soon Christine was ceasing to listen to her.

By now Michael and Thomas had begun, as on that previous occasion, to talk to each other in low voices in German. Meanwhile Ludwig and Klaus were staring at the two women with childish expressions of pleasure on their faces. From time to time Klaus would put a hand over his mouth and emit a hollow, rattling cough until tears began to fill his eyes. Eventually Michael, breaking off his conversation with Thomas, jumped up and went across to him. He put a hand on his shoulder and said quietly in German: 'You shouldn't be coughing like this, Klaus. Have you seen the doctor?'

Klaus shook his head. His large, white teeth flashed as he smiled. 'It's nothing. Only my wound.' He tapped on his chest. To Christine his Prussian dialect sounded like a different language from Michael's formal German. 'It's often like this in this weather.'

Michael remained standing beside Klaus for several seconds, glumly silent. Then he repeated, this time in English, as though not for Klaus but for the others: 'You shouldn't be coughing like that.'

Miss Bollinger put her hands on her knees. 'Well, I suppose Ludwig and I must be hitting the road. I want to see that new flick with Anna Neagle and Michael Wilding, but Ludwig is dead keen to go to the *thé dansant* at the Forum, so I've given in – as per usual. Talk of a busman's holiday! Still …' She sighed as she pulled on her gloves. 'A *thé dansant* is really more up the poor dear's street. Apparently, they never have a hop at the camp.'

Ludwig slipped a proprietorial arm through hers. He grinned at them. 'Back in Berlin I once won a dance contest – Viennese waltz.'

A few seconds after the two had left the room, Ludwig was back. He crossed over to Michael and asked in a confidential whisper loud enough for the others to hear: 'Please, could you let me have some money? I'm sorry. A friend owes me money but he can't pay me for the moment.'

Michael hesitated. Then with an irritable shrug, he twitched a ten-shilling note out of his wallet and held it out, insultingly, between thumb and forefinger.

'Oh, this is too much!' But so far from making any effort to return the note, Ludwig was already stuffing it inside his tunic. 'Thank you, thank you, thank you.' He gave a little bow each time that he came out with the thanks.

When Ludwig had gone, Michael turned to Christine: 'In a rash moment I once told Ludwig that, if he ever needed anything, he must never hesitate to ask me. One tends to fling about that sort of invitation without really meaning it, doesn't one? I suppose it's salutary when someone has the courage to call one's bluff.' He turned to Thomas: 'Now you and Klaus go to the opposite extreme. I never know what you both need because you'd never dream of telling me.'

Klaus once again began to cough, doubling over, hands on knees, as he gasped for breath. 'Are you all right?' Michael asked sharply in German.

'Of course.' Klaus straightened, face congested, and grinned. 'I'm very strong. I never fall ill.' His mouth was agape and with each breath his nostrils distended. Suddenly he sank on to the sofa. He lay back in it, hands dangling, like some mute animal unable to understand the extent of its sufferings.

'How is the music going?' But Michael was still so much concerned about Klaus that he was not really listening to Thomas's reply.

'I think – well. My hand's already stronger. It's very kind of Miss Holliday –'

'Oh, call me Christine, please!' She did not wish Michael to know that Thomas had already been doing that.

'Thank you.' Thomas gave her a small nod. 'It's very kind of – of Christine to allow me to use her piano. You know, she plays very, very well herself.'

'Yes, I know,' Michael said vaguely, still preoccupied with Klaus. He pulled a gold cigarette case out from a jacket pocket and, without offering it to any of his guests, helped himself to a cigarette. The cigarette remained unlit between his lips until Thomas, having noticed, produced a lighter. 'Thank you.' Michael puffed twice. Then he exclaimed: 'Oh, I'm so sorry. You must think me very rude.' He held out the case to Christine, who shook her head, and then to Thomas, who also shook his head. Deliberately he did not hold out the case to Klaus.

Eventually Klaus produced a battered Oxo tin and drew from it the misshapen chipolata of a hand-rolled cigarette.

'Do you think you really ought to smoke?' Michael asked him in German. 'I didn't offer you one of mine because I thought it better for you not to have one. Didn't the doctor tell you –?'

Klaus gave a deprecating smile. 'One cigarette? It can't hurt me, Michael. How can one cigarette hurt me? Come on!'

'Nicotine's the worst possible thing for your lung.'

'There are so many things bad for one's health. Why live if one cannot do any of them?'

'Yes. But in your case, well, it really is crazy to smoke.'

'No, please. Listen.' He got up and went to crouch on his haunches beside Michael. 'I tell you, I'm strong. You can see how strong I am. It'll take more than one cigarette' – he held it up – 'to finish me off. You mustn't worry. Oh, Michael, please, you mustn't worry if I smoke this one small cigarette. See?'

'Oh, very well.' Michael spoke the German words with a petulance that was merely a screen for his continuing concern. 'In that case take one of these State Express. There's less danger from them than from those home-made gaspers of yours.'

Still squatting, Klaus took one. Then he put a hand on Michael's shoulder. 'Don't worry about me. Please.' He scrambled to his feet and seated himself in one of the armchairs. As, head back on its cushion and legs thrust out ahead of him, he inhaled the smoke deep into his lungs, from time to time he would smile or nod at the incomprehensible things that the others were saying in English around him. Then another ferocious spasm of coughing convulsed him. They all broke off their conversation to watch in alarm as the dry, hollow sound reverberated from what appeared to be the centre of his being. Eventually he jumped up, crossed over to the mantelpiece and, still coughing, thumped with his fist on its polished wood. His face was blotched with scarlet; tears welled from his eyes. He jerked up, put a hand to his mouth, and rushed from the room.

'Is he all right?' Christine asked. From the next-door bedroom the horrible coughing reverberated like a powerful machine that could not be switched off.

'I'll go and see.'

As Michael opened the bedroom door, they now heard sounds of violent retching.

'Are you all right?'

Klaus was supporting himself against the edge of the

washbasin, his head bent over it. The blond hair at the back of his neck was dark and damp with sweat. He straightened and attempted a smile. His face, recently so flushed from the effort of coughing, now had a greenish tinge around eyes and mouth. One hand went out to the tap and turned it off. Water swished round the basin as he said in German: 'Now I feel better. Much better. I'm sorry to have made such a scene.'

Michael noticed the single drop of bright arterial blood, high up on the basin, where the water had not reached it.

'Have you been coughing blood?'

Klaus gave a reassuring smile. 'It's nothing.'

'Klaus – have you been coughing blood?'

'A little. But I'm better now. See, I'm all right. It's always like that.'

'What? Does this often happen?'

'Not often. But when I cough badly, then I spit a little blood, and then I feel better. Nothing to worry about. Only my wound.'

'Of course it's something to worry about it. You're ill. *Ill*. I told you that you were ill. Oh, you're so stupid, Klaus. You must go straight back to the camp and see the doctor. At once!'

Klaus was bewildered and fearful. 'But there's nothing wrong with me. I told you. I'm quite well, Michael. You mustn't worry so much.'

'Oh, don't argue! I told you, told you not to smoke that cigarette. You're just a child. You don't know what you're doing.' A crisis of illness always flustered and exasperated Michael, as no other crises did.

Klaus hung his head, as though about to burst into tears.

'Well, let's get moving.'

'All right, Michael … Michael – I'm sorry.'

'Klaus's not at all well. He must get back to the camp and see the doctor.' Michael reverted to German as he turned to Klaus: 'Wrap that scarf of mine around you.' He pointed to where it hung from a peg on the door. 'And put on my overcoat.' He pointed again, and then himself rushed over to fetch it. Klaus stared at him in incredulity. 'Do as I tell you! It's madness your going about in this weather without even a sweater. I'm going to order a taxi and take you back myself.'

'But, Michael ...' In his amazement Klaus all but dropped the coat just thrust at him. 'There's no need for a taxi. I can walk.'

'In this weather? Are you crazy? Of course you can't walk. Do you realise how many degrees below zero it is?'

'But I tell you, Michael, there's nothing wrong with me! I've had this cough for many weeks now and I've been working every day in the fields – eight or nine hours. Tomorrow morning, if you wish, I'll see the doctor. He'll give me some medicine –'

'You're going to see him *now!*'

'But that's impossible. Unless it's urgent, very urgent, we're not allowed to see the doctor except in the morning.'

'I'm going to take you to see him at once. I'm going to go with you in the taxi to the camp and I'm going to see that you get the urgent attention you need.' Michael crossed to the telephone and began to ring for the taxi.

Klaus turned to Thomas: 'What's he doing? What does he mean? How can he come to the camp? It's forbidden. I'm not ill. Tell him, Thomas, tell him.'

'Michael knows what he's doing. You must trust him. He'll see that you get the best treatment.'

'I'm not ill,' Klaus repeated in a flat, peevish voice, more to himself than to Thomas. 'There's nothing wrong with me. I'm not ill.'

Michael put down the receiver. 'Come on, Klaus! The taxi will be round straightaway.' He turned to Thomas and said in English: 'You'd better come with us. You might as well save yourself the walk.'

Thomas hesitated. 'OK. Thank you.'

Michael now turned to Christine. 'Sorry to leave you like this. But you do see …'

'Of course. Is there nothing I can do?'

He shook his head. 'I don't think so, thank you.' Then with a fierceness that he rarely displayed, he went on: 'I'm going to kick up such a hell of a fuss that they'll have to send him straight to hospital. It's outrageous that he should be working in his condition. Fortunately the Commandant was also at Winchester – though not in my house. I've met him once or twice at ghastly old boy dinners. He wants to get his son into the college.'

Thomas crossed over to Christine. 'Goodbye, Christine. I'll see you tomorrow? Blenheim?'

'Yes, tomorrow, of course. Everything as we arranged.'

Now Klaus crossed over to her. He held out his hand, eyes lowered and a look of utter wretchedness on his face. '*Auf Wiedersehen,*' he muttered.

Suddenly, on an impulse, she turned to Michael: 'Oh, Michael, before he goes, do please tell him how beautiful I think that model of the red two-decker bus.'

'*What?*'

'Tell him in German for me. He won't understand in English.'

Exasperated – idiot woman, he thought, to hold them up at a moment like this – he hurriedly delivered the message.

Transformed, Klaus raised his head, beamed at her, and then, laughing with delight, rushed over to throw his arms around her. '*Danke, danke, danke!*'

'Now come on! Let's get going!'

Reluctantly Christine stepped back. '*Auf Wiedersehen*, Klaus. Good luck!'

His face had resumed its anxious, harried expression. She looked at him and gave a coaxing smile, as to a child in fear or distress. But he would not smile back. '*Auf Wiedersehen,*' he eventually returned, as though uncertain of her identity. With his left hand he jerked Michael's expensive scarf over his mouth. Then he turned away and hurried to the door. With a look of intense impatience, Michael had been holding it open for him.

X

When, on her return from Michael's disastrous tea party, Christine hurried out of the cold into the warmth of the Wellington Square house, Mrs Albert's son halted on his way up the stairs and stared down balefully at her through the horn-rimmed glasses always worn low on the bridge of his nose. 'Is that you, Miss Holliday?'

Ever since Thomas had started to visit the house, Ralph's attitude to Christine had changed from jaunty friendliness to glum hostility. He now rarely said good morning to her, often failed to pass on messages and on one occasion had deliberately slammed the front door shut when she was about to enter behind him.

'Yes. What is it?'

'A bloke's been asking for you. I told him he could wait in your room. Called Maxwell. I thought it safe to allow him in. I've met him once or twice at the Model Railway Club.'

'Thank you.'

'That's OK.' He continued up the stairs, whistling horribly out of tune to himself.

When, puzzled as to who this unexpected visitor might be, Christine entered her sitting room, it was to find a bulging rucksack on one of the two armchairs, a pile of books on the other, and Bill lying full length on the sofa, his feet up. He was reading a copy of *Lilliput*, picked up off her desk.

'Oh, it's you! My landlady's son told me that someone called Maxwell was waiting for me and I had no idea who it was, since I remember you only as Bill.' She stared at him. 'You've shaven off your lovely moustache.'

'Removing it was part of my effort to come to terms with the peacetime world. I can't be a perpetual fighter pilot. I hope it's all right my popping in unannounced. Damn cheek, I'm afraid. But I was passing this way on my journey up from the station and I suddenly thought, well, I might look up such an attractive girl. I hope you don't mind?'

'Of course not.'

'I ought really to have given you some warning. I've been wanting to come ever since I played such havoc with your feet on the dance floor at Branksome.'

'Well, why didn't you?' As she began to take off her coat, he rushed forward to help her.

'Oh, I don't know. I wasn't sure if you'd welcome a visit.' Having hung up the coat, he went across to the armchair on which the rucksack was resting. She cried out: 'What have you done with your shoes?' She had now noticed for the first time that he was in only his socks.

'They got soaked in the slush – just in the short walk from where I parked the old bus to the house. I hope you don't mind. Regard their removal as an act of respect, as in Japan.' He began to rummage in the rucksack. 'I've brought you a birthday present.'

She laughed. 'But it's not my birthday! Not until August – a long time away.'

'Never mind. Think of it as an unbirthday present. Or – if you prefer – you can keep it unopened until August. Dash it! Where's the bally thing got to?' He pulled out two crushed shirts and a pair of slippers, downtrodden at the heels, and dropped them to the floor. 'It must be somewhere here. I've been up to London. I meant to go for the weekend, that's why I took up all this clobber, but then I suddenly remembered that I had an essay to write for Monday. Well, I didn't remember, I knew all along, but my conscience pricked me – belatedly. Is your conscience like that? It's like having a stone in one's shoe. At first it doesn't worry one but then gradually ...' He was still rummaging in the rucksack. 'Ah, here it is!' He held up a small object untidily swathed in tissue paper. 'I hope you'll like it.'

'What is it?'

'Open it and see.'

Having pulled off the tissue paper, Christine peered down 'It's very beautiful. What is it exactly?'

'Well, I don't know how truthful the chap in the Kensington Church Street antique shop was being when he sold it to me, but he told me it was a Ming period snuff bottle. Who knows? Anyway I bought it. Do you really like it? I thought it suited you. Beautiful. Elegant.'

She turned it over in her hands. 'But I – I couldn't possibly...'

'Why not?'

'Well, we hardly know each other.'

'Oh, don't say that! Anyway – what possible use can it be to me? I've nowhere to put it.'

'Oh, come on! It's not all *that* large.'

'As soon as I saw it, I wanted to buy it not for myself but for you. And as for the money, I'm for once wonderfully rich. You see they pay me for my lost leg – not a lot but something – and then I have my grant. Again not a lot but something. Cheques for both came in last week.'

'But you should be saving. You seem to be terribly extravagant.'

'My last girlfriend came from a banking family and had

oodles of cash. But she was terribly mean. Not that that was why our relationship ended. She met an actor johnny and, understandably, she thought him a better bet than me.'

'What a sad story.'

'Yes. But, strangely, I wasn't sad for long.' He perched himself on the arm of the sofa, swinging his feet in their furry woollen socks. 'I'm not going to have you refuse my birthday present. It's very rude and hurtful of you. In any case I once borrowed some money off Ben in a pub and never had the chance to bung it back. So I'm trying to do so now.'

'Well, in that case … Thank you, thank you so much.' She stared at him. 'You know, I can hardly believe it's the same person. And I don't mean the death of the moustache. You're so different from last time.'

'Worse, you mean?'

'No, of course not worse. Just … different.'

'I have my ups and downs.' He fastened the straps of the rucksack, looked up and grinned. 'Which of us hasn't? But mine are more extreme than most people's, I imagine.' He again perched on the arm of the sofa. 'Today – don't ask me why – I feel on top of the world. Tomorrow – who knows? … Mind if I smoke my pipe?'

She shook her head.

He felt in his pockets. 'No matches.'

She fetched him a box of Swan Vestas from the mantelpiece. 'Here you are.'

'Thanks.' He began to light the pipe. 'Know anything about Gower?'

'Who?'

'No, you wouldn't. No sensible person would. He's the chap I've got to write my essay about. You know, after two years in a prison camp, reading non-stop, I thought I knew all about English literature. And then I came here and found that these professor johnnies had discovered a whole gaggle of writers I'd never even heard about. Gower! Oh, blast Gower!'

He attempted to lob the box of matches back on to the mantelpiece, misaimed, and hit the snuff bottle, which tottered and then crashed on to the tiled hearth below. 'Oh, lordy, lordy!' he groaned as it shattered. Then he burst into laughter. 'Eight pounds gone west!'

Christine stooped to pick up the fragments. She held some out on the palm of her hand. 'I'm afraid it can't be mended. Oh, dear! It was such a lovely thing.'

'People are always saying, "Something will always come along." But it would be more truthful to say, "Something will always go." And the more you value that something, the quicker the going happens.'

'Oh, don't be such a pessimist.'

'Well, then, let me be an optimist and invite you out to dinner.'

'Dinner? When?'

'No time like the present. Tonight. Now. Why not? Are you doing something?'

'No.'

'Good. Great. Poppet awaits us.'

'Poppet?'

'My jeep. I thought we could drive out to a place I know. On the river, near Abingdon. How about that?'

'Won't it be very cold?'

'No colder than the gardens of Branksome. When we arrive we can have lots and lots to drink. In fact, we can have lots and lots to drink before that. I have a whole bottle of Scotch in Poppet.'

Christine hesitated.

'Oh, do say yes!'

'All right.' The idea was crazy, with the temperature once again several degrees below zero; but she welcomed a possible relief from the depression that had enveloped her after the tea party.

When Bill had helped her up into the jeep and had arranged a tartan rug about her, he produced the promised bottle of Scotch. 'I should have a good swig now.'

'Neat?'

'That's the best way.'

She took a gulp and at once gagged and began to cough. Perhaps it was the coughing that reminded her of Klaus. All at once she was again thinking of him: where was he now, how ill was he, would he recover? Her own mother had died of TB, only a few months after a famous Scottish consultant, noted for his frankness as much as for his skill, had made the brutal diagnosis. The bottle still in her hands, she stared out at the few leafless trees around the Wellington Square gardens, while Bill attempted to start up the jeep's engine by hand, the snow falling around him. Poor Klaus! But if she continued to think about him, remembering above all that bleakly muttered '*Auf Wiedersehen*' as he had said goodbye to her, she would spoil the whole evening. Once again she put the bottle to her lips, threw back her head, and this time took gulp after gulp.

'Bravo! Good girl!' Bill, having at last succeeded in starting the engine, was now clambering into the jeep beside her.

In a miraculously short space of time, even as they were quitting the outskirts of Oxford, all her nagging thoughts of Klaus, Thomas and the other prisoners had been anaesthetised. Bumping and swaying through the February night, she even began to feel exhilarated.

'Cold?'

'No, not in the least. It's wonderful, absolutely wonderful.'

'I'm going to let Poppet have her head.'

As they roared down a straight, glimmering avenue of silver birches, Christine began to shout: 'Faster, faster, faster!' Her hand went out from under the rug and gripped his arm.

At last they drove into the silent, deserted yard of the 'place' that Bill knew. 'Well, well! Not a single banger in sight,' he commented. Christine swayed as they began to walk up the narrow path to the entrance. She giggled: 'Oh, dear, I think I'm a little tipsy. And this path's so slippery, isn't it? Oh, hell!' Her high heel had just splintered the ice sealing a puddle and water had splashed up over her ankle. 'This keeps happening to me in this hideous weather.'

'You'd better let me help you.'

She suffered him to put an arm round her waist, experiencing in this proximity of their two bodies a vague arousal.

In the summer this pub by the river would be crammed with people, many of them undergraduates. Cars would be parked, nose to tail, in the yard, in the lane and along the riverbank. But now, except for a subdued buzz of voices from the public bar and a solitary white van, blazoned 'Wilson and Daughter Quality Butchers' by the entrance, there was no sign of anyone.

Since the open fire in the dining room had not been lit, the elderly waitress, in black dress, white frilly apron and mob cap, laid their meal for them in the saloon bar, tenantless except for a single old man, who slept in a corner, with a half-drunk pint on the table before him. He opened an eye as they were shown in, and then went back to his snoring.

Gradually, as she made her way through a plate of roast duck, Christine sobered, and Bill's high spirits ebbed. Their conversation trickled, an all but exhausted spring, then dwindled and dried up. There followed a long silence, unbroken except by an occasional voice raised in the public bar and the sounds of their own dogged eating. Glancing up, as he removed a splinter of bone from between his teeth. Bill noticed the look of abstraction on Christine's face. 'Penny for your thoughts.'

'Oh, you'll have to pay more than that for them in these days of inflation.'

'Something's worrying you. Tell me.'

'It's nothing.'

'No. Do tell me. It may help. Or perhaps I can help.'

He spoke so gently and his sympathy was so manifest, his plain, irregular features expressing only the desire somehow to come to her aid, that she began to tell him not merely about Klaus, for whom her anxiety was still uppermost in her mind, but also, eventually, about Thomas. Then she broke off. 'What *has* come over me? I'm telling you things I've been reluctant to admit even to myself.'

'I'm flattered. And glad.'

'Perhaps the whole thing rather shocks you?'

'Shocks me? What does shock me is that you've put that question. Why should I be shocked?'

'Well, you were one of their prisoners, weren't you?'

'Yes. And it wasn't much of a picnic. I must admit that. But,' – he put out a hand and began to fidget with the cruet stand between them – 'after knowing so well what that sort of life can do to a chap, I' d hate to condemn even a Jerry to it. Because, you know, from my own experience at least, the real fun begins not *while* you're a prisoner but when it all ought to be behind you. Through the days of confinement something keeps you going – don't ask me what. But when you come out, you suddenly realise just how exhausted – not merely mentally but physically – you are.' He halted, and then pushed on. 'You know, sometimes, just sometimes, I wonder if I'll ever get back to normal.'

'Oh, you've got back to it already.'

He shook his head. 'It's like being in hospital for a major operation. Your body braces itself for the ordeal, and later you appear to have got through it unscathed. But then you go home and your convalescence starts. And you realise how weak and listless – and desperate – you really are.'

She gazed at him, at a loss what to say.

He shifted, then picked up his glass of draft cider and gulped at it. 'I can't pretend to be able to advise. But this – for what it is worth – is what I think. It may seem tough to you, but I have to tell it as I see it. If you do at last get married – if that does somehow happen – then don't imagine that'll be an end of your problems. It won't. There'll be other problems – perhaps even worse ones.' He shook his head. 'I'm not trying to discourage you, far from it. But, unlike Gower, this is something I do know far more about than most people. Of course, if he has you waiting for him, through thick and thin, then that'll be more than half the battle. But even so …'

'You're finding it difficult now, aren't you?'

He rested his short, nicotine-stained fingers on the edge of the tablecloth and stared down at them. Then he looked up. 'Yep. I don't know why it is. When they amputated the leg, I sometimes think that they also amputated some essential part of me up here.' He tapped his forehead. 'But then, perhaps it all has nothing whatever to do with the war. Perhaps the war has become merely a convenient excuse for me. I suppose I was always a bit of a drifter. And the fact that my father was a successful insurance agent made the drifting easy and comfortable for me. I can't stick to things. I just give up.' He grinned. 'This essay now. I came back from London with the intention of doing it. But I know now that I won't. Tomorrow I'll get out all the books, perhaps I'll even work on them for an hour or two. Then … I'll decide I want a drink – oh, just to oil the works, you understand. So I'll pop over to the boozer – the Lamb and Flag or whatever takes my fancy – and I'll meet some of the chaps and we'll have a ploughman's together – and talk – and talk. And then I may even take two or three of them for an airing in Poppet. And the essay? Another tutorial will be a washout on Monday morning.'

'But how long can that go on? Won't the college eventually make a row?'

'Of course. Eventually. The Warden, my tutor, the dean – they're all very understanding. I'm an ex-serviceman, a former POW – that makes a difference. They feel guilty that I was going through all that while they were – most of them – reading and writing about Gower or doing whatever other civvy jobs their reserved occupations or their asthma or varicose veins allowed them to pursue.'

She was surprised, even shocked by the bitterness with which he spoke the last sentence.

He went on: 'I think the Warden – Bowra – must have taken some sort of shine to me, God knows why. He's not generally regarded as a kindly or tolerant sort of chap. But with me he puts up with so much.'

'Michael knows him well. He says he would betray even a close friend for a joke.'

'Well, at least the jokes are good. When he eventually kicks me out, no doubt there will be a joke to explain why he has done so. Anyway – sooner or later, probably sooner, he will make that decision. But as things are at present,' – he laughed gleefully – 'they've decided in their infinite wisdom that I must see an elderly female trick cyclist somewhere in the remotest arctic wastes of Headington. That must mean that they really are near the end of their patience.'

'And then? After you leave?'

'Oh, lord knows. Why think about it? I'd rather like to become the sort of hermit that used to be so common in the eighteenth century. For an aristo to keep a pet hermit then was an even classier act than having a black pageboy or a baboon. Some hugely wealthy and cultivated landowner would provide me with a hovel with all mod cons and some scraps from the kitchen. No responsibility, no brainwork, no work of any kind in fact – and, best of all, no need to see anyone I didn't wish to see … It's weird. You know, before the war, I was tremendously ambitious. I was as crazy about earning money, lots and lots of it, as my dear old dad. And now – I just couldn't care less.'

'You must learn to care again.'

In his shabby Harris tweed jacket, its cuffs and elbows patched with leather, his grey RAF shirt and his grubby, creaseless flannels, so that, even when he stood up, she could see his thick, grey woollen socks, he had, from that first sight of him sprawled on the sofa earlier that evening, struck Christine as a pathetic figure. Now, with his searing frankness about his own inadequacies, he had intensified that impression.

'I must, must take a good pull on myself,' he said at last. 'But I've tried often enough. No success. There was once a girl – before the one I've already told you about. Waited all the time I was a prisoner, wrote every week. When I came back she at once noticed the change. Told me so. I promised to buckle down to things, work hard, give her the things she wanted. Somehow all those resolutions came to damn all. I drifted up to Oxford and she decided I no longer cared for her. Perhaps she was right? Who knows? Anyway the whole thing fizzled out. She's now married to a man at least twenty years older and the two of them run a small bed and break-fast in Torquay. Perhaps she sometimes now wonders if she ought not to have stuck with me? I doubt it.' He lumbered to his feet. 'Some coffee?'

'Lovely.'

He gave the order through the hatch and then returned, swaying between the tables as though it were now he, and not she, who was tipsy.

'Tell me. Be frank. If you were given the chance – if he wanted it and it was possible – would you marry this chap?'

'Of course.' She spoke without hesitation. 'What else? I love him very much.'

'Good for you!' Suddenly he had emerged from his mood of mournful introspection. 'Oh, I like your guts, I really do. You know, Ben once said that about you – he liked your guts.'

'I wonder what he'd say about Thomas.'

'"Good luck" – I hope.'

'These last few days I've kept thinking – am I letting him down? After all – he *was* killed fighting against them.'

'There I can't help you, I'm afraid. I've not an atom of feeling about the dead – apart of course from a sadness that they've vanished. They're dead – so what? We're alive. One's loyalties to the living are complicated enough without worrying about our loyalties to the dead. Does that sound callous? I suppose I had to make myself think like that during those years when friends – many even younger than myself – kept getting picked off.'

He got up, crossed to the wireless at the other end of the room, and twiddled with its knobs. The old man who had been dribbling peacefully in his sleep in the farthest corner – a tobacco-stained stream has coursed down his chin and then left slug trails on his waistcoat – stirred, grunted and sat up. The whole of the lower half of his face was covered in short, whitish bristles. He scowled first at the wireless and then at Christine and Bill. Eventually, having picked up his tankard, he limped through to the public bar.

'Oh, what a shame! We've turned him out.'

'Does it matter? Let's dance.'

'Here?'

'Why not? I can push these tables to one side. I want to show you how much I've improved. I've been taking lessons.'

'Not at the Oxford School of Dancing?'

'Yes. How did you guess?'

'From Miss Bollinger?'

'From Miss Bollinger. A real bottle of fizz. None other.'

She laughed and began to tell him about meeting with her at one of Michael's tea parties.

'I'm very grateful to Miss Bollinger,' he said, as they now began to move around the deserted room. 'I've learned a lot from her. Don't you think so?'

'You certainly have. Last time you held me as though I were a time bomb.'

'If you'd been Miss Bollinger, you'd have said "Tighter, duckie" – as she did at my first lesson. Now I'm often her duckie – or ducks.'

Next time that they passed the wide, uncurtained window, they stopped, as if by mutual consent, to peer out into the night. On the terrace, a tarpaulin covering some stacked chairs and tables was luminous with frost. The lawn, on which in summer teas were served, glimmered empty under a sky crowded with stars. Beyond it, there was a constant flash and sparkle from the swollen river as the wind ruffled it.

They drifted on again: towards the fire, the untidy, casual remnants of their meal, the boom and buzz of voices and the clink of glasses through the open hatch; towards things safe and familiar after that desolate view beyond the window. They were now dancing close, without saying a word. Anyone who saw them might think that they were lovers.

Suddenly she experienced a flare of resentment that this man who held her so closely, with such a palpable tenderness, was not that other man who had never once held her in any way whatever. At that she had to resist the temptation to push him away from her, to leave the warm, shabby, comfortable room, and to go out, alone, through the French windows into the dark and cold.

He was saying something.

'What? I'm afraid I wasn't listening.'

'I said, I can't help envying that German. He's a damned lucky chap.'

XI

Michael had been wonderful. Thomas had nothing but praise for the way in which he had handled the whole situation. Klaus had left the camp that morning, no one knew for what hospital. Poor Klaus! He could not understand all the fuss.

'What do you think is the matter with him?'

'Michael's sure that it must be tuberculosis. He says it's criminal that they didn't notice sooner. Perhaps he has given it to others.' He laughed. 'Perhaps to me. He was always coughing over me.'

'Oh, God, I hope not!'

He crossed to the window and peered out, tapping with the fingers of his left hand on the frosty glass. 'I ought to have realised that he was so ill.'

'But he himself didn't realise it!'

'I know I was not in the same hut, but yet … I was his friend. I heard him cough, I knew he was often in pain, and I did nothing, nothing at all. It was an Englishman who did something.'

Moved by the desolation of his guilt, Christine went across to him and put an arm round his shoulder. 'Oh, Thomas, it's absurd to blame yourself. If anyone is to blame, it's Klaus himself. That's obvious.'

He swung round in anger. 'Do you blame your dog if he is ill, terribly ill, and you don't notice?' Once again he turned to stare out of the window. He shrugged. 'But maybe – maybe you are right. In the camp every man must fight for himself.

That is how it is. Each day – a battle.' He turned. 'Well … Do we go to Blenheim?'

'It's just as you wish. If you'd rather not …'

'No, no!' He picked up the soft, brown trilby that Michael had lent him and put it on before the mirror. 'I'm not used to such a hat. I think that I look funny perhaps?' He turned to show himself to her, hand to brim.

'Well, yes … Perhaps just a little. Pull it more over one eye. Like this!' She went over and showed him what she meant. As she did so, she felt an almost irresistible impulse to slip her hand down from the brim along the smooth surface of his temple and his cheek. She broke away. 'Where did I put my coat?'

The gloom in which their talk of Klaus had enveloped them remained throughout the bus ride to Woodstock, keeping them silent. In any case, Thomas preferred not to make himself conspicuous by talking in an accent so obviously German. Michael's clothes, which had seemed so grotesque on Klaus, fitted him well. True, his shoulders were a little too broad and he had to wear the trousers low on his hips, but otherwise it would be hard to guess that the suit had not been tailored expressly for him. He looked like any ex-service undergraduate, and if from time to time people glanced at him, it was not because they suspected him of being an impostor, but merely because of his good looks.

When they reached Blenheim the sun was already foundering. Momentarily, the windows of the palace caught its oblique rays and brimmed with fire, each becoming a peephole into the conflagration, so that it seemed as if, even while they watched, the flames would burst through, the roof would collapse, and the whole great edifice would tumble, subside and then disintegrate into a million particles of light.

But in a few seconds all was over. The sun descended into mist; the fire ebbed; the windows were once more windows. Everything was bare, moist and chill.

All that day it had been thawing, so that, as they tramped through the solitary park, the slush wet their feet and the trees wet their clothes. Noises of invisible dripping were all around them. Far off, they could hear a roar of water descending into Capability Brown's artificial lake. Yet, for all its dampness, dimness and melancholy, the place retained its beauty. The dying light, the lake, stretching out into the mist, the wavering, barely perceptible outlines of the trees and, beyond, the fantastic outline of the palace – all these things, despite the evanescence of their presences, combined to make an overwhelming impression on them, so that their sadness over Klaus seemed all at once to have taken on an external form, desolate and yet also strangely comforting.

As they stopped to gaze at the bridge, Christine edged closer to Thomas and slipped an arm through his. But to this gesture he made neither repudiation nor response. When they walked on, her arm remained where she had placed it.

He was speaking now about the scenery around his home. But Christine had ceased to listen. There were so many other things that she must somehow get to discuss with him. But how would she dare? And, having dared, what would she gain from it? This was the man, of all men, for whom she would be willing to sacrifice herself not once but a thousand times; but – yes, she was certain of it – he would never want or allow that. Oh, how she wished that she could be rid of her obsession, manifested as much in her constant longing to clutch his arm, to stroke his hair or to run a hand down a cheek or across his forehead, as in her desperate waiting for each weekend that would bring him back to her for a few brief hours.

How it then happened she did not know. Sometimes, thinking about it later, she decided that she must have willed it to happen. But was it possible to simulate a fall so neatly? – the foot touching the ice, slipping, the hand flung out, the whirl around, each intricate movement timed as precisely as June's in a ballet, until his arm came across to save her.

Then they were clutching each other, her face first against his coat and then raised questingly upwards to his. She could hear him mutter something in German, incomprehensible to her.

'What are you saying?'

'I'm asking myself – why am I so lucky?'

His saliva tasted bitter as his mouth closed on hers, but strangely that did not disgust her. She only felt a deep pang of pity for him, knowing about the wretched diet on which the prisoners subsisted.

'Is that right?' he asked

'Is what right?'

'For me to love you. What future for us?'

'Oh, don't talk about the future!'

'But some time we must talk about the future!'

'But not now.'

'Oh, Christine, you must understand that I am –'

'No, not now. Not now.'

She put a hand over his lips. Then, removing it, she again sought his mouth with her own, once more tasting the saliva that seemed to have in it all the accumulated bitterness of his captivity.

'I live only for the present.' She slipped an arm through his. 'You must learn to do the same. Only for the present.'

'Only for the present?' He shook his head, smiling. 'I will try.'

He said the last three words on a note of weariness that made her feel anxious and ashamed.

'This way?' He pointed. Arm in arm, so close that sometimes they stumbled over each other, they had neither of them heeded in which direction they were walking. Now they had lost themselves. 'Yes, I think so.'

'But surely the village is over there?' Christine pointed to the left.

'No. This way, I think.'

She laughed. 'Does it matter anyway?'

'A little. You forget – we must catch the bus. And I must be back at the camp in time.'

'Heavens! How prosaic you are!'

'Prosaic?'

'Unromantic.'

'It is not good for a prisoner to be too romantic. See what has happened to me.'

Again she felt a sharp twinge of anxiety and guilt. 'Poor Thomas!'

'Do you know when I first realised?'

'Realised what?'

'That I love you, of course.'

'*Do* you love me?'

'Of course.'

She had put the question playfully; now the calm reply had brought her not joy but a foreboding chill.

'Well, it was the first time I saw you,' he went on. 'Do you remember how my face became red and I could say so little?' Yes, she remembered. In his coarse clothing and cumbersome boots, he had struck her as being himself coarse and cumbersome. 'I think it was then that I fully realised what it was to be a prisoner. I left the room ashamed of my uniform, my heavy boots, my dirty cap, my – my embarrassment, my English. Everything. You looked so – so *clean*.' He laughed, pressing her close against him as he did so. 'Yes, that's a funny thing to tell a girl. But nothing at the camp – and no one – ever seems truly clean. Even the guards, the officers … We wash, wash, wash – floors, clothes, toilets, our bodies. But the dirt stays, always stays. A smell. Spots. Stains.' He broke off, swivelling his body from side to side as he sought in vain for some landmark. 'Now truly we are lost!' He peered again into the mist.

'No, we're not. Listen. I can hear traffic on the main road. Beyond those fields there.'

'That's no traffic.'

'Don't be silly! Of course it is. We've only to walk across the fields. We can slip through the barbed wire here.'

He looked unconvinced.

'You don't believe me?'

He smiled and shook his head.

'I bet you five bob. Do you take me on?'

'If you win, I won't be able to pay you.' All at once a look of humiliation came over his face. 'You're with a man who can't pay even his own bus fare.'

'I wish you wouldn't talk like that. You keep going on and on about not being able to pay for this or that. Naturally you can't pay for things. That's understood. Forget it.'

'Still …' He raised his shoulders in resignation. Then he burst out: 'Perhaps I'm stupid, but I don't like always eating other person's food, always spending other people's money. First it was Michael. Now it's also you.'

Shouts battered at them through the mist; vague figures

emerged only to disappear again. A football materialised in mid-air and thudded to the ground with a whisk of slush. Three boys, with bare, red knees, red faces and cropped hair, collided together as they ran towards it; then they saw Christine and Thomas and skidded to a halt.

Christine approached them. 'I wonder if you could tell us – is the main road over there?'

'It is. But you can't go through this way.' The tallest of the boys, who must have been ten or eleven, had picked up the football and placed it under his arm. His raw face, saddle-nose covered in freckles, expressed an overweening hostility.

'Oh, why not?'

'Because this is private land, that's why. Didn't you see the barbed wire? Or the notice? All this land belongs to my father. It's his farm.'

'But surely he wouldn't mind –? You see, we've been stupid and got lost. And we're afraid we might miss our bus if we don't get to Woodstock soon.'

The boy put his hands on his hips, dropping the ball to the ground. 'You can't go through,' he repeated.

'But that's ridiculous. We can't turn back. We don't even know the way. It'll be dark quite soon.'

'That's your lookout. Shouldn't have come through in the first place.'

The other two, smaller boys, their stockings rucked about their ankles and their shorts pinched in at the waists by identical snake belts, had so far only scowled at the intruders. But at this point one of them chimed in, in a shrilly girlish voice: 'Serves you right for trespassing.'

'We're not trespassing,' Christine snapped back. 'We've done no harm.'

'Well, you're jolly well not going a step farther. That's flat.

Otherwise I'll go and tell my father. He'll see you off. And damn quick too!'

Thomas, who had so far refrained from joining in the argument, touched Christine's elbow. 'We'd better turn back.'

'Certainly not! And let these little creatures boss us around? Come on. Don't take any notice of them.' Thomas hesitated, looking from her to the boys and then back again. 'Come *on*!'

'We don't want any trouble. While I'm wearing these clothes,' he added in a low voice, 'and I'm more than five miles from the camp, outside the zone allowed.'

'What trouble *can* we get into?' His caution maddened her.

She had said this loud enough for the boys to hear. 'You'll soon see,' the oldest threatened. The three of them had tightened into a close, menacing group.

Christine strode forward and Thomas, after a second or two, followed. As she moved, the boy sprang out to bar her path, but she pushed him aside. He raised a hand to strike at her, but then thought better of it. 'I'll tell my father,' he shouted. 'You attacked me!'

'Oh, go to hell!' Thomas called out over his shoulder.

'Go to hell yourself!' one of the two younger boys screamed, and the other then added: 'Bloody foreigner!'

As Christine and Thomas hurried over the mist-blanketed field, they could hear the boys behind them, jabbering excitedly among themselves or raising a voice to shout an occasional insult. Something splashed a short distance away from them. 'What was that?' Christine asked. Again there was a splash as a snowball exploded at her feet, drenching her shoes and stockings. 'That'll teach you!' an invisible voice jeered.

Looking over her shoulder Christine had a glimpse of a barbarically triumphant face before the hat borrowed from Michael was knocked off Thomas's head. As he picked it up, attempting to brush away the granules of coffee-coloured ice with the sleeve of his coat, he swore in German under his breath. Then he said: 'Wait for me. I'm going back to them.'

'What can you do? What's the good? I suppose we're in the wrong. In any case we don't want a row. Oh, come on!'

Again and again snowballs hit them. Their clothes were soaked; the muddy slush stung their faces and melted on their shoulders. At last they saw the roadway glimmering ahead. 'The beasts! The filthy little beasts!' Christine gasped. At the rim of the field Thomas held the barbed wire up for her as she attempted to squeeze through; but such were her exasperation and haste that the hem of her dress got caught, she tugged and a large rent appeared. At the same moment more slush spattered outwards from the hard surface of the road.

As they hurried off, they heard behind them: 'Go on! Get out of it! Beat it!'

'Oh, Thomas, Thomas, Thomas!' Now that they had turned the corner of the road and could no longer hear their persecutors, Christine clung to him, sobbing with hatred and humiliation. His own face was pinched and grey, as he gasped again and again for breath. 'How cruel, how needlessly cruel! And my legs are drenched!'

'I wish you'd let me go back.'

'To do what?'

'To punish them.'

'Oh, what would have been the good? It would probably have ended in the police court, and you, being a prisoner, in civilian clothes … Oh, how unjust it all is!'

'Michael's suit will have to be cleaned. How can I explain to him?'

'Tell him what happened. He'll understand.' He shook his head. 'Why not?'

'Because …' He paused. 'No, I'll tell him something else.'

'But why? Why?'

'I feel – *beschämt* – ashamed. That those three – three *children* …'

'Ashamed?'

'Yes, *yes!*' he repeated in a sudden access of fury. 'See what they do to you. And I? I do nothing, nothing at all. We run away.'

'But what else could we do?'

'I don't know.'

'Then what's the point of talking about it?' she demanded, all at once exasperated.

'No.' He drew away from her, the arm that had been around her shoulder falling limply to his side. 'You haven't understood me.'

They trudged on in silence until they came to the bus stop, and there, still in silence, hunched deep in their soaking clothes, they waited until they saw the blurred lights of the bus moving slowly down from the crest of the hill.

'Oh, how I wish I'd been with you!' Michael exclaimed. He had clearly been amused, not shocked or angered, by Christine's narration, even though in the course of it he had from time to time made some such interjection as 'Oh, you poor things!' or 'Oh, what brutes!'

'I can assure you, you wouldn't have enjoyed it.'

'Oh, I don't know. Tell me more about these little savages.'

'There's nothing more *to* tell. Let's drop the subject. It was a thoroughly nasty experience but, now, thank God, it's all over.'

'Yes, but what did they look like?'

Reluctantly Christine described them as best she could, while he exclaimed: 'Yes! Oh, of course, of course!' Then, when she had finished: 'Yes, I can just see them … The football, the grey flannel shirts, the snake-belts … It's all just right. Perfect in every detail. But tell me about their accents?'

'Their accents?'

'Well, were they proles? Or were they, as they say, out of the handkerchief drawer?'

Christine had had enough. 'I don't know.'

Thomas had been glancing at his watch. 'Michael, I think I must go.' Instead of at once getting into his uniform, he had been sitting before the fire, feet bare, in the flannel pyjamas and dressing gown that Michael had insisted that he put on, telling him 'We don't want you to catch a chill.'

When Thomas now went into the bedroom, Michael jumped up and followed him. Christine all but followed too; then she retreated back to the chair in which she had been sitting. That she too had been drenched had caused Michael little concern. 'If you sit by the fire – next to Thomas – you'll dry out more quickly,' he had told her. He had then produced a towel. That was all.

All at once she was consumed with the desire to know precisely what it was that was passing between them. She went out into the hall and stood there, straining to listen. There was a laugh from Michael, followed by an odd word or phrase here and there from one or the other. Nothing more. The thickness of the college walls frustrated any effective eavesdropping.

Ashamed of her failed attempt, she returned to the

sitting room. There, she reached out for the book lying, face downwards, on the table beside her. *Tales of the Hasidim* by Martin Buber. Was there any subject to which Michael did not extend his omnivorous – or should it be dilettante? – interest.

Now she felt not merely exasperation but also anger at their prolonged absence. Could it be that she resented their obvious affection for each other? She had always despised possessive women – those who wished to open every door and ransack every cupboard in the lives of their men folk. Was she herself now becoming such a woman?

'So you poor things had rather a miserable afternoon?'

She started at the voice. Michael had returned, by himself.

'Well, that incident wasn't all that pleasant. But otherwise – I really enjoyed it. I love Blenheim in winter. No people, that superb architecture seen through a mist, those beautiful, bare trees.'

Michael sat down at the farther of two desks, picked up a letter and began to read it. She had a strange feeling that she must on no account watch him and turned her head aside.

Then he put down the letter and she heard: 'He's a nice chap. Isn't he?' He might have been referring to anyone, even the writer of the letter, but she knew that he was referring to Thomas.

'I like him. We get on well. We have the music in common.'

'Yes, of course. There's that.' Abruptly he jumped to his feet. 'You know – you're both somehow – somehow *changed*.'

'Changed? I don't get you. In what way?'

'That's what I'm trying to puzzle out for myself. Unless, of course, you tell me.'

'Tell you? Tell you what?'

'Oh, never mind!'

'I wish I knew what you were driving at.' But she thought that she could guess. She laughed. 'Sometimes you can be really maddening, you know.'

He shrugged. 'Forget it.'

At that moment Thomas returned. For some reason, he had parted his long, dark hair in the middle. Christine decided that it did not suit him that way and almost said so.

'You know, Thomas, I almost think you look better in that grubby uniform of yours than in my civvies. What do you think, Christine?'

'I prefer civilian clothes. I've never found uniforms in the least exciting. I always hated it when Ben wore his.'

'I thought a woman could never resist a uniform.' He jumped up. 'Thomas, I must tell you, your English has so much improved. Even Ludwig must be impressed by how much better your accent is.'

'Well …' Thomas smiled across at Christine. 'Now I have practice with Christine. Often she corrects me. She can be severe, you know.'

'It's wonderful you've found such a good mistress.'

To Christine that last word administered a sudden, unnerving jolt. Surely most people would have said 'such a good teacher'? Had he used 'mistress' as a snide indication of what he imagined now to be the nature of their relationship with each other?

Unaware of any possible nuance between the one word and its alternative, Thomas glanced from Christine to Michael, bewildered by an animosity that he sensed but could not define. 'I think I must go.' He looked at his watch. 'I'm late already. I'll probably have to find a way through the barbed wire.'

'Oh, I hope no one will see you,' Christine said.

He smiled. 'I did it many times.'

'I've done it many times,' she corrected. 'Do remember that.' She was constantly telling him that he must not muddle his tenses.

'I've done it many times.'

Michael patted him on the boulder. 'Bravo, old chap! You're getting the hang of it.' He turned to Christine. 'You mustn't worry too much about your pupil.'

Christine walked part of the way to the camp with Thomas, through narrow, unlit streets and alleys where there was less chance of anyone noticing his prisoner's uniform so late in the evening. They moved swiftly and did not talk to each other. As though in celebration of the end of the blackout, many of the curtains on the windows of the houses that they passed still remained undrawn, to provide momentary glimpses of a table laid for supper, a head bowed over needlework or a newspaper, two people in conversation before a fire or leaning forward to listen to a wireless set on a table between them: things that now seemed oddly remote, oddly unfamiliar to Christine.

Thomas had halted. 'Here we must say goodbye.'

'Oh, but I'll come a little further with you.'

'It's better not. I must take the short way across fields, not to be late. It'll be difficult for you to find your way back. And, besides, it's very rough. You've got wet once already today.'

She drew him into the unlit doorway of a small house that, to judge from its state of advanced dilapidation, must be uninhabited, perhaps even condemned. She put her hands on his shoulders and pulled him towards her. She held him tight, thrillingly aware of his growing erection.

Eventually, he broke off their kiss with an abrupt jerk of his head. 'Goodbye,' he muttered. But he was still reluctant to let her go, pressing still hard against her.

'When shall I see you again? Can't you possibly come during the week?'

'Impossible. Sorry. I'm working now. Have you forgotten? No more Brussels sprouts. Tomorrow, I must help to dig the new road.'

'Then it'll have to be Saturday. Oh, dear!'

'No, not Saturday. Sorry. I have Michael on Saturday. But perhaps you can also come – ?'

'Does Michael matter all that much?'

He gazed out over her shoulder into the distance. Then he looked down at her and smiled. 'Okay! I come to you on Saturday.'

'I'*ll* come to you on Saturday,' she corrected, suddenly remembering that rebarbative phrase 'a good mistress'. 'Oh, it seems such a long, long time. But – never mind.' She sighed. 'Oh, well, goodbye, sweetie.'

'Goodbye.'

Again they kissed, even more ardently than before, and again she felt his erection hardening against her. Then he was moving off at a slow trot, like an exhausted runner completing a marathon, into the dark and cold. Motionless, gloved hands clasped before her, she peered down the alley with its gleaming cobbles, its dustbins and its smells of cats and urine, until he vanished round a corner. Then she looked around her, in vain, for someone to ask for the nearest bus stop.

Saturday. He would come on Saturday. He would come to her and not to Michael. To her, to her. Her victory filled her with a crude sense of triumph.

XII

As soon as they had embraced, Christine stood back and stared.

'What's the matter?' she asked.

'Nothing's the matter. What do you mean?'

She shook her head. 'Oh, I don't know.' But she did know, even if she would have been at a loss to explain how she did. Their relationship had altered as decisively as it had during their visit to Blenheim. 'You – you look so worried.'

'Maybe I'm tired.' He slouched, shoulders hunched, over to the door and hung his cap on one of its hooks. He moved to the sofa, peered down at it, and perched himself on its edge. She had an impulse to put out a hand and push him back into a more comfortable position.

'Have you been working hard?'

'Oh, yes. Very hard.'

'Put your feet up. That cover's so shabby and grubby that it doesn't matter. Here. Let me help you.' She stooped to lift up one of his clumsy army boots, but he pulled the leg away.

'No, no! I don't want to dirty your sofa.'

'But I can put a newspaper there.'

'Not necessary.'

She gave up. She flung a cushion down by his feet and lowered herself, cross-legged, on to it. 'Tell me your news. What's been happening to you?'

'You must never ask a prisoner for his news. He has no news. Everything is always the same. No change. Tea still without milk and sugar. Still bugs in the hut. Still snow and cold. All, all the same.'

Disturbed, she gazed up at him. 'Poor Thomas! Is it beginning to get you down?'

'Beginning! A long beginning.' Tilting his head on to the back of the sofa, he closed his eyes for four or five seconds.

'The only consolation is that life might be even more horrible in Germany.'

'That's no consolation.' Silence. Then: 'And you? What have you been doing?'

'Oh, nothing special.' She did not have the heart to go through her week. Uneventful and unexciting as most of it had been, it must certainly have been better than his.

'Tell me, please. Tell me.'

'Well, if you'd really like to hear …'

'Yes, I wish to hear. Tell me.'

'Oh, all right then.'

On one afternoon, she began, Bill had come to see her but she had been out; he had left a bunch of flowers wrapped in cellophane, which for some unaccountable reason she did not pick up from the table where he had left them, until Margaret came in, exclaimed, 'What a huge bunch! They must have cost a fortune', and offered to arrange them.

On another afternoon, alone at a Playhouse matinee, she had seen Michael, forlornly slumped ahead of her in the half-empty stalls. Having overcome a reluctance to seek him out in the interval, she had found him surprisingly sympathetic and friendly. As they sipped cups of lukewarm, bitter tea and crunched Marie biscuits, it seemed absurd that they should so recently have been so disagreeable with each other.

On Thursday she had heard from her widower father. He

wrote incoherently, referring to information that he had forgotten ever to give her, and scratching out whole paragraphs so cursorily that she was still able to read them. He was worried about money (was he ever not worried about money, despite his pension and investments?); the doctor had started to give him some different injections for blood pressure; and he was once more considering whether to resign from the presidency of the local branch of the British Legion. This letter Christine had still not answered, although she knew that the delay would upset him.

On Friday there had been a tutorial, with Mrs Dunne yet again showing displeasure, this time over an inadequate Latin prose. 'Are you really quite well?' she had once again asked. Christine had wanted to reply: 'No. I'm lovesick.'

Through all this Thomas listened with what she was sure was a genuine, if surprising, interest. From time to time he asked a question – how old was Bill, what was the play to which she had gone, had her father been an army officer, did Mrs Dunne have children? – as though any information about her life would more closely knit together a relationship that was in danger of unravelling. Sometimes, if he did not understand some word or phrase, he would interrupt her to ask its meaning.

Having finished her account, she realised, with sudden dismay, that in fact she had revealed to him nothing of what had been happening to her at a far more profound level than that of these trivial, tedious incidents: nothing of the alternating excitement and boredom, joy and despair, in which she had passed the interminable days that had separated her from him. There were periods when she had been totally indifferent to the world around her, moving in a meandering, intoxicating dream, and others when she had lain on the sofa brooding about the future, *their* future, in a darkness from which there seemed to be no possibility of ever emerging. Last night she had fallen asleep thinking joyously 'He loves me, I love him'; but the night before, restlessly awake through the desolate early hours, she had asked herself all those questions – how, when, where? – with which, she had persuaded herself, their lives would be increasingly tormented.

But of all this she made no mention. At any other time she might have done so, but today she felt afraid of revealing to him the obsessive, unwearying impetus of her love, guessing, she could not have said why, that by doing so she would further darken the gloom in which she had found him.

Thomas had begun to caress her. But as his hands moved over her body, she became despairingly convinced that all this tenderness was no more than his way of putting out of his mind, in a transient stimulation of the senses, all the difficulties and decisions that were weighing on him.

Unable to remain motionless any longer under his increasingly exploratory touch, she twisted round with a small groan, placing her arms around him, her head in his lap. Now even his uniform, with its stale, sour smell and its abrasiveness against her cheek, added to the anguished pleasure of their contact. He in turn put his arms around her, pressing her closer and closer, until, overcome by physical discomfort, he finally released her. But still she clung on to him, as they had clung on to each other that afternoon at Blenheim under the ceaselessly dripping trees, waiting as if for some unseen disaster – a bomb, an earthquake, a stroke of lightning.

'No! No!' He had jumped to his feet. 'Better if I go now.'

Still crouched on the floor, she began clumsily to button the front of her blouse. 'Go? What on earth do you mean?'

'Sorry. Mistake. My mistake.' The way in which he isolated each of these words, speaking them as if he had learned them by rote in a tongue unknown to him, imbued them with a peculiarly desperate emphasis. He extended his arms towards her. 'Forgive me, Christine. I love you – truly I love you. Of course. But. No.' He shook his head. 'Best I never come again. Believe me – that is best. Forget me, forget me, Christine.' He turned away, reaching out for the cap that he had thrown on to a chair

'What *is* all this? What are you talking about? Have you gone crazy?'

'No, it's life that's crazy.' He blinked, blinked again. He pointed to the sofa. 'Sit. Not on the floor. Here. Sit.'

She obeyed him. 'Well?'

'I've been thinking. All week I've been thinking.' He spoke quietly, almost meditatively. 'What happened at Blenheim, what has happened to us. For that, yes, I am happy. But also, also sad.'

'Oh, but, Thomas –'

He put a hand over her mouth, so roughly that she felt the sharp impact of his forefinger on her upper lip, pressing it against her teeth. 'No, listen to me. Listen. I'm a prisoner, yes? No home, no money, no future. Yes? I'm a prisoner here for another year, maybe two years. And after that? In Germany – no family, no work, nothing. And you – if you come with me – what happen?' Under the stress of what he was struggling to tell her, his command of English began to disintegrate. 'You leave friends here in England – Michael, Margaret, this Bill – and in Germany you find – what? Coldness, suspicion, maybe hate, yes, hate. Here you live in comfortable house, have clothes, books, good food.'

Suddenly she could no longer listen, gazing intently into his louring face. 'Oh, how little you understand me. As if I really cared about all those things! I'm lucky to have them, I'm happy to have them. Bu I don't *need* them, not at all! Things like that don't matter, not a bit.'

'Not now,' he said softly. 'But later. Now we are like – like people who are drunk. Or like people who are, are – *Droge beigemischt* – drugged. We're frightened of nothing. But it can't always be so. We wake. We see it is a dream.'

Suddenly rage consumed her. She jumped off the sofa, crossed over to the mantelpiece and, with agitated fingers pulled a cigarette from the packet that she had left there and struggled to light it. 'Are you absolutely without any spine?'

'Spine?'

'Courage.'

Her desire had been to wound him. She saw now, with dismay, that she had wholly succeeded. He hung his head; a flush mounted to his cheeks and forehead.

She once more sat down on the sofa and rested the cigarette in an ashtray beside it. 'Thomas, listen.' She reached for his hand and, yet again a mother reasoning gently with a frightened, despondent child, took it in hers. 'I know the future's pretty black for us. Of course it is. But we love each other.' She tilted her head upwards and stared into his eyes. 'Don't we? Don't we?'

At the second time she put the question, he nodded slowly.

'Well, then. In that case, all those other things are trivial, meaningless, wholly unimportant. You have me, I have you. That's all we need. All we should want.'

His tongue moved over lips chapped by the icy east wind

in which he had been working on the new road. 'You don't understand.' His tone was sullen and petulant.

'You're always telling me that I don't understand things. What don't I understand?'

'Something you don't know. Something I've never told you. That was my mistake.'

'Well? Tell me now.'

Again his tongue moved over the chapped lips, again he blinked, this time repeatedly, as though a gust of wind had blown some grit into his eyes. 'I'm married.' It was so soft that she wondered for a moment if she had heard him correctly.

'*Married*?'

Hands tightly clasped, he nodded.

A silence followed. As she stared at him, willing him to raise his downcast eyes, she had a sense of all the objects in the frowsty, comfortable room – the piano, the chairs, the tables, the cupboard, the bookcases, the desk – all, all colliding, smashing together, splintering in the same delirious, dizzying vortex. When at last she spoke, she was surprised by her calmness. 'Why didn't you tell me earlier?'

At last he looked up. 'Because, as you just told me, I have no – no *spine*.' He spat out the unfamiliar word.

In a weary voice she said: 'It makes no difference.'

'How can you say that?'

'Because it happens to be true. We've started on this road and I'm happy to go along it with you. Wherever it takes us.' Looking at his slumped body, his head tilted forward so that she could not see his face, she now felt only the desire to communicate to him her own resolution. His weakness only lent her more strength; his indecision only made her path clearer. She had seen the major flaw in his character, a fatal lack of what she had called spine, and it no longer frightened or repelled her.

She waited for him to say something. Head still lowered, nothing came.

'Do you still love your wife?'

'No. Only you.'

'Does she love you?'

He gave a brief, bitter laugh. Then he raised his head. He swung round and faced her. 'Oh, Christine, you do believe that she is now nothing for me? Nothing, nothing! You do believe that I hid my marriage not because I wished to cheat you but because I was afraid – so afraid I lose you?'

'Of course!'

'I wished to tell you at Blenheim. And I was a coward, I couldn't do it. Then I was going to write to you. And then too – I was afraid. This afternoon I was going to tell you and after that leave your life. And this afternoon too …'

'Don't let's go all over that. You *have* told me. That's what matters now. Now tell me about your wife. What is she like? When did you marry her? Tell me. I must know.' Even as she pressed the questions on him, she thought: *Oh, this dreadful curiosity of mine*! She jumped up and fetched two cigarettes. She lit one and placed it in his mouth; then she lit another for herself. She dragged the smoke of her cigarette deep into her lungs. 'Tell me.' It was an order.

Reluctantly, he began. He sat far back in his chair, his face averted. She leaned forward, elbow on knee and her first cigarette and then another constantly raised to her mouth. Repeatedly she interrupted him, asking for some information about something still not revealed or for some clarification of something still not fully understood. By this stern, sometimes even implacable imposing of some sort of

144

coherence on the narrative that he reluctantly brought out with so much incoherence, she at last came to a measure of understanding of his destructive and finally desperate marriage.

He began with the difference between the ages of his wife and himself, since he clearly felt that to be the key to their whole relationship. Ilse was seven years older than he was. They had first met when, as the daughter of new neighbours in the farm next-door to his family one, she had come over to look after him at times when his parents were too busy to lavish on their beloved only child all the attention that they thought he needed and deserved. For this service they gave her what they always called 'pocket money'. His memories of that period were only happy ones. The robust blonde girl, with her already maternally large breasts, would join in his childhood games, buy sweets for him, and constantly subject him to friendly teasing about such things as his precociously adult vocabulary, his frequent inability to catch a ball thrown to him and the dreamily withdrawn state into which he would so often retreat. After she got married and left the neighbourhood to move into her husband's farm, five hours away by the slow train that halted at the village stop only once each day, he was overcome by a sense of abandonment. His teachers then complained to his parents of his lack of interest in his studies and asked him if he were unhappy about something. Indignantly he replied, 'Of course not.'

Half-a-dozen years later she returned to her old home, a childless widow, after the death of her husband, a man in his fifties, in a road collision involving his tractor and a carelessly driven bus in a narrow lane. Now thirteen, the pubescent boy was at once attracted by the mature woman and, to his delight and amazement, she returned his feelings. Soon they began to arrange meetings that would appear to their respective parents to be wholly accidental. In the corner of some remote field or in the kitchen or barns of one of the two farmhouses when everyone was out, she would allow him to become intimate with her firm, strong body, even if she would irritably push his hand away whenever it threatened to explore too far. Eventually she began first to masturbate him and then to go down on her knees to fellate him. Each of them became insatiable for this last act.

He went away to university in Göttingen. Here he flirted with girls attracted by his grave good looks. Under some bushes in a park, while rain spattered down on them, he even had hurried, furtive sex with one of these, a Czech science student with a face of astonishing pallor and desperate eyes. But he never ceased to think of Ilse and to long for the vacation. Soon after he was back home, he had achieved with her all that he had ever dreamed.

When the next vacation brought him home, she suddenly put it to him, out of the blue, not when they were making love but while they were listening to Richard Strauss's *Alpine Symphony* on the wireless in Thomas's parents' otherwise empty house, 'Why don't we get married?'

He pondered, brows puckered, for a moment. 'Yes. But later. Not now. It's too soon. First I must get my degree and get a job.'

'I have some money. No need to worry about a job. You know, I'm not a poor woman now. I inherited money from my husband. Not a lot of course, but enough. When we're married, you can live with my parents when you're not in Göttingen. Then, after you have your degree and your job, we'll buy a house. With my money. Of course.' She had worked it all out.

He graduated, he got a job teaching English at a secondary school, and she bought a comfortable little house on the edge of the town in which he was employed.

Then, within a few months, he realised that he had made a terrible mistake. There was something both crude and bullying about her, so that her clamorous personality began first to get on his nerves and then to disturb and disgust him. She had failed to have a child by her first husband ('He was past it,' she would say contemptuously, always putting the blame on to him) and she had now become obsessed with having one by Thomas. He would return exhausted from a hard day at the school only to have her demand, as soon as they had eaten one of the dreadful meals that she would prepare for him with hasty indifference, that they must at once go upstairs. When, despite all his efforts, her menses occurred with unfailing regularity, she would always then put the blame on him. What was the matter with him? Wasn't he a real man?'

Eventually he decided that he must tell her that he wanted a divorce to release him from this hell. After all, what was the point of her sticking to a man whom she despised, or of his sticking to a woman who had become physically and emotionally repellent to him? But Ilse was adamant. The staunchest of Roman Catholics, often deploring his refusal to convert to her faith, she told him implacably that she could never agree to such a 'sin'. He was hers, just as the German shepherd dog that barked ceaselessly at the end of its chain outside their house was hers. She was never going to release either of them from their bondage.

At the end of the story, Christine asked, 'And what has become of her now?'

He shrugged. He did not know. The last that he had heard,

from an aunt of hers almost three years ago, was that she was nursing in the casualty ward of a Berlin hospital. Now all over Germany people were desperately searching for their lost loved ones. Why should he begin a probably fruitless search for a lost unloved one? But he feared that eventually she would find him. She had that kind of obsessive persistence; and once she had found him, she was not the sort of person to give away her recovered possession, however little she herself wanted or needed it. Of one thing he was absolutely certain: she would never agree to a divorce.

He pressed his hands between his knees and gave a sigh that was almost a groan. 'Now you will understand why we must stop seeing each other.'

Christine shook her head. 'Certainly not. No. No one is going to keep you from me. No one, no one, no one. Never.' The obstacles, to him insurmountable, that he had revealed to her, had merely fortified her determination and love.

As Thomas tried repeatedly to argue, he felt both amazed and diminished by her steadfastness.

At their goodbye, she put a hand to each of his shoulders and looked for a long time into his eyes. He had to make an effort of will not to let his own eyes waver or retreat from her gaze. 'We must stick together,' she said at last. 'Whatever happens.' She shook him. 'Nothing must stop us. Thomas, are you listening to me?'

He gave a weak smile and shrugged his shoulders.

She shook him again.

Later, as he was trudging back alone to the camp through the chill of a gathering mist, something strange – even miraculous, he was to think later – happened. It was as though, while the distance between the lodging house and the camp was decreasing pace by pace, so at the same time Christine's serene, undeviating confidence in their ability to make a future together was filling him like cold, clear water rising up and up in a previously stagnant cistern. Yes, she was right. To continue with the relationship in circumstances of illegality, secrecy and stress was infinitely better than to abandon it. Each time that they met, it would continue to be for a few brief, clandestine hours over a weekend. When they parted it would be without knowing for certain when next they would see each other. But all that did not matter. It did not matter in the least.

XIII

The next Saturday, Thomas left early, having decided not to risk slipping back through the barbed wire of the camp for two weekends running. Christine accompanied him. Since it was raining and he had with him neither umbrella nor coat, she shared her own umbrella, her arm linked in his. All that afternoon they had made love, from time to time breaking off to smoke a single cigarette between them. At one moment there had been a knock at the locked door and then a succession of even louder knocks, followed by a frenzied rattling of the handle. They had frozen in silence. Margaret, Mrs Albert, her obnoxious son Ralph? When Christine had begun to giggle, Thomas had put a hand over her mouth.

Bicycle bells rang impatiently; cars swished past; figures flitted through the moist, melancholy twilight with heads lowered. But they themselves did not hurry, abstracted in a long, leisurely dream. As they passed the New Theatre, a figure waiting on the steps peered out at them through the rain. It was, Christine realised with a shock, Mrs Dunne, in a soiled, beltless white raincoat and a beret pulled down low over her forehead. In one hand she was holding an open umbrella, not over her head but outwards from her body, as though to ward off any possible assailant, while with the other hand she struggled to tuck an errant wisp of damp hair back under the beret. Christine glanced at her; Mrs Dunne stared back with narrowed eyes. Then Christine and Thomas had passed on, into the jostling crowds, the rain and the darkness, and Mrs Dunne could no longer see them. She was meeting her husband, manager of a bank in the High, to see *The Gondoliers*. He, not she, was a lover of Gilbert and Sullivan. As he approached, she greeted him: 'Such an odd thing has just happened …'

Meanwhile Christine had told Thomas: 'That was my tutor. Oh, hell!'

'I guessed it was.'

'How could you guess?'

He shook his head. 'I *felt*. She saw us together. Maybe that's bad for you.'

'Don't let's think about it.'

'Maybe she wonders why you're with –'

'Don't let's think about it. *Please*.'

'Okay.'

They walked on in silence. Then, as they approached the station, Thomas said: 'Here you must turn back.'

'Why?'

'It's too long a walk for you. It's not … pleasant from now on.'

'No, I'll come with you. I want to see the camp. Even if it's only from outside.'

'But then you'll have to go back all this way alone. There are bad streets. And you're becoming very wet. Let's say goodbye here.'

'Oh, no. No!'

They trudged on, over a gravel-strewn road pitted with holes brimming with water, past lots where machinery rusted in rank grass, sodden front gardens of stunted red-brick bungalows, and an occasional field enclosed in a jumble of wooden stakes and barbed wire.

From time to time other prisoners, muffled in long,

dark-blue overcoats, would hurry past, some of them momentarily turning to stare at the well-dressed, beautiful English girl splashing through puddles on the arm of one of their fellows. Often these prisoners would themselves have women with them, young girls for the most part, with mud-stained stockings and hair on which the raindrops corus-cated. When these girls peered at Christine, she imagined that their faces assumed an air of mockery or disdain. Such girls could be found haunting any camp where troops were stationed or, failing that, where POWs were penned.

Eventually one particularly noisy group passed them, composed of at least half-a-dozen prisoners and even more girls. One of the girls was belting out 'She Wore a Little Jacket of Blue' in a powerful but erratic contralto. She was enormously fat and, as she waddled along, her head shaking from side to side under a scarlet pixie-hood, a prisoner, far slighter than she was and only a little taller, suddenly scooped her up in his arms and ran ahead with her. Break-ing off from the song, she kicked out, giggled shrilly, and then emitted one piercing screech after another.

'She sounds like a pig being killed. And looks like one.'

Christine felt genuinely sorry for her. 'Poor thing. One might imagine that every juvenile delinquent girl in Oxford trekked out here on Saturday and Sunday evenings.'

'Horrible.' He spoke with a puritanical distaste.

'Well, if you think of the sort of lives that most of them must lead – '

'Horrible,' he repeated with a little shudder. 'Prisoners boast – they have made love to girls of thirteen, fourteen, fifteen. They think all English women are similar. For me – better to go without.'

'What can the poor things hope for in return?'

'A baby!' He gave a contemptuous laugh.

'Oh, don't be so censorious. Please, Thomas. It's not like you.'

'Prisoners have no money. But such girls don't want much. Perhaps a ring made from a spoon. A brooch perhaps, made from an empty sardine tin. Not romantic.'

'You're awfully priggish about the wretched creatures.' She pressed the arm linked with hers, to take the sting out of the reproof. 'There can't be much fun in their lives.'

'If I speak strongly, maybe it's because … Sometimes I myself feel … Maybe you can't understand this. Maybe I shock you.' He turned his head away from her.

'Of course not. No.' So far from shocking her, the thought that from time to time one of these girls had excited him and perhaps – who knows? – had even had sex with him, made her feel a vicarious thrill.

'It's not so much that you wish to make love with a woman. But you wish to have a woman – any woman – close to you. To look at, to talk to. Like now with you.' Once again he turned to stare at her. 'Do you prefer me not to tell you such things?'

'Of course not. I want to know everything about you and your life.'

He sighed. 'But such solutions are always *ersatz*. All of us know that. That makes us feel ashamed.'

'Am I also an *ersatz* solution?'

'You?' He stopped in his tracks, shocked and furious. His grip on her arm tightened painfully. 'You're not one of these prostitute girls. Please – don't talk like that.'

'Is there so much difference?'

'Christine!' He shook her arm. 'I told you – don't talk like that!'

She laughed; but, lips compressed and brows contracted, he did not laugh with her.

They were now on the last and steepest curve of the road before it reached the camp. She halted for breath, forcing him to halt too. 'I'd never realised how far it was.'

'I make myself hurry by thinking of how I'll be punished if I'm late. Once Horst and I returned too late from Michael. A week in the calaboose.'

'How is Horst?' she asked as they resumed their by now effortful trudging.

'Oh, he's okay.' As on previous occasions when she had asked about Horst, she had a sense of doors being shut and blinds being pulled down.

'Did he leave the camp this Saturday?'

'No.'

'I thought he might have gone to Michael's tea party.'

'He doesn't go to Michael. You know that, Christine.'

'Life must be boring for him.'

'He has many things to do. He's always, always busy. He doesn't often leave the camp.'

Oh, but why were they having this absurd, prolonged conversation about a man whom she disliked, when already ahead she could see the entrance to the camp? It was as if, a ghostly presence, Horst had intruded on them.

Thomas had put a hand up to her cheek, gently stroking it. Seeing how raw and swollen it was in the glare of the spotlight high up on one of the observation towers, she cursed herself for having once again forgotten to press on him a pair of the woollen gloves knitted for her by her aunt, to replace a pair, given to him by Michael, and yet again 'borrowed'.

'We must say goodbye here. We don't want the guards to see us.'

'The other girls have gone right up to the gate.'

'You're not one of the other girls. I've already told you that, *Liebling*.'

As he took her clumsily in his arms and kissed her, first on the cheek and then on the mouth, forcing her lips open with his tongue, she was all the time conscious of nothing but the sweaty smell of the greatcoat in which he was muffled.

'Until tomorrow?'

She nodded, her eyes suddenly making out, over his shoulder, a couple clutching each other under a rowan tree further down the slope. Did she and Thomas look as graceless as they did?

With a final, abrupt kiss and a wave of the hand, he turned and strode off; and she at once experienced a baffling sense of relief. She took a few steps and then halted under an insistently dripping tree. From there she watched while he trudged up the few yards that now remained between him and the entrance. When he did not look back, she herself turned away. As she descended the hill, her previous relief suddenly began to surge into a no less baffling exhilaration.

The couple farther down the road had separated and the German was thrusting towards her, shaved head lowered, with long, impatient strides. A farm labourer, she decided, as he came closer; and therefore better able to endure this sort of life than poor educated Thomas was. He passed her without even glancing in her direction, his wide face tensed into the exasperated concentration of a child worrying over a lesson he cannot master. The girl was already running away down the hill, trailed by a thin, shaggy mongrel dog. But soon her headlong pace slackened; she halted to pick up a stick to throw to the dog and, when she moved again, it was not at a run but with draggingly indecisive footsteps that brought Christine nearer and nearer to her with each stride.

They were now both on a footpath crossing a triangle of wasteland covered in brambles, old clothing, rusty tins and sodden newspapers. A brook, swollen with melted snow, raced alongside, washing clean the roots of the stunted thorn trees bristling along its banks. Eventually this brook thrust under a bridge, where the girl halted, to gaze down into the frothy, mud-stained waters; her dog sat leaning against her legs. Hanging over the rickety balustrade, her bosom pressed up against her thin arms, she struck Christine as being no more than fourteen or fifteen. Her hair had probably once been curled, but the damp now made it hang in wispy ringlets to her hunched shoulders. She wore an overlarge mackintosh blotched with oil stains, a crocheted beret and platform-heeled shoes each with two wide straps across the instep.

She turned from her contemplation of the brook just as Christine passed her. 'Excuse me!'

'Yes?'

'You couldn't spare a fag, could you? I gave my last to my bloke.'

Christine hunted for her cigarette case in the pockets of her coat; then, as she held it out, she suffered a moment of irrational panic – suppose this girl-child were to snatch it and make off with it? It had been Ben's last gift to her.

'Ta. Got a light?'

Christine was already pulling out a box of Swan Vestas.

The girl sucked greedily on the cigarette, as Christine did up her coat and pulled on her gloves. 'Cor – I really needed this.' She sucked again. Then, as Christine began to walk on, she called after her: 'Say!' Reluctantly Christine halted and turned.

'Who was that one with you? Was that Thomas?'

Christine swung away and, head lowered, continued to hurry on.

'Say! Wait a mo! There was something ...'

In her haste Christine yet again splashed into a puddle and yet again icy water spurted up her leg; but on this occasion she hardly noticed. To herself she was saying all the angry, ungenerous things that she had wanted to shout back at the girl but had not dared to. *Get away. Don't talk to me. Leave me alone. I'm not one of your sort. I want nothing to do with you.*

As she turned into the main road, she heard a voice: 'Where are you off to in such a hurry?'

It was Bill, screeching to a halt in his battered, rain-streaked jeep.

'Oh, just trying to get out of this cold and drizzle.'

'Jump in!' He pushed the door open for her. 'Now, madam, where do you want your chauffeur to drive you?'

'Well, where are you going?'

'Nowhere in particular.'

She laughed. 'You must be going *somewhere*. No one would go out in this weather just for the fun of it.'

'No one except me. My plans always tend to be fluid – like this ghastly winter ... Why don't we go and have a bite at the Randolph?'

'I don't think I really have the time. I've so much work to do. Thanks all the same.'

'Ah, well ... Some other time perhaps. At least let me drive you home.'

'If it's no bother.'

'I'm always at your service, as you know.'

He was wearing a khaki balaclava helmet, a leather jacket

157

tied round the waist with a length of string, and some RAF flying boots.

'Where have you been?'

'Seeing my German back to the camp. I've always wondered what people mean when they talk of "the sticks". Now I know.'

'How are things going between you two?'

Christine hesitated and then told him, without any cautious or craven editing of her story.

At the close, he whistled through his teeth. 'Not too good for you. I'm sorry.'

'There's really nothing to be sorry about. I know now that he loves me. That's the only thing that matters.'

'Well, if that's really how you feel … Oh, gosh! I don't know why I'm butting in like this. You know your own business best. But, well, it seems to me that you may be going to have a pretty rough time of it.'

She shook her head, staring out through the windscreen at the lights of the oncoming traffic. 'Not really.'

'Well, I always thought you had guts. But still … The fact that the poor bastard is *married* …'

'You're not being very encouraging.'

'Sorry … It's just that I hate to think of you … Waste. I hate *waste*.' It was like Michael saying, as he so often did: 'Mess. I hate *mess*.'

She continued to stare out, now dizzied by the onward rush of approaching headlights.

'You realise that, if there is anything that I can do, any way I can help you, then, well, you've only got to ask? I mean that.'

'Thank you.'

When they reached the Wellington Square house, Christine said reluctantly: 'Come in for a drink.'

'No, I won't do that. Ta ever so, all the same,' he added in a parody of female gentility.

'But I thought you said –'

'Well, when I invited you to dinner at the Randolph, I was preparing to cut a meeting of the Liberal Club. The other day they elected me treasurer. God knows why, since I've always been hopeless with money. So, on second thoughts, perhaps I really ought to go along.'

'Of course you ought! … How's the work going?'

He pulled a comic face. 'Ghastly! I've had an ultimatum. I was hauled before Bowra yesterday. He told me I'd have to take two sections next term – Old English and Shakespeare. If I don't pass, I might as well stop wasting my own and the College's time – as he charmingly put it.'

'So now you're going to settle down to a really hard slog?'

'I doubt it. A really hard snog would be preferable.' He sighed and then blew out his cheeks. 'No, this means I've had my ticket. I'll just get into Poppet and drive away the day before the first exam starts.'

'Don't be an ass. If you do a little work, you can quite easily wriggle through two sections.'

'Perhaps. The trouble is I'm getting pretty browned off with Oxford. I think it's time I moved on.'

'What'll you do with yourself?'

'Oh, God knows! Sufficient unto the day …' He began to clamber out of the jeep. 'You know, on second thoughts, I think I'll give that meeting a miss after all.'

'No, no! You can come and have a drink some other time.' She put her hands to his shoulders and gave him a gentle push. 'You *must* go to the meeting.'

'What a bully you are!' He began to clamber back. 'Did you like the flowers?'

'Oh, crumbs! I never thanked you for them. Yes, they were lovely. You must think me very rude.'

'I expect you've had lots and lots of things to think about.' Suddenly he was glum. 'Well, since you insist, I'd better be on my way. When shall I see you again?'

'Whenever you like.'

'How about lunch tomorrow? At the Kemp – or anywhere else you fancy.'

'All right. Thanks.'

'One o'clock. OK?'

'OK.'

As he moved off, he turned to shout: 'I like you very much.'

'I like you,' Christine shouted back.

'What's that?'

'I – like – you,' she shouted even louder. 'I – like – you.'

He had been grinning back at her in the light of a solitary lamp post. But the grin faded and he began to shake his head when at last he heard what she was shouting.

XIV

'Ah, Christine! You've come just at the right moment! We've been talking about Thomas's song. This is Chris Reid-Falconer, president of the College musical society,' – Michael pointed to a stooped, bespectacled youth in a shiny, dark blue serge suit – 'who is really quite enthusiastic about it. And this is Nick Meredith, who wants to sing it. He's also at Balliol.'

Reid-Falconer gave a jerky, little bow, hand to the bridge of his glasses. Meredith turned a handsome, vaguely dissolute face, the protuberant eyes giving it a perpetual look of faint surprise, towards Christine, as he drawled: 'I'm not sure I'm really the person for the job. But it was a choice between me and the Jew Meyerstein, and I really don't think that your German pal would regard it as a compliment if a member of the hooked-nose fraternity were to be chosen as his singer.'

'Thomas wouldn't have minded in the least. He's in no way anti-Semitic.'

Meredith raised his eyebrows and grinned. 'Oh, you bet he is! They all are.' He was either genuinely unaware of Christine's indignation or had decided to pretend that he was. 'Of course just at the moment it's worth their while to keep their traps shut. I don't blame them. But if you'd talked to as many as I have – '

'Oh, I've talked to quite as many as you have,' Michael intervened sharply. 'I still haven't met a single confirmed Nazi, not one.'

'Oh, my dear Michael, when people are in trouble, they tend to say what is likely to get them out of it. Surely you know that?' From his coolly *de haut en bas* tone it might have been he who was the tutor and Michael the student. 'You're a good, old-fashioned liberal, so of course they trim their sails accordingly. Whereas to me – since I'm none of those things – they are, well, shall we say, a little more *frank*.'

'Are you saying that all my Germans lie to me?'

Meredith ran fingers through his thick, corrugated blond hair. 'You can accuse them of that if you like. But "lie" has such a whiff of moral disapproval. Let's face it. If our positions were reversed, with our being wholly at the mercy of the Germans instead of the other way about, well, I wonder how many of us would have the courage to a say a good word of the Jews – or a bad word of the Holocaust?'

'Oh, Nick!' Hand once again to spectacles, Reid-Falconer cleared his throat. 'Why do you always have to be so perverse – and silly?' His disagreement was no more than mildly plaintive. 'Why do you keep spouting the very ideas that caused the war?'

Meredith swung his legs over an arm of his chair, and looked down at his suede shoes as though inspecting them for any scuffing. 'Come on, come on! Or – better – come off it! Ideas never cause wars. If only they did! What causes wars is economic necessity or economic greed. You're clever enough – and educated enough – to know that, dear boy.'

Reid-Falconer lowered his head, frowning in exasperation. Then he looked up. 'Oh, I don't want a row. You know how I hate them. And I'm sure Michael doesn't want to have one, or hear one, either. But all you say makes such a farce out of those years of horror – and sacrifice – and suffering. How *can* you, Nick?'

'Those years were a farce anyway.'

'The war a farce!' Christine exclaimed.

'Of a particularly dismal kind – yes. Admittedly not the sort of sunny, imbecilic, Tom Walls and Ralph Lynn farce that used to fill the dear old Aldwych Theatre.' Meredith now turned back to Reid-Falconer, like a cat pouncing on a fledgling. 'Incidentally, Chris, before we continue to argue about the war, let me remind you that I served in it and you didn't.'

Reid-Falconer drew himself up until he was almost on tiptoe, with arms held rigid to his sides, as though at a challenge to a fight. His prominent Adam's apple jerked up and subsided. 'That was hardly my fault.'

'Of course not! No fault at all.' The tone was brutal in its sarcasm.

'Let's drop this subject,' Michael interposed.

But Meredith continued, in the same coolly derisive voice as before: 'I'm sure, dear chap, that you did everything expected of you. Burrowing away at your research – if one can burrow away at a retort or a test tube. Firewatching on the roof of Bodley. First-aid lessons. And so forth, and so forth. An admirable war! But when you tell me why I fought it – why I was at Dunkirk, Salerno and Normandy – I just want to say "Oh, bloody well, *fuck off*, dearie!"'

Christine had hoped that Michael would intervene. When unaccountably he failed to do so, she did so herself. 'If you feel as you do, why on earth did you fight?'

'Oh, God knows! I was clever enough to get exemption as a conchie at a tribunal, I imagine. But, well, I was a bloody fool and I never tried. At eighteen one thinks that that sort of bloodbath is going to be as much *fun* as a dive into a swimming pool during a heatwave. And yes, I must admit, a lot of it *was* fun. And there's also the herd instinct – isn't there? The young can rarely resist it.'

Reid-Falconer, body slumped, was staring gloomily into the fire. Suddenly Meredith leapt to his feet with a crow of laughter, rushed at him, and began to thump him on the back as though he were burping a baby. 'Cheer up, old chap! I'm not really as rotten as you think.'

Reid-Falconer ducked away from under Meredith's arm and stood up. He turned to Michael. 'I must be getting back to the labs.' He gave a little, formal bow. 'I apologise for having started this argument in your rooms. Please forgive me.'

'Oh, don't worry! Don't worry! In any case, Nick started it, not you.' Michael looked over to Meredith and, in a voice the geniality of which exasperated Christine, told him: 'And now, Nick, perhaps you'd better go too.' He laughed. 'For today I think I've had enough of you.'

'You can never have enough of a good thing. But no matter. I'll toddle off to White's for a drink.'

Once alone with Michael, Christine turned on him. 'You treated all that disgusting nonsense as though it were just a joke. How could you? How could you?'

'Oh, you really mustn't take him too seriously. The young always *exaggerate* so much. Not you, but most of them. Dear Nick can be utterly maddening. As he's just shown. Amazingly for someone so intelligent, he's become besotted with Mosley. The only thing is to laugh at his childish antics.'

'I wish I could.'

'How about a glass of sherry? I got this really rather good Tio Pepe from the Buttery. Unobtainable for ages.' He began to pour out the sherry, then looked up with a smile, decanter in hand. 'The funny thing is that there's really something attractive about Nick – underneath all that Byronic posing and posturing. Isn't there?'

She took the glass that he was now holding out to her, and firmly shook her head. 'Balls!'

Disconcerted by her vehemence, he sipped from his glass. 'He has a very distinguished war record. He sings well, has a blue for cricket. He is also – so John Austen tells me – quite a good philosopher. And he has looks and charm, as I'm sure you'd agree. If only he hadn't got mixed up with all this Mosley business! That really worries me.'

'I love your fatherly attitude to your pupils – even the most repellent of them. Women dons are never really motherly. They regard one as no more than a possible name high up on an Honours list.'

'Oh, I'm sure Mrs Dunne must take a motherly interest in you.'

'Don't you believe it!'

'The last time I ran into her, she did nothing but talk about you.'

'Really?'

'She said you were the most brilliant pupil she'd had since – oh, I can't remember whom, but it was ages back.'

'Exactly. That proves my point. So long as she thought I might win a fellowship, she was interested in me. But now!'

'What's happened between you both? Haven't you been a good girl?'

'Oh, I don't know. I don't seem to be able to concentrate this term. I suppose I'm losing interest.'

'What's the trouble? What's on your mind?'

She shrugged and turned her head away. She might confide in him another time but she was in no mood to do so now.

He crossed over to his desk and picked up the two sheets of paper on which Thomas had written out his setting of Isaac Rosenberg's 'Returning We Hear the Larks'. It was Christine who had suggested both the poem to him and the performance to the Balliol Music Society. He smiled as he tapped the sheets against his chin. 'I'm glad they're going to do this. It may encourage poor old Thomas to embark on something else. I wonder if Nick realised that the poem was by a member of what he calls the hooked-nose fraternity.' He again looked down at the score, absorbed. 'Yes. It's good. Not all that distinctive but he's really got something. If only he doesn't lose it picking Brussels sprouts that no one likes or digging that wretched road that no one needs or wants. He should have some lessons of course. Perhaps Tommy Armstrong – I might have a word with him. The trouble is that those poor devils have so little spare time – and what they have is rarely to themselves.' He threw the sheets down and began to fuss over the ink-bottles and pens on his desk. 'I suppose Thomas uses every spare moment he's got at your piano. It's an age since I saw him.'

'He was thinking of coming here next Sunday,' Christine lied.

'Then I hope you'll come too. I look forward to that. Without him and Klaus my weekend gatherings have now become really rather dreary. Ludwig will bring that ghastly Miss Bollinger, and last week a man turned up who had been a hairdresser in Berlin and was so camp that he might have been the Jerry equivalent of one of the performers in those forces drag-shows – *Soldiers in Skirts* or *Fig Leaves and Apple Sauce*, you know the sort of thing.' He took Christine's glass from her and began to refill it. 'By the way, do you ever see Thomas's chum – Horst?'

She shook her head. 'No. Why? Do you?'

'An odd thing happened. He came here last Sunday – late, when the others had gone. I've been meaning to tell you about it.'

She felt a sudden foreboding. 'And?'

'There was something frightening about him – though he was in no way aggressive or rude – as there is about so many people with that degree of self-control. He asked for Thomas, that was his reason for coming – or so he said. When I told him that I hadn't seen him for weeks, he seemed to imply that I'd hidden him somewhere. Then he said he wanted to talk to me, so I asked him to sit down. But he wouldn't do that, so we both remained standing – not the best position from which to conduct an amiable conversation. He told me he was worried about Thomas – quite why he didn't really make clear – and in some way he seemed to imply that I was to blame. It was my "influence" – that was the word he used – as far as I could gather.'

'Your *influence*?'

'Well, you can see at once how crazy all of it was. When I repeated that it was weeks, literally weeks, since Thomas had been here, it was obvious that he didn't believe me. In fact, he as good as told me I was lying.'

'And what did you say to that?' Her foreboding had intensified.

'Well, I told him that, as far as I knew, he spent the weekends over at your place, practising the piano.'

'You *told* him that?'

'Yes. Does it matter? I'm only surprised that Thomas had never told him himself. They always seemed so close.'

'And how did he respond?'

'Well, at first he said that he didn't believe me. So I just shrugged my shoulders and said "Well, why don't you ask Thomas then?" That shut him up. All through the interview his face had been totally expressionless – rather alarming. It remained like that as he bowed – clicking his heels in that awful German manner – apologised for causing me trouble, thanked me, and left.'

'How strange!'

'Very. What I can't understand is why Thomas never told him about using your piano so often? Why did it have to be secret? You know, I have a hunch. I think that Thomas may have told him that he was coming here when he was really going over to you.'

'Why on earth should he do that?'

'Search me!'

'Oh, I do wish you hadn't said anything about the visits to me! The last thing I want is a visit from him.'

'Perhaps that was a mistake. Sorry, old girl. But you and I both tend to tell the truth. It comes naturally to us. Anyway, I was so anxious to clear myself. At your expense, I'm afraid. Typically selfish of me! Anyway we must have a word with Thomas about it all.'

'Do you really think we should?' Secretly she had already resolved to question Thomas; but she did not want Michael also to be involved. 'One's got to be so careful. I mean, small things take on so much importance for them. Living cooped up like that, isolated, away from their familiar worlds. A recipe for paranoia, I'd have thought. You know what I mean?'

'Good God, yes! Because that's exactly what I felt when Horst was grilling me – aha, paranoia! So stiff, so outwardly polite, but with such an obsessive intensity over something so trivial. Yes, perhaps it would be better if we didn't get involved.' He crossed over to the window, glass in hand, and looked out. 'Amazing! I can see the first snowdrops.'

She went across to join him. He pointed. 'There – under that tree.'

'Yes, yes!'

'They are really rather mean little flowers, I always feel. But the first sight of them makes me happy. It announces that this ghastly winter must at last be nearly over. Do you know what John Clare called them? "The gentle midwives of the nascent year". Rather absurd. But I like it.'

As they returned to their seats, she asked, 'What news of Klaus?' At unexpected moments – boarding a bus, brushing her teeth, opening a newspaper – she had often thought of him.

'Klaus? Oh, I have a letter from him somewhere here.' He pulled out his wallet and then replaced it. 'It's in German, so there isn't much point in showing it to you. In any case he gives so little news. Says he hopes to be back in a week or two. A week or two! Poor Klaus. More like a year or two, I'd guess. They've sent him to a military sanatorium some-where in Scotland. I want to visit him, but of course there are the usual difficulties with red tape. Everyone kind and helpful but, well, as they keep telling me, I'm "not family". As though any of his family could ever get here, even if I sent them the fare. Still, I hope to fiddle it somehow or other – the usual strings!'

'I'm sure you'll succeed. You have so many strings and you always pull them so skilfully. Have you heard what's wrong with him?'

'What I thought. TB.'

'Oh, dear! That's awful. Even those two letters fill me with dread. Mother died of it so quickly and so horribly.'

'I want to find out what are his chances. I suppose I'll have to wait until I can speak to the doctor in Scotland. If I can ever do that.'

'How sad it all is!'

'Yes. Sad. Sad.' He was staring out over her shoulder, his face frozen. 'I might no longer be here,' she thought.

On an impulse, she leant forward and touched him on a knee. He started as if aroused from a dream. 'May I ask you something private? Don't answer if you don't want to do so.'

'Why not?' His voice and his body both seemed to sink under a burden of overwhelming fatigue. 'We have never had any secrets between us. That's why I've always so much valued our friendship. I've always had to keep so many secrets from others. So – what is it?' he prompted, sensing her hesitation.

'Well … Am I right in thinking you've fallen for Klaus?'

'I love him. Yes.' The words were chilling in their undramatic directness and desolation. 'But what use is it? I could never tell him. The poor creature would be horrified. He might even beat me up. In any case, how could we have any sort of life together? Can you imagine him coming with me to listen to Walton at the Sheldonian or to look at Piper at the Ashmolean? And, with no English, what work could he do? Oh, he'd hate it here. So, that's that.' He tapped his knees each with a hand, a gesture of finality.

'Oh, Michael, I feel so sorry for you.'

Mouth compressed into a line, he again stared out over her shoulder with woebegone eyes.

'Do you know, for a time I thought it was Thomas in whom you were interested.'

He stared at her, and then shook himself and even managed a fleeting smile. 'Not a chance. Though of course it would have been far easier if it had been Thomas and not Klaus. We'd have been able to have some sort of life together – if he had wanted that. But of course he wouldn't have, not in the least. Yes, I'm fond of him, who wouldn't be? But, sadly – even if he were interested, which he certainly isn't – he's just not my type. You must know what my type is by now. Don't you remember how besotted I was with your father's gardener? I once even helped him empty a cesspit – something I'd never done before and, thankfully, have never had to do since. And yet, do you know, at this precise moment his name totally escapes me. Well, that's everlasting love for you.'

'Tony. That was his name – Tony Blythe.'

'Yes. Tony. What wasted hours, and wasted presents!'

Soon after that, she got up to go.

'Goodbye, old girl,' he said, suddenly jolly. 'Your friendship has always meant a lot to me – even if we hardly ever agree about a single thing.'

'As yours to me.'

Like many close intimates, whether members of the same family or friends, he and she were undemonstrative with each other. But now she put her arms around him and kissed him first on one cheek and then the other. She smelled Caron Pour Un Homme – at once thinking 'Funny – Peter uses that.' She felt the cold, smooth flesh on her lips.

XV

How well Christine knew the first sign. 'So it's you again,' she felt like saying to the small, jagged piece of glass that had appeared in the centre of the book. The glass began to revolve with hypnotic rapidity; it grew and grew. Now came that moment of useless panic when her eyes went from the book to the window, from the window to its curtains, from the curtains to the stove, in the hope that somewhere they might alight on a place where the glass did not exist. But that was useless. The glass was already covering and distorting everything about her. She glanced across at the librarian and found that it had covered the whole of the right side of his face; her own hand seemed unaccountably to have lost two of its fingers; and now, as she stared once again at the book, she could see only a blurred swirl of letters. Yes, it was one of the usual, dreaded attacks. Only a moment now, and she would feel the invisible thumb pressing on the right eyeball. Ah, there it was. Again and yet again the nerves behind the eye contracted in agony.

Clumsily she made a pile of her books, put them under her arm, and stumbled through the echoing hall of the Ashmolean and out into the street. As she turned right, the front of the Worcester looked like a badly executed daub – smeared, indistinct and covered in greasy, yellowish patches … Oh, God! And of course it would happen at the weekend, when she was expecting Thomas.

Somehow she found her way back to Wellington Square, the landscape jerking and shredding as on an ancient film, dragged herself upstairs and pushed open Margaret's door.

Margaret lumbered up from the mat before the gas fire, where she had been squatting to read an ancient issue of *Country Life* abandoned in a refuse bin by another of the tenants. She put an arm round Christine. 'Straight to bed!' she commanded. No one more enjoyed such crises; no one was more effective at dealing with them. 'Come along, dear!' She half led and half dragged Christine into her bedroom, laid her on the bed, and began to tug at the curtains.

'Oh, let me have a little light!' Christine moaned.

'You know Dr Watson said that complete darkness was the best thing. But if you like, I'll put a scarf over the reading lamp and then you can have it on. How about that?' Having extracted a silk scarf from a drawer, she padded across the room with it trailing from a hand. 'Feeling sick?' She adjusted the scarf over the lamp.

'Hm.'

'Well, let me get the pills. Here we are!' She crossed to the washbasin and ran some water into a tooth mug. 'Swallow these and then have a good zizz.' Coaxingly she put an arm under Christine's shoulders and, breathing heavily, raised her until her lips met the rim of the glass. 'Swallow! *Swallow!*'

'It's such a bloody nuisance. It's an age since I last had one as foul as this.'

'I wonder what brought it on. It can't be the sun, as that goofy neurologist at the Radcliffe seemed to think. We haven't had any sun for the last week.'

'Stress.'

'*Stress?* What stress?'

'Oh, never mind!'

'Come on! Spill the beans.'

'Not now.'

'Well, in that case …' Margaret gave a sigh. 'If madam doesn't want to tell me, I'll make myself scarce.'

'Oh, don't get huffy. I'll tell you another time, when I feel better.'

'Very well. I'll just have to wait till then. Won't I?' Margaret was not placated. 'Anyway, just give me a shout if you need anything. I'll be next door, mending that curtain. No hope of Mrs A. doing anything about it, I'm afraid.'

Yes, of course it was stress, Christine told herself, as Margaret closed the door.

Ever since Michael had told her about Horst's visit, her mind, afflicted with a kind of agonising cramp, had refused to let go of it. She had decided to write – telephoning was, of course, impossible – to Thomas to ask him what it all meant but had then decided to wait until she next saw him; and, yes, all that Saturday morning, even at the second when the small, jagged piece of glass had first appeared in the centre of her book, she had been rehearsing how she must speak of it. It was a matter so trivial and yet one that nagged at her, like a medical diagnosis awaited with unrelenting apprehension. Repeatedly she told herself that, if indeed Thomas had pretended to Horst that he was visiting Michael, rather than her, then there must be some perfectly ordinary explanation. But nonetheless … She remembered now how she had once asked Thomas, 'Have you told Horst yet?' and he had replied with unexpected irritability, 'Told him? Told him what?'

'About us, silly.'

He had nodded and muttered, face grim: 'Yes, yes, he knows.'

'What does he think?' she had persisted – foolishly, she was now convinced.

His answer was perfunctory and dismissive: 'Oh, you know Horst!' He had then begun to talk about something else.

She clawed at her left temple as though to trap and then squeeze to extinction the nerve that thump, thump, thump, was battering it like a bird trapped in a closed room. No use. Oh, she must take into consideration that, like most good conversationalists, Michael always carried around with him the invisible paintbox of his imagination to make humdrum reality more vivid and startling. Much of what he had told her about Horst's visit must certainly have been touched up; some of it might even have been pure invention. Horst had probably come in to ask for Thomas merely because he had forgotten that that afternoon he would be, not with Michael, but with her. That had then at once caused Michael to recreate the whole trivial event into something far more dramatic and lurid.

Margaret was back. 'Would you like a cold flannel?'

'Oh, no. Thank you.'

'You know that sometimes it helps.'

Christine closed her eyes, making no response.

'Well, just an idea. No matter. Just try to have a snooze.'

'What about Thomas?'

Margaret squinted down at the watch that, like a hospital sister, she wore pinned to her bosom. 'Well, he won't be here for another three hours – if he comes at the usual time. We can see what you feel like. If the worse comes to the worst I can always give him a cuppa. I've got rather a lot to do but I can always put it off till tomorrow – or do it after he's gone.' This was a lie. Margaret had been wondering through an empty morning how she would fill an empty afternoon.

'Oh, I expect I'll be all right by then. But thank you all the same.'

'Well, you never know.'

No sooner had Margaret shut the door behind her than Christine heard her greet someone on the staircase. 'Well, well, hello! You're quite the stranger. It's yonks since you – '

'Oh, didn't Christine tell you?' It was Peter's resonant, over-confident voice. 'The FO sent me over to Prague for a month – for my sins.'

'What gorgeous flowers!'

'Yes, they are rather nice, aren't they? Cost a bomb at this time of year, but there you are! Nothing's too good – or expensive – for my girl. Is she in?'

'Well … yes, she is. But the poor darling's not feeling at all good. In fact, she's thoroughly seedy. One of her beastly migraines. I've just put her to bed.'

'Can I slip in and take a quick shufti?'

'Well, I'm not really sure …' Hadn't Christine told her, after the ball, that she never wished to see Peter again? 'But I'll go in and check with her, if you like.'

'Would you? That would be angelic.'

As soon as Margaret opened the door, Christine raised herself on an elbow and, with a grimace, frantically shook her head. Margaret flashed a gratified smile, nodded and pulled the door shut. Christine could hear her explain that the poor dear was already fast asleep. 'Shall I take the flowers?'

'Would you? They'll need to be put in water. And there's some sort of sachet with them – you'll have to add that. Don't absent-mindedly drop it in her tea!'

She was affronted. 'I'd never dream of such a thing.'

'I was only joking! Perhaps I can call back some time this evening?'

'No promises. But no harm in trying.'

Silence. Christine relapsed into a throbbing half doze.

When she re-emerged, still drugged from the pills, she fancied but could not be certain that a figure was seated on the uncomfortable straight-backed chair at the other end of the room. She closed her eyes again, deciding that this was no more than a delusion of her migraine. But when, after some minutes, she once more roused herself, the motion-less, shadowy form was still there. 'Who's that?'

'Me. Thomas.' His voice sounded oddly thick, as though he needed to clear his throat.

'Oh, Thomas! Have you been there long?'

'Not long.'

'Aren't you going to come over to say hello to me?'

He got up and began to walk slowly and stiffly towards the bed. She felt an immediate apprehension. He halted a few feet away from her. He stood there, silent, looking down at her.

'What is it? What's the matter?' How easily each of them could now intuit the other's moods!

His hands, which had so far remained to his sides, rose and met in a small, flustered gesture. He gave a dry cough. 'Horst. Horst is dead.'

'*Dead*!' She sounded incredulous and aghast. But curi-ously the news had come as no surprise to her. It was some-thing that, subconsciously, she had known would eventually – perhaps even soon – happen, she could not have said why.

He nodded. There was a long pause, while she waited. Then he muttered: 'Killed himself. Last night.'

'But that's horrible!'

She held out her arms to him, the kimono that she was wearing falling away from them to leave them bare. But he did not go to her. Instead he sat down on the edge of the bed, his body and face rigid. In the light that filtered through the silk scarf thrown by Margaret over the shade of the bedside lamp it was impossible to see the full extent of his desolation. She jerked herself up. As she did so, the pain pierced through her right eyeball; she almost cried out with it.

'How did it happen?' He shook his head, biting his lower lip. 'How did it happen?' she repeated, even more insistent.

In a barely audible voice, his head turned down and away from her, he told her what he knew. Horst had disappeared when the time came for him and his fellow workers to return to the camp the previous evening. There had been a search – a hurried one since the guards had been eager, as always, to go off duty as quickly as they could – and he had then been posted missing. At a nearby farm, the nine-year-old daughter of the household had found him hanging from a beam in a barn when she had entered it late in the evening with a torch, looking for her cat. So far, apart from these bare facts, nothing else had been revealed. But, inevitably, a gale of rumours was swirling round the camp and there was a general air of excitement and horror. Wherever prisoners gathered, it was noticeable how the babble of their voices resonated more and more loudly as they yet again went over every detail. They all agreed that Horst was the last person they would have expected to do such a thing. There were even suggestions that he might have been murdered.

Having finished his bare, halting account, Thomas got to his feet with a deep sigh, crossed over to the washbasin and, with trembling hands, poured himself out a glass of water. He swallowed it in two gulps, grimacing after each as though it were some bitter medicine. Then he remained there, head lowered as he stared down into the empty glass.

'But why did he do it?'

He shrugged, still staring down into the glass.

'There must have been some reason.'

He looked up at her. He hesitated. 'Today I found a letter. From him, from Horst. He left it in my locker.'

'A letter? What about?'

He fumbled in the breast pocket of his tunic and pulled it out. He half held out to her the thin, lined sheet of paper with the scrawled German characters on it.

'Please – translate it for me.'

'If you wish.' He squinted down at it, as if for the first time.

'Come and sit over here.' She extended a hand and patted the seat of the chair beside her bed. 'I'll put on the light.' She did so and the raw glare after the consoling darkness made her raise a hand to shield her eyes. When she looked across at him again, it was to find him staring at her with what was almost an expression of hostility.

'He begins "*Mein – mein sehr lieber Freund*". My very dear friend. You must forgive me for what I have already done when you have this letter."' He screwed up his eyes, frowning down at it. Then, with the exasperation of a child urged to perform a task too difficult for it, he announced: 'Impossible. My English is too bad.'

'Why not just give me the gist then?'

'The gist?'

'In your own words. Briefly. Simply.'

'Well …' Again he stared down at the fragile sheet of paper. 'I'll try. He begins – no one is to blame, I am not to blame. What we discussed yesterday evening – that has nothing to do with it.'

'What did you discuss yesterday evening?'

'What we often discuss. The past. The future. Our lives.'

'Go on.'

'He writes – for a long time he thought that maybe he would do this thing. But he always thought of his daughter Annette. Maybe she was still alive. If she was still alive, he must continue for her. But now …' He broke off. 'He gave up hope. Or hope gave up him.'

'Is there nothing else?'

Another long pause. 'Only – he thanks me. Nothing more.'

'May I see it?'

'What's the use? It's in German.' He again held up the sheet before her, as though she might not believe him.

'Terrible,' she said. And yes, in a weird way the whole incident had filled her with what she could only describe as terror similar to that induced in her each time that she had heard a V1 sputtering above her to its fatal and wholly arbitrary rendezvous with its victims.

'And I'm to blame.' He said it in a flat, barely audible voice, at the same time playing with the tassel of the dressing gown that lay across the foot of the bed.

'You're to blame? What do you mean?'

'First Klaus. Now Horst.' He shook his head. 'I bring bad luck. And I'm a bad friend.'

'But what more could you have done for him?'

'Much. Much. I knew that he was unhappy. Needed me. And I – I did so little. Said so little. Took little notice. Now, I feel so ashamed.'

'Well, in that case, I suppose I'm also to blame. I've taken up so much of your free time these last weeks.'

He did not contradict her. Head bowed, speaking almost to himself, he went on: 'I should have told him straightaway. I lied to him. I pretended that I was visiting Michael, not you. And then – he found out the truth – that I was lying to him.'

'I'd begun to wonder if you'd told him.' All at once she

wanted to strike out at him, withholding that comfort with which in the past she had always been so generous.

He tugged viciously at the tassel of the dressing gown cord until finally it broke. He held out the tassel in the palm of his hand. 'See what I've done. Sorry.'

Just as she had ignored the breaking, so she now ignored the perfunctory apology for it. 'So I was right in my suspicion – you didn't tell him.'

He tossed the tassel down on to the bed. 'I didn't tell him.'

'Why on earth not?'

He shrugged and looked away. 'I don't know.'

'But there must have been some reason.'

'Perhaps – perhaps I didn't wish to hurt him.'

'Hurt him?'

'You know how he feels about prisoners and English girls.'

'But that's absurd. Surely it's your own business if you –'

Roughly he broke in: 'He was my friend! Don't you understand? *My friend*!'

'No, I don't understand. I'm sorry.'

His anger ebbed. With a fatalistic melancholy, he said all but inaudibly: 'You cannot understand. You're right. Only a prisoner can understand.'

'But can't you explain?'

'There will be a – what do you call it? In court. *Untersuchung*.'

'An inquest.'

He nodded. 'An inquest. And they will then decide – what was wrong with him, why he did such a thing. He was depressed. He thought too much about his daughter – all, all the time. Maybe she was dead, maybe she was homeless, maybe she was starving. He hated the camp. He wished to return to his country. Oh, they'll find reasons, many reasons. They will explain, of course they will explain. But,' – suddenly his voice became relentless – 'they cannot know. They cannot know *anything*.' He put his head in his hands. '*Ach*, poor Horst!'

There were no more questions she could put, no more comments she could make. Implacably she had driven him, a hunted animal, from covert to covert in her desire to know all; but he had escaped her. He was a man, he was a prisoner; she was a woman, she was free. She could guess at the complexities of the relationship between the two men, and she could discuss them with Michael, with Bill, and even with Thomas himself, but she would never know, much less understand, except always at one remove.

'Well, if you think you're to blame, then so – in part at least – am I,' she said quietly, more to herself than to him. 'But most of all the whole stupid, cruel system that keeps you all here – merely because we want to stuff ourselves with more Brussels sprouts and drive our cars too fast on a new trunk road,' she added in sudden, unreasonable anger.

He stretched himself out on the bed beside her, his face buried in the dressing gown. 'Oh, Christine! How often you save me!' He turned over and put his cheek against hers.

After that for a long time they lay facing each other in a serene sadness, no longer touching. Christine had already put out a hand and switched off the lamp. Her head ceased to pound and, when she looked into his face, there too all tension was relaxed. Minute followed minute until, in that cold, unlit Oxford bedroom, she all at once had an illusion of Thomas and herself lying out on some vast, empty, tropical beach, with the sun blazing above them and the sea glittering out and out before them, and his breath, as now, gently fanning her cheek …

A brief shiver passed through his body. He put out a hand and rested it on her left breast. His forefinger circled the nipple. All at once that illusion of beach, sun and sea was obliterated. She groaned. Involuntarily her lips moved towards his and his towards hers.

At the end: 'What have I done? What have I done?' he whispered, one conspirator to the other. She stopped any further utterance by once more pressing her lips against his.

Much later, as they lay half-asleep and still naked in each other's arms, a knock aroused them. Christine jerked up. 'Oh, lord, I forgot to lock the door!' Thomas leapt off the bed and began to pull on his trousers. She drew sheet and blankets up to her chin. She shouted: 'Wait a moment! *Wait*!' Thomas was buttoning up his fly. His feet were only in their socks.

The door handle turned. 'Oh, gosh! I'm sorry. Sorry, sorry, sorry!' It was Peter, staring at them with a mixture of shock and disbelief. He made an attempt to show neither of these emotions. He even forced a placatory smile. 'Margaret didn't tell me ... I brought you some flowers before lunch but she then said you weren't well enough to see anyone. I thought that by now the migraine would have ...' It was the first time that Christine had seen him fazed by anything. 'I hope you'll be better soon.'

Christine steadied her voice and attempted to present the incident as a perfectly normal one. 'I was just about to get up. Won't you wait for a cup of tea? If you and Thomas would like to go down to the sitting room I'll get myself ready and join you in a moment. You know Thomas, don't you? From the night of the ball? He's just dropped in.' Even while, a hand still clutching the bedclothes up to her chin, she was babbling all this, she realised its absurdity. With an effort, she swallowed the laughter that was now beginning to well up in her throat.

Thomas was reaching down to pick his shirt off the floor.

Peter backed towards the door. 'Well … As a matter of fact, I've got to meet someone. I'm in Oxford for the whole of the weekend, so perhaps – some time tomorrow? Some time tomorrow,' he repeated, having received no response. 'Goodbye, Christine. Sorry about …' He ignored Thomas. Having placed the flowers on the dressing table, he hurried through the door and then pulled it decisively shut behind him.

Now at last Christine could laugh. She did so for several seconds while Thomas, stricken, stared at her. Then he exclaimed: 'Oh, Christine! This is terrible! See what I've caused you.'

'What does it matter? Who cares? Anyway, he's unlikely to talk. He learned a lot of things at Oxford but – unlike Michael – never how to gossip.'

'But he must have realised …'

'Of course he realised. One would hardly expect to find a German POW in a girl's bedroom in only his trousers, while she was lying in the bed with the sheet pulled up to her chin. Forget about it!'

'How can I forget?'

'Don't worry. I'm not worried. I don't care a damn.'

Before going to bed, Christine and Margaret sat silent at the scratched, wobbly kitchen table, their mugs of cocoa between them. Christine mused: all that had happened had been such an extraordinary mix of tragedy, passion and absurdity.

Then, suddenly, like a violent gust of wind, the thought hit her: *We made love over a corpse.*

XVI

That terrible winter was at last drawing to a close. So was the term.

Already Bill had tried to put his plan of escape into effect. On the eve of his exam, he came to say goodbye to Christine, left a number of his more valuable possessions with her, and drove off into a night as obscure as his own future. Goodbye, Oxford, a long goodbye! But on Headington Hill Poppet had broken down and Bill, having cursed, attempted to mend her and watched someone from the RAC attempting to mend her, at last got a lift in a lorry back to Wadham, where he spent the night. His impetus had been stemmed; and though he failed to appear at the Examination Schools the following morning, and though he talked of a new departure – to France, Italy, Egypt – in Oxford he then remained. Having soon been asked to vacate his college room, he had rented a squalid bedsitter in Jericho, emerging from it every morning at eight-thirty to sell books at Blackwell's. Was he happy? Christine asked. Grinning he replied: 'Well, at least I'm living in the same town as you.'

Michael was preparing for a British Council lecture tour. 'I've never much liked the *idea* of Sweden. But it'll be wonderful to enjoy all that comfort, plenty and efficiency. So unlike dear old Blighty!' Then he asked: 'Shall you stay in Oxford?'

'I don't know.' Christine and her father were still arguing as to whether she should spend her vacation in Oxford or at home.

'If you are going to be here, I wonder if you would do something for me?'

'That depends what it is.' But already she knew.

'It's my little family – the Germans. I'll be away for three weeks and that may make them feel rather lost. Do you think you could possibly have them in to tea on a Saturday or a Sunday? Not all of them of course, just two or three – Ludwig, say, and a nice boy called Werner, who's been coming recently. It seems awful to abandon them. I'm planning to send them parcels from Sweden. That would help to tide them over, wouldn't it?'

'You're so kind, Michael.' She meant it. 'Yes, of course I'll have a little party for them – if I'm not back at home in Wimbledon. By the way, it's interesting that you should refer to them as your "little family". When I'm with any of them – even with Thomas – I feel as if I were a parent with a child, whom one must simultaneously guide, cherish and console. I get the feeling that the parental role is not merely one that unconsciously adopts oneself. It's one that they themselves *want* one to adopt.'

'Strange. I was thinking that myself while I was shaving. No wonder I cut myself!' He put a forefinger to a small plaster on his chin. 'With so many prisoners dependent on me, I've become another old woman who lives in a shoe.'

'Not all that old. And the shoe is a remarkably roomy and beautiful one. They're lucky in that. And so are you.'

The next day Christine had her last tutorial of the term.

Mrs Dunne took a square of chamois leather out of her desk drawer and began to wipe her glasses on it. 'It hasn't been a good term for you, has it?' Without their glasses, the eyes fixed on Christine looked surprisingly small and weak.

She sighed. 'You know, you've been a great disappointment to me, I don't mind telling you.'

'I'm sorry.'

'Clearly other things have been occupying your mind. I'm not going to ask you – or try to guess – what they are. But I sincerely hope that by next term you'll have passed through this – this crisis – or diversion – whatever it is, and be able once again to get back into your stride. It's rather tragic to see potentialities like yours squandered without a thought.'

'That was not what I intended, Mrs Dunne.'

'Well, you're the best judge of that.' The voice was cutting. Mrs Dunne replaced the glasses across the broad, fleshy bridge of her nose. She leaned forward. 'I do wish you weren't so buttoned up.'

'How do you mean?'

'Uncommunicative. So many of you girls seem to be the same these days. Good heavens, it's much better to speak out if something's on your mind. After all, that's one of the things I'm here for.'

Later Christine realised Mrs Dunne had been making a genuine attempt to establish some sort of communication between them. But it had come too late; and the manner of it had been too clumsy.

'Well, I hope you have a good vacation.'

'The same to you, Mrs Dunne.'

That afternoon Margaret and Christine walked back home through an early spring afternoon that had all the evanescent, end-of-chapter radiance of an autumn one. Margaret was in a state of exaltation. She kept running ahead of Christine, eventually to stop, breathless, for her to catch up; her plump cheeks were flushed; her small, hooded eyes shone. 'Oh, I feel quite mad today,' she exclaimed more than once. In her excess of high spirits, she totally failed to notice Christine's depression.

Margaret's mood was so euphoric because she had succeeded in securing a vacation job that would keep her away from the Birmingham chemist's shop owned by her elderly, widower father. She was to look after an epileptic child in a country mansion, owned by a rich industrialist, not far from Leeds. Slipping her arm through Christine's and trying to drag her into a run, she explained: 'I'm to have a bedroom *and* a sitting room – all to myself, just imagine. And all meals with the family.' She gave a brief, whinnying laugh. 'Oh, it's going to be super. And apparently the little girl – Mavis – is perfectly normal but for her health problem. I imagine I'll get used to that after the first two or three attacks. What do you think? I'm not at all squeamish, as you know. Oh, and there's a large, formal garden, a paddock with two horses, and some beehives. I'm actually terrified of bees, but never mind. Oh, Chrissie, don't you think I'm lucky?'

'Yes, that's wonderful.' Although Margaret had never revealed anything about her home life, Christine had long ago decided that it was even more unsatisfactory than her own.

As soon as they had re-entered the house, Margaret cried out: 'Now how about some tea?' and, without waiting for an answer, rushed up the stairs. Christine walked into her sitting room, sat down at her desk, and once again attempted to answer a letter from her father. Even the thought of having to do so made her feel exhausted. He had written, not for the first time, to ask about her plans for the vacation. She crossed to the window with the two stiff, white sheets of paper, each dye-stamped 'United Forces Club', and began once more to read them. Poor Father! Even when he wished to be affectionate, what he finally produced read like a business letter. Nonetheless, under the formal, stereotyped phrases, she detected his chagrin at her pretext that she must spend the vacation in Oxford to work. Through a maze of hints and circumlocutions, at first no less difficult to decipher than his scratchy handwriting, he made it clear that he had not been taken in. After all, he pointed out, library facilities in London were at least as good as those in Oxford.

Christine threw the letter down on to the desk, putting off for another day the decision that she must sooner or later make. She looked out of the window. Below her in the street, two German prisoners – evidently posted sick, since this was a Friday, a workday for them – were wandering round the square at an aimlessly dragging pace. One of them picked up a short stick, which he then rattled against the area railings. On an impulse Christine threw up the window.

'Would you like to come up for some tea?'

They both craned up, startled and uncomprehending.

'Tea! Tea!' She mimed, lifting a cup to her mouth, little finger daintily extended, and then beckoned.

At that they grinned up and nodded. They were men in their mid-forties, with grey, creased faces and the sturdy, squat, slightly bow-legged physique of manual labourers. Neither of them could speak a word of English. Again with signs, Christine indicated that she would come down to open the door. As she was rushing out to do this, she all but bumped into Margaret with the tea tray. 'Oh, Chrissie!' Margaret exclaimed when Christine hurriedly revealed the invitation. 'We don't know a single thing about them. And in any case,' – she indicated the tray with a bob of her head – 'there are only three cakes.'

Not answering, Christine began to hurry down the stairs. Margaret shouted after her: 'I don't mind going without, I'd just as soon have some bread and butter.' Again Christine did not answer.

After tea – at which the two women divided one of the three cakes between them and gave the other two to the men – they all sat down on the floor before the fire and embarked on a jigsaw puzzle, since any sort of conversation was clearly out of the question. Margaret and the Germans giggled incessantly as they attempted to force together pieces that obviously did not fit. Christine grew increasingly bored and restless. At one point the larger and jollier of the men demonstrated a trick. He had a wound, like a deep dent, below his left eye. He pointed to it, grinning, and inhaled vigorously from a cigarette that Christine had just given to him. Two or three seconds later a puff of the smoke wreathed up, alarmingly, out of the hole. This was followed by a tear, which slowly trickled down his cheek until he raised the back of a hand to wipe it away. The whole display struck Christine as being not merely grotesque but repellent; but he was clearly immensely proud of it, repeating it again and then again.

'I think that they enjoyed that, don't you?' Margaret said after their departure. 'It was really rather fun.'

'Yes. Up to a point. But I could have done without the eye trick.' For Christine it had not been fun. A constantly intensifying depression had begun to descend on her. Perhaps its cause was the recent tutorial or the letter from her father; perhaps the autumnal melancholy of the March evening light; perhaps no more than the bizarre recollection of that tear coursing down the German's grinning face.

Margaret having left with the tray, Christine sat down at

her desk and pulled a sheet of paper towards her. She dipped her pen in the inkwell 'My dear Father …' She pushed that sheet aside and began another. 'Thomas, my dearest …' For the first time that day she felt completely happy as her pen hurried on and on.

Christine stayed in Oxford for a further five days. Then, after yet more letters, one even threatening to cut off her allowance, had rained down on her, she decided that, yes, she would have to obey her father and go home for at least a long weekend, leaving both Oxford and Thomas. That night she lay sleepless as she tried to prepare herself for her reluctant return to the melancholy, dilapidated Wimbledon house, hung with frayed rep curtains and massive Victorian and Edwardian pictures in battered gilt frames, and choked with tarnished sporting trophies won by her father in games of squash and rackets. Through this mock-Elizabethan pile, her father and her aunt, both now suffering from the deafness of old age, pursued each other from one cold, cavernous room to another, waging a constant war of mutual recrimination. Only the third floor, now abandoned to a staff of cook and housemaid, and the attic floor were free from their presences. Here neither of them penetrated, unless it were for an ascent to turn out a cabin-trunk, a wicker basket or a wardrobe – expeditions from which they would all too often return breathless and full of indignation against some innocent former servant who, their failing memories had persuaded them, had 'pinched' something in fact long ago mislaid, sold or junked.

'You *will* write every day?'
Christine and Thomas were in Fuller's, having their last

Sunday tea together, away from Margaret. Thomas was wearing some of the clothes that Michael had left behind for any of the prisoners who wished to make use of them.

'If I can. We work very late. I become tired.'

As so often, his melancholy resignation simultaneously touched and exasperated her. 'Yes, I know, I know.' At once she regretted her irritable tone. 'Anyway I'll write to you – every day – even if you're unable to answer.' As a perfunctory act of contrition for speaking as she had, she put out her hand and placed it over his, where it rested on the edge of the table. 'I'll try to get back just as soon as I can. Everything seems to be going wrong at home. Father and Aunt Eva hardly on speaking terms, not enough coke to run the boiler all day, the cook giving notice and then changing her mind. These crises always seem to blow up at the start of a vacation. I think they must plan them in order to force me to come home.' There were shoppers queuing for tables. As a harassed waitress swept past Thomas with a laden tray, she halted to ask: 'Ready for the bill, sir?'

Thomas looked up at her, startled.

'Let me have it,' Christine told the waitress.

Thomas's face was reddening. 'I am a man who cannot pay for his own cake and coffee – never mind his girlfriend's.'

'Oh, don't keep returning to that! I'm happy to pay for you. You know that. Sometimes you drive me crazy.'

After she had paid the waitress, Christine drew out two ten-shilling notes from her bag and pushed them across the table. 'These may come in useful while I'm away. I don't like to think of you short of money.'

'No, no!'

'Please.' Obstinately he shook his head. 'It'll make me happy.'

Again he shook his head, this time leaning back in his narrow gilt chair, as though to distance himself from the two crumpled notes lying between them.

'Come on, Thomas! There may be an emergency.'

Frowning, he sighed. Reluctantly he began to smooth out the two notes. Watched anxiously by her, he took up one, and then the other. After a second or two, he put both into the breast pocket of Michael's Savile Row jacket.

At Balliol, he changed back into his uniform and she then again walked with him up to the camp. Everything had altered. Instead of the former snow or rain, there was now a clear sky, with no more than a hint of frost to suggest that this was still early March. The once desolate strip of wasteland that they had to traverse looked surprisingly green; and the girls, previously so often cowed and morose as an icy wind battered them, now giggled and squawked even more loudly on the arms of their Germans.

Although she would not be seeing Thomas for some time, Christine was happy and even exhilarated until the moment when they turned off the main path and began to mount the steep track that led up to the camp. Then, for some reason that later, brooding alone on it, she was still unable to fathom, an overwhelming panic struck her. She halted, turned to him and threw her arms around him. She closed her eyes. Tighter and tighter she clung to him.

'Christine! What is it? Come on! Tell me!' His astonishment at her behaviour was turning to anger.

'I – I feel so frightened,' she whispered.

'Why? What has frightened you?'

'I don't know. I just don't know. I can't bear to say goodbye.'

'But it's such a short time. Only a few days. In such a time, what can happen?'

By now some of her panic had communicated itself to him. Though still holding her, he was looking about him, distraught. Other prisoners, other girls, paused for a moment as they passed, to stare at a couple so clearly in distress. Christine loosened her grip. She looked up at Thomas and attempted to smile. Then, as suddenly as it had engulfed her, the panic subsided. She felt only shame that she had attracted the attention of those passers-by. Who knew how much mockery he might not now suffer in the camp? And she would be the cause. 'I'm sorry. I'm afraid I've disgraced you.'

'Oh, such people don't matter.' He looked over his shoulder at the couples toiling up the slope. 'But you. I'm worried for you. What is it, Christine? What upset you? So sudden. We were happy, yes?'

'Yes, we were happy. Very happy. And we still are.' That was the truth. 'I was just being hysterical, that's all. I'm not usually like that. Sorry. Please forgive me.'

He remained bewildered and disturbed. 'If there's anything …?'

'No, nothing. Nothing at all.'

She put up a hand to his face. 'Now – now, my dear, I'm afraid we must say *Auf Wiedersehen.*'

XVII

'I can't think where your father's put *The Times*. It's so thoughtless of him. He knows I always like to do the cross-word after breakfast. Hardly a day passes when I don't have this sort of hunt.' Aunt Eva pulled open one desk drawer and then another. Baulked, she tugged at a cumbersome armchair in an attempt to see if the newspaper might not somehow have slipped under it.

Christine looked up from the letter that she was writing to Thomas.

'Oh, do give me a hand, Christine. You can see that this chair is too much for me.'

'It can't be there. How could it be?'

Aunt Eva raised hands to her ears. 'Please, dear, please. *Not so loud*! I'm not as deaf as you're determined to imagine.'

'Oh, sorry, sorry.'

Aunt Eva picked up one of Christine's books from the top of a pile, and then, satisfied that it had not been concealing the paper, replaced it with a sigh.

'Why don't you just ask Father?'

'Oh, don't be silly, dear. You know that for donkey's years your father has insisted that he must not be disturbed when dealing with business.'

'Business? What business?'

'Well, his letters then.'

'If I remember rightly, the only letters he had this morning were two circulars and a reminder that the laundry bill had still not been paid.'

Aunt Eva was now looking behind the sofa, having already thrown its cushions on to the floor.

Christine got to her feet. 'I'll go and ask him.'

'Oh, leave it, please leave it. He'll only go off the deep end. You know what he's like. I sometimes wonder these days if he's really quite all there.'

Having reached the door, Christine returned to retrieve her half-written letter. She knew that her aunt was perfectly capable of reading it. A former Senior Wrangler at Cambridge, a cryptographer during the two wars, and senior maths mistress at a well-known girls public school between them, she had once always struck people as a model of intellectual and moral distinction. Now she had disintegrated into this pitiful, shrunken woman, shuffling around either in agitated search of something wholly trivial or surreptitiously reading communications not meant for her eyes.

Colonel Holliday had been staring out of the window at two Norland nurses who were perched on a bench beside the bus stop, each extending a hand to restrain their huge landaulets from rolling down the hill. They were not an attractive or even youthful couple, but from such a distance his short sight had deluded him into believing that they were both those things. Christine's knock sounded precisely at the moment when he had decided to fetch his binoculars from the cloakroom. Hurriedly he lowered himself into the chair behind his desk and picked up his pen. Then he shouted: 'Yes? What is it? Oh, come in, come in!'

'I'm sorry to disturb you, Father. Aunt Eva wants *The Times*.'

'Well, she can't have it. I haven't finished with it.'

'But you're not even reading it.'

'True. But the rule in this house is that she reads it after

I've done so. I pay the newsagent and so that's my privilege. Like it or not.'

'I do think that's awfully selfish.'

He ignored the comment. 'As soon as she gets her paws on that bloody paper, it's the end for me. Always cutting things out. Always getting the pages crumpled and mixed up. Interested in nothing but the matches, hatches and des-patches – and the adverts, of course. It's a marvel that she managed to survive even a week at Bletchley.'

Christine turned away with a sigh. 'I can see it's no good.'

'You're bloody right.'

Out in the corridor Christine found Aunt Eva waiting for her. 'Well? Did he let you have it?'

'He hasn't finished with it. In fact, he hasn't started on it.'

'What did I tell you? He never really reads it. He just gets pleasure in keeping it from me. Oh, what a mistake I made when I agreed, out of the sheer kindness of my heart, to come and live with him after your mother's death. Didn't someone once say that a good deed never went unpunished? I'd be so much happier on my own in that little Brighton flat – poky though it was.'

Suddenly Christine saw that Aunt Eva was tugging a tiny, lace-fringed handkerchief out of a sleeve. She put it to her nose and sniffed. Then tears began to appear along her lower eyelids. 'Oh, don't cry! Please!' As Christine put an arm around her aunt's bony shoulders, her nostrils filled with the earthy smell that had emanated from her ever since, in the last year of the war, she had had what she would call 'my big op'.

'Forgive me. It's silly of me, I know. But I get so depressed. I feel so lonely so much of the time. So many dear friends gone – or imprisoned in ghastly nursing-homes miles and miles away. And my brain is not what it was – not by a long chalk. I used to finish those *Times* crosswords regularly, day after day. Oh, and of course there's also the constant worry about money – or, rather, the lack of it – largely thanks to your father. I was such an idiot to agree to his offer to handle my investments after brave little Edna died. A right old mess he's made of that!' Edna had been her closest friend both at the school at which the two of them had taught and then during those exhausting yet exhilarating wartime years when they had worked together in willing harness as cryptographers at Bletchley. 'You don't know how lucky you are to be young.'

Christine was filled with pity; and yet at the same time she longed to get away. Oh, the horrible inanity of old age! It was terrible to think that a once brilliant, commanding woman should now be reduced to *this*.

As soon as she had retreated to her bedroom, she told herself: 'I must, must be patient with the poor old dear. And with father – though he deserves patience far less.' But to have that patience was hard, and particularly hard at that moment. For days now she had been in a state of growing tension, her sensibilities so raw that the slightest intrusion on them made her want to scream.

Her period was now more than a month overdue.

XVIII

Her first decision was to go and see Dr Walsh. After all he had attended to her ever since he had decided, merely because she had suffered two severe sore throats in rapid succession at the age of barely five, that she must have her tonsils removed. Within only two or three hours he was performing the operation on the kitchen table, having first ordered one of the two cowering maids to scrub it with Lysol. In his brooding, melancholic way, he exuded sympathy – whether real or fake, she had never been sure. He, a widower, and her mother, the constant victim of a husband of erratic moods and impulses, had been close friends – perhaps even secret lovers, Christine sometimes thought.

Eventually, however, having made an appointment with him, she cancelled it, to go instead to a woman doctor of whom she knew only because Michael, a friend of her husband, had spoken of her. Michael's friend had been an Austrian refugee student at the Slade when Dr O'Neill – as she then was – had met him at one of Michael's parties. He was twelve years younger than she was, and he was already, as she had at once recognised, suffering from multiple sclerosis. He himself was unaware of the nature of his illness, since the specialist who had made the first, tentative diagnosis had decided that for the moment it would be more merciful not to tell him.

At once the couple had fallen in love. Eventually he had proposed to her and, without any hesitation, she had accepted him. For a while he had continued at the Slade.

Then a relapse had obliged him to leave. In the course of a remission he had gone back there and graduated, only once again to become so ill that much of his time was spent in bed. Dr Graff – as she now was – frequently buckled under the stress and herself became exhausted and ill. Her practice was beginning to disintegrate and she had spent most of her savings on 'cures' that she knew, at heart, to be useless. From time to time Michael would help the couple financially – once commenting to Christine, 'I feel that with each cheque she hates me even more.'

One morning, without saying anything to her father or her aunt, Christine set off for the surgery in a cul-de-sac at the Fulham end of the King's Road. A bomb, she decided, must have fallen in the street during the war. It was odd that so little had since been done to repair the damage to the tall, narrow house. A thick dust clogged the corners of the steps, and above the portico a length of tarpaulin, having worked loose, flapped in with a grating sound at each gust of March wind. A postcard was pinned above the bell: 'Out of order, Please knock.' The letters had faded and run.

Eventually, an emaciated, chalk-faced woman in a flowered apron opened the door. She smiled wanly. 'Yes?' Her cheekbones seemed to be pushing through the puckered surface of the skin like fists in a too tight pair of gloves.

Christine assumed her to be a cleaner. Michael had spoken of Dr Graff as a large woman of inexhaustible vitality.

'I have an appointment with the doctor.'

'That's me.' Again she gave the wan smile. 'And you must be Miss Holliday. A patient has cancelled, so I can see you at once.'

Christine followed her down a dark corridor into a waiting room looking out over a narrow tongue of garden furred with long grass and weeds. There were three wicker chairs, a wooden table covered in oilcloth, and another, smaller table on which old copies of *Picture Post* and *Punch* were untidily stacked. Mysteriously, there were no radiants in the gas fire. No wonder the rooms felt so bleak.

'I must take some soup up to my husband. He's not all that well. In fact, he's in bed. I'll be back in a sec.' Dr Graff sniffed. Christine had already become aware of something burning. 'Oh, lordy, lordy! I hope it hasn't boiled over. I must fly!'

Christine turned over the pages of ancient magazine after ancient magazine as the 'sec' extended itself to almost half an hour. At last Dr Graff returned. 'I'm terribly sorry. He wanted one thing, he wanted another thing, he wanted something else. You know what it's like when people are ill. Would you like to come through to my consulting room?'

'Fine.'

'I'm afraid it's an awful mess in here.' Dr Graff went across to the washbasin and began to soap her hands. 'I've no help at present, so what with looking after my husband, my patients and the house …' She cleared a space on her desk, pushing piles of papers now to one side and now to the other. Then she picked a card out of a wooden index box and began to jot down some of Christine's particulars. Her mind clearly occupied with other things, she repeatedly had to go back to alter or erase something already written.

Christine recoiled involuntarily at the touch of her spidery fingers. Dr Walsh first pulled on a pair of pink, rubber gloves before touching her so intimately. 'Sorry. I'm afraid my fingers are cold. Poor circulation.' There was an abstracted look in her eyes, as though her mind was still busy, not with this patient, but with the far more important one upstairs. When she asked Christine an abrupt question, she seemed hardly to be listening to the answer. Eventually, one hand brushing away a wisp of grey hair sticking damply to her forehead, she glanced down at the card on the desk and then, slightly pursing her lips, looked up.

'I suppose you must have guessed what might be the matter with you?'

'Guessed?'

'Hadn't it occurred to you that you might be pregnant? You've told me that, before this episode, you've never once suffered from amenorrhoea. That in itself is indicative.'

For days Christine had been brooding on the possibility. But now it seemed unbelievable. 'But that's out of the question. We always took so much care.'

'Not enough, I'm afraid. All those thousands and thousands of spermatozoa can be amazingly persistent. I take it you're not married?'

'I'm afraid not.' Christine's voice was faint. She turned her head away and leaned her cheek against the back of the cracked leather couch on which she had been lying.

'Won't he marry you?'

Christine shook her head.

'Can't he marry you?'

There was no answer. Christine's eyes were shut. She might have been asleep or even unconscious.

'I see.' Dr Graff gave an impatient sigh.

At that, Christine opened her eyes and jerked up violently. 'You've got to help me. Do something. *Please!*'

'That's what I'm here for. But the question is what?'

'Can't you help me get rid of it? Give me something – or do something? Can't you do that?'

Dr Graff looked down at her hands, which now rested

inert, one on top of the other, in her lap. Then she looked up. She shook her head. 'Sorry, my dear. Anything like that is impossible. Put it right out of your mind. I couldn't do it.'

'But surely – *surely* … Of course I'll pay whatever has to be paid. Don't worry about that. I think you know my cousin – Michael – Michael Spencer. He's a friend of yours, isn't he? He can vouch for me, guarantee me.'

Dr Graff frowned and shifted in her chair. 'I'm not going to pretend I don't need your money. At this moment, when a hefty rent bill has just come in, I badly need money – anyone's money. But …' She shook her head vigorously. 'Out of the question. Sorry.'

Christine considered. Then she ventured: 'Perhaps someone else? Perhaps you could give me – refer me to someone else? How about that?'

'No.' Dr Graff's face and voice had both suddenly hardened. 'I'm afraid I couldn't possibly be party to a criminal act. It would be even worse than stealing money to pay that rent bill. Let's end this conversation. I'm sorry for you, of course I am, as I'd be sorry for any woman in your predicament. But – there it is.' Stiffly she got up from her chair. Then she softened. 'Why not go through with it? I've had a number of patients who've done that. Oh, of course, there can sometimes be a certain amount of gossip and scandal, but usually it doesn't last for long. People can rarely be bothered to be malicious for any length of time. They're lazy and it requires too much effort.' Christine found herself unable to look at her interlocutor. She stared down at the cracked linoleum that covered the floor beneath Dr Graff's feet. 'You could always go away. And then, afterwards, there's always the possibility of adoption.' She leaned forward. 'I could help you over that.' She hesitated. 'You see – two years ago my husband and I adopted a child. But – unfortunately – again our luck was out. We lost it.' She blinked rapidly two or three times. 'Anyway – I'll do anything possible to make the journey easier for you. Except for that one thing ...' She looked with an awkward tenderness into Christine's eyes and then once again shook her head.

'I don't understand. The baby's mine. What does it matter to you if I get rid of it now or later?'

'Well, the difference is between life and death, isn't it? And between what the law forbids and what it allows. Please, let's drop the idea that I might help you in that way. I've told you. It's out of the question. I just can't. Impossible. That's it.'

Somewhere, from an upstairs floor, a hand-bell tinkled and then, more peremptorily, tinkled again.

'Oh, dear! Excuse me for a moment. That's my husband. I'll just see to him.'

But Christine did not wait. She took two five-pound notes from her bag, slipped them into an empty envelope that she saw lying on the desk, and wrote across it in her firm, neat hand: 'I hope this covers things. I am truly sorry to have troubled you.' She was about to add: 'Please don't say anything to Michael.' Then she realised that Dr Graff would never do so.

Out in the street, she was overcome with a shame so acute that for a brief while she was morbidly convinced that every passer-by must be able to see it on her face. Wasn't it Auden who wrote: 'Motives, like stowaways, are found too late'? Too late she had now, this very moment, stumbled on the stowaway motive that had led her to opt for Dr Graff instead of for Dr Marsh. Michael had so often spoke pityingly of the brilliant art historian's degenerative illness, his wife's failing practice, and their constantly increasing rent – often eventually paid by him to save them from eviction. A successful physician like Dr Marsh, with his three junior partners and his rich wife, would be immune to corruption. But desperate, beleaguered Dr Graff ...?

Yes, though hardly conscious of it, she had made that crude, cruel calculation.

XIX

Aunt Eva had just returned from church. Standing before her dressing table, with its clutter of medicine bottles and scent bottles, pin cushions, silver-backed brushes and family photographs, many of them sepia-coloured, in their silver frames, she emitted a tremulous sigh as she carefully peeled off first one and then the other of her black leather gloves. She emitted a similar sigh as she twitched back her veil. The friend beside whom she usually sat in church was gravely ill, perhaps dying, and she still had not been able to summon up enough resolution to go and see her in the cottage hospital at the end of the road. They had known each other for forty-seven years. She shuddered. These days she felt increasingly like some disintegrating vessel beached in total isolation by a rapidly ebbing tide.

From the far end of the garden, gusts of blue smoke rolled towards her window. Someone – Christine or her father – must have made a bonfire. Oh, how inconsiderate it was! Surely they must have realised that the direction of the wind would send all that thick smoke billowing over to the house? The last thing that one wanted was that awful autumn smell to spoil such a beautiful spring day. She straightened, went close to the window and peered out. The skin round her short-sighted, watery eyes gathered into miniscule tucks, she tried to discern something through the swirls. Impossible. But then, suddenly, in the break between one swirl and the next, she saw them. Oh, heavens!

She hurried out on to the landing and approached the

window there; then she was at the window of the next-door guestroom and finally at that of the lavatory, a small room dominated by a mahogany throne with a flush that resembled an old-fashioned bell-pull.

'Henry! Henry! *Henry!*' Now she was calling to her brother, as she searched for him in his bedroom, his study, the dining room, the sitting room and even the drawing room – her preserve, seldom entered by him – where she held her weekly tea parties. From her brother's workshop down in the basement her dulled hearing at long last detected the screech of a saw. She hurried down, all but twisting a narrow ankle on the unlit stairs, fumbled for the switch at the bottom but could not find it, and eventually groped her way to the door and knocked. Henry never liked to be surprised down there. It was his private domain. He did not even like Mary, the maid of all work, to bustle in with her Hoover, scrubbing brush, pail and sour-smelling cloths.

'Yes!' It was the bark of a guard dog warning off any intruder.

'Only me!' She turned the handle of the door and put her head round it.

'Oh, it's you, is it? I've told you umpteen times …' He was in his shirtsleeves, his face even redder than usual because of his exertion. 'Well, what is it this time? Don't complain to me yet again about that ropy switch at the top of the stairs. I haven't forgotten.'

'No, no! This is something far more important.' As she hurried over to him, her nose wrinkled fastidiously at the fish-like stink of boiling glue. 'Christine has some men in the garden. Two of them.'

'Some men?'

'I can't think what they're doing in our garden on a Sunday morning.'

'What *are* you fussing about? I can't see that it's any of your business – or my business, for that matter – if Christine decides to entertain two of her chums, female or male.'

'They're *Germans*! German prisoners of war. I recognised at once those uniforms and those awful caps they all wear.'

'You're imagining things! Why on earth should Christine have some German prisoners with her? Or any Germans. She hates the whole bloody tribe.'

'I'm not yet totally blind – or dotty, for that matter. Well, if you don't mind having German prisoners mucking around in the garden, I suppose that's none of my business, is it? I'm sorry I disturbed you.'

'Hang on, hang on!' He walked round his workbench. 'Wait a mo!' He threw down his fretsaw, wiped his hand on a cloth and slipped on his green Harris tweed jacket with the leather patches at the elbows. Then, mopping at the beads of sweat on his forehead with a handkerchief jerked out of a trouser-pocket, he preceded her out into the hall. In silence the two of them made the slow ascent, he still in the lead. At the top he tried the light switch, a crooked forefinger flicking it back and forth with increasing impatience. 'Yes. The bloody thing's still kaput.'

'Look! From here you can see them. Perfectly.' Aunt Eva pulled back the net curtain over one of the three drawing-room windows.

'My God! You're right!'

'Yes, I *am* sometimes right. But you never believe anything I tell you.'

They stood side by side, peering out through the smoke at the figures of the two men in uniform and the girl in slacks, raking up the brownish-black, impacted leaves once sealed off for weeks by the freeze but now revealed by the sudden thaw, and throwing them on to a bonfire at the far end of the garden.

With a muttered 'Oh, hell!' he strode purposefully to the door.

'Where are you going? What are you going to do?'

He took no notice as, now in the hall, he snatched up first his walking stick and then his tweed cap, which he tugged down low over his forehead.

'Are you going out to them? Do you think that's wise?'

Without answering, he pulled open the front door and walked out.

'Don't do anything rash! Be careful!' One could never, she thought, be certain how creatures like that might react to a challenge. She stood at the open door, half screening herself behind it.

'Christine!'

Christine turned, rake in hand. 'Yes?'

'Just one moment please. Perhaps you could kindly explain to me. Just who the hell *are* these men? Forgive me for asking but their presence here does seem to be just a little odd. And unwelcome,' he added, turning his head to glare at the intruders. Waving his stick, he advanced on them. 'Gentlemen, I want you to go. At once!' They stared at him, one holding a rake and the other a broom. 'Vamoose!' He pointed with the stick at the gate.

The Germans backed away. They gazed at each other, glanced nervously at this irate old man and his beautiful daughter, and once again gazed at each other. In sudden, simultaneous panic they dropped rake and broom and rushed to the gate.

'Don't go!' Christine commanded. Then she repeated, 'Don't go!' as one of them fiddled with the latch with nervously clumsy fingers. The gate at last open, they dashed through it, all but colliding with each other, and then began to run helter-skelter down the narrow, grass-choked lane that would eventually bring them to the thunderous main road.

Christine hurried to the gate. 'Hey!' she shouted. 'Hey! Come back!' Probably they could not hear her. If they did, they paid no attention, still running on and on without a backward glance.

She turned. 'Why did you have to do that? What was it to do with you? I asked them in for a cup of coffee – when I saw them strolling aimlessly in the high street with nothing to do but window-shop. They offered to sweep up the leaves for me. In fact, insisted. They wanted to make a return for the coffee and cake. Why not? What's wrong in that?'

'What's wrong in that? I'll tell you, my dear. I do not – repeat, do *not* – want German prisoners wandering around *my* garden, much less entering *my* house. You didn't even have the courtesy to ask if I minded. That's the least you could have done. Bloody cheek!'

Christine hesitated. Then she began to walk, with slow purposefulness, towards him. In a quiet but implacable voice, she said: 'What an awful man you are! Do you ever realise that? I don't mind that you humiliated me. I'm used to that. But to shout at those men as – as if they were nothing better than straying cattle – that, that was unforgivable. And I'll never forgive it. Never.' Suddenly, to her own amazement as much as to his, she raised her arm and slapped him across the face.

He stared at her, rubbing his cheek with one hand.

Aunt Eva, who had all the time been watching and listening from her redoubt behind the front door, now hurried over. 'Christine dear, what *are* you doing? You should be ashamed. What's come over you? Surely you both can discuss this matter in a civilised way? I must admit that I don't myself feel that having those two men here was, well, quite the right thing but all the same –'

'The right thing! What do you both imagine to be the *right* thing?' Christine felt an explosive rage detonate within her. But her voice remained calm. 'For years – ever since mother died – you two have led your sheltered, useless lives, without one generous impulse, one thought of anyone but yourselves. For years now I've watched you and had to put up with you. It's all hate, hate, hate …'

'Christine – please!' Her father's tone was surprisingly restrained. 'You really mustn't speak to me and your aunt in that wild, insulting fashion. I think I can truthfully say that we've always tried to do our best by you. And by the world at large. Difficult though that sometimes has been. But I must now make something absolutely clear.' His voice hardened into ice. 'I forbid, absolutely forbid, you to invite any more of these prisoners into this house or even the garden. House and garden are both *mine*, let me remind you. Do you understand?'

'While I live here, I'll ask whom I please.'

'You'll do nothing of the sort. The privilege of living here brings with it certain obligations and conditions. Like most privileges.'

'Then I shan't live here any longer. That's simple enough. I'm afraid that, at the age of twenty-five, I must have the freedom to live the life I want.'

'I don't care what age you are. You're behaving like a child.'

'Now just listen to me. Listen! I'm going to tell you something. Once you've heard it, I don't care what you think, I don't care what you say. When you humiliated me in front of those Germans, you didn't realise something. Something important. Now I'm going to tell you.'

'Well, tell me!'

'In six or seven months I'm going to have a child.'

'What?'

She nodded. 'And it's by a German prisoner.'

'Christine!' Aunt Eva hurried forward. 'Stop these silly jokes! That isn't true, is it? You're telling us that just to upset us? Aren't you?'

'I'm afraid not. I had to tell you some time. Now you know.'

'And have you married the creature?'

'No, Father. Not yet. Perhaps never.'

'Are you talking of one of those two wretches?'

'Of course not! I told you – I met that couple for the first time this afternoon in the high street.'

'You're shameless.' There was a quavering note of wonder in his voice. 'I can hardly believe you're the daughter I thought I knew.'

'You never knew me. You never bothered to get to know me.'

He hesitated, staring at her with red-rimmed, prominent eyes. Then he said huskily: 'I think you'd better go. I can't take all this. And your aunt can't take it. Perhaps we're too old. Too set in our ways. But there it is.' He turned away.

'Fine. I'll go just as soon as I can make arrangements for somewhere to go to. Excuse me, please.' She put her hand on his shoulders and pushed him gently but inexorably away from her.

Christine stooped and dragged her suitcase out from under the bed. Having placed it on the bed, she clicked open the hasps and stood motionless, hands resting on their cold metal. She felt exhilarated, she felt ashamed. She had won a victory but she wished that the means of doing so had not been so brutal. Suddenly exhausted, she threw herself on to the bed beside the suitcase and stared up at the ceiling.

When she was a child she would often be woken in the middle of the night by incoherent yelps and screams. In violent gusts, the sounds whirled up from the room in which her mother and father slept below her own. She would try to make out words but rarely could do so. Most often, if she could make out a word, it was 'No!', either screamed by itself or constantly reiterated on a note of rising panic. Later, she had decided that it represented the rejection of some experience too devastating to be relived in sleep, much less in life itself. Repeatedly she had crept out on to the landing and even ventured down to the lower floor, to ask her mother 'What's the matter, Mummy?'

The reply was always along the same lines: Nothing. There was nothing the matter. Her father had just had one of his nightmares.

With her desperate eyes and hollow cheeks, her mother would then order: 'Back to bed. It's nothing important. Go on!'

'I'm frightened.'

'Don't be silly. There's nothing to be frightened about. You heard what I told you – back to bed!'

On these occasions she never saw her father. She would imagine him sprawled or stretched rigid on the canopied double bed that her parents always shared, recovering from whatever it was that had caused that terrible uproar in the middle of the night.

When she was older, she asked her mother, 'What does he dream about?'

'Oh, the war.' The tone was strangely casual, almost bored.

'The war?'

'He went through things – awful things. He can't speak about them. It would be better if he could. But the poor old buffalo can't.'

At the memory of those final words, Christine jumped to her feet. She felt an overwhelming contrition, followed by a no less overwhelming pity. She went to the door, hesitated and then opened it. She hurried, faster and faster, down the stairs.

When she knocked at her father's study, there was no answer. But somehow she knew that he was in there, perhaps silently cursing her, perhaps labouring in his mind to devise some way of reasserting his domination over her. She knocked again. Then she turned the handle of the door and walked in.

He lay on a chaise longue under the window. He had kicked off his shoes, which lay far apart from each other. There was a glass of what she knew must be whisky, his habitual drink, on the floor beside him. He scowled across, saying nothing, almost as though he were trying to remember who she was.

'Father ... I'm sorry about all that.'

He made no reaction, continuing to scowl at her with the same puzzled intensity. Did she imagine it or was his left cheek still red from the slap?

She took a step forward, then another. 'I'm sorry about all that,' she repeated.

At last he spoke: 'Why do you think that's of any interest to me? Please go. Please leave the house as soon as you can. I'll go on paying your allowance but otherwise ... Please go.'

'If that's what you wish.'

'Yes, that's what I wish.' He lowered his hand and picked up the glass of whisky. He put it to his lips and sipped at it, his eyes still fixed contemptuously on her face.

As she was about to leave the room, he called out: 'Oh, by the way, old girl – don't forget to give your keys to your aunt before you go. We don't want to have you smuggling any Tom, Dick or Harry into our old sweet home.'

That was the last time that Christine saw her father.

Five days later this holder of a DSO and an MC with bar had once again been asked to speak at a British Legion dinner. The note that went out with the invitations described the occasion as one in which a hero of World War One would introduce a hero of Word War Two.

A practised and fluent orator, he had just told an ancient but well-received joke about two tommies arguing in the trenches as bombs rained down on them, when he had faltered, with a sudden look of bewilderment. 'Now where was I?' He looked down at his notes and then out over the heads of the audience. 'I'm sorry … Lost my place … My eyes …' With a groan, he tottered and fell forward across the table, knocking over the glass filled with his usual whisky.

A few minutes later, as a retired army doctor was clumsily attempting to loosen his old-fashioned wing-collar, he died.

XX

Mrs Dunne had just returned from Wales the previous afternoon, with regret certainly that her all too brief holiday was over but also with an eagerness to settle once more to her book on Virgil. It was only in strenuous exercise of her body or her mind that she was ever truly happy. She had put off beginning that sixth and most important chapter on the *Georgics* ('Good Husbandry' should be its title, she had all but decided) until the holiday was over, partly because she had been a full-time companion to her husband, as she rarely was, and partly from the perverse desire for self-torment that impels lovers to defer from hour to hour the telephone conversation, letter or visit that will bring them together.

She had woken with exhilaration, her husband still snoring beside her, thinking: 'Today I start.' Already she had shaped the opening sentence, and at intervals, as she had her bath and dressed, she repeated it over and over to herself, testing it out, like a sip of vintage claret on her tongue at one of the Somerville wine tastings. She smoked one of her Gitanes, glanced through the *Manchester Guardian*, and then drew herself up at her desk, touched in turn the pens of various thicknesses, the inkwell, the blotter and the heap of high-quality foolscap, like a general reviewing his forces before a battle, and began to write.

Only a few minutes seemed to have passed – although in fact it was almost an hour – when there was a knock at the door. Oh, lord, she had completely forgotten that Holliday girl's telephone call the previous afternoon, asking for an urgent appointment. One did not expect to be badgered by pupils during the vacation, when one was seldom in College and in any case had better things to get on with.

'I met a boy on the doorstep and he let me in.'

'That must have been my grandson. He's staying with us while his parents are in Cyprus. That's where his mother comes from.' Mrs Dunne was brisk, almost impatient. 'Now what can I do for you?'

On her walk over, Christine had felt calm; but now, with those fierce eyes fixed on her with what seemed to be disdain, she wondered if she would ever be able to come out with what she must say.

'Well?'

Christine blinked and jerked her head sideways, as though to avoid the blow of the monosyllable.

'What is it, Christine?' Mrs Dunne softened. 'Come on!'

'Well, what I wanted to tell you – had to tell you – is that – I don't think I can come back next term. It's impossible. I'll have to leave.'

'What are you saying? Has something happened? I don't get it.'

'It's a question of money.' Christine had already planned her story. 'My father died only a short time ago. Suddenly. It seems that his finances are in a terrible mess. He made all sorts of risky investments. Now my aunt and I – well, we must cut down on all our expenses.'

'Oh, I'm so sorry to hear about your father. Someone once told me that he'd been a hero in World War One. Isn't that right? I must have missed his obit.' The perfunctory tone indicated no real concern. Briskly she went on: 'Anyway, as far as the university is concerned, you've nothing to worry about. There are all sorts of college and university funds for a scholar of your calibre. And with my recommendation … I like to think that after all these years I can exert a certain pull.' She smiled. 'I honestly don't think you need worry. In fact I'm on the committee of the Henschel Trust. You're exactly the sort of person we help.'

'Oh, that's kind of you, I'm grateful. But – well …' Christine's voice trailed away, with none of the relief and gratitude that Mrs Dunne had expected.

'Christine, what *is* all this? Come on! Tell me! Do you still have a problem?' Mrs Dunne was shrewd. There was clearly something amiss other than lack of money. She drew a cigarette out of the packet on her desk, lit it, and then squinted, small eyes narrowed, through the smoke exhaled. 'Buck up! Nothing's ever as bad as it seems. Particularly if one's prepared to face up to things.'

'I'm sorry.'

'There's no need to apologise. Just tell me what's the matter. What's upset you?' Christine did not answer. 'It's not just your father's death and financial problems? Is it?'

Christine shook her head.

'Then?'

To hell with it! Why shouldn't she hear the truth, if she was so eager to ferret it out? 'I'm going to have a baby.'

Mrs Dunne blew out some more smoke. She stared at Christine. 'Married?'

'No.'

'Going to get married?'

'No.'

'I see.' Mrs Dunne lumbered up from her chair, wincing as she did so, and crossed over to fetch an ashtray from the mantelpiece, even though there was already one on her desk.

There was a silence as she stubbed out her half-smoked cigarette. 'What a damned fool thing to allow to happen! Can't you see that your career –?'

'I don't care about my career.'

What an idiot of a girl, for all her intellect! Then she changed her mind. 'Well, perhaps you're right. Who knows?' She slumped back into her chair and looked up at the ceiling. A thought came to her. 'It's not that – that –? Oh, it couldn't be!'

'Couldn't be what?'

'Just for a moment the crazy idea came to me that it might be that German – that prisoner – I saw you with last term.' Christine lowered her head. 'Is it?' When, head still lowered, Christine did not answer, Mrs Dunne knew that she was right. She jumped to her feet. 'Well, at least that shows guts! Real guts! I admire that.' She strode across the room, stooped to a cupboard and extracted a bottle of whisky. 'How about some of this?' She held up the bottle. 'The best malt. My husband would love to get his greedy hands on it.'

'No, thank you, Mrs Dunne.'

'Oh, come on. Do you good. Do both of us good.'

Forlornly, Christine shook her head. 'Thanks.' She had not the heart to tell Mrs Dunne that she had loathed whisky ever since, still a small child, she had struggled to get away from her father as he had tried to enfold her in his whisky-sodden presence.

'Well, perhaps you're right. Too early in the day. My better half would certainly disapprove.' As she poured out a glass of Kia-ora orange squash for Christine and some whisky for herself, she looked up. 'You know, I can't get over this news. I ought to disapprove, of course, but somehow … I always felt that one day you'd do something out of the ordinary.

Well now you have, even if it's not quite the sort of thing I hoped for and expected. You never seemed to be an ordinary sort of girl. Perhaps that's why I took to you from the very beginning – not just because you're so bright, which of course you are. But damn me – I never thought you'd do something like this.' She handed Christine her glass, then raised her own. 'Cheers!'

'Cheers.' Christine mumbled it. She felt far from cheerful.

'So … how long will it be now?'

'Seven months.'

'No good for Schools.'

'But I don't want to take Schools.'

'If it can be arranged, why on earth not? Look, I'm going to be frank with you.' She drew up a chair to face Christine's; their knees almost touched. 'It's years and years – twelve to be precise – since I last had a pupil as good as you. I mean that. Of course these past few months you rather went to pieces – and now I understand why – but your work before that was outstanding – what every don hopes for and all too rarely gets. Yes, really, it was a joy. I'm not one to dish out undeserved – or only half deserved – praise, and I'd never have told you all this but for this bombshell of yours. Whatever else happens, you must keep up your Classics. You must!'

Christine shook her head.

'With a little thought and trouble, the whole thing can be arranged.' She got up and began to pace the room as she talked. 'Obviously you'll have to leave College until you've pupped. No one must even guess what's going on,' – she smiled – 'as much for my good name as for yours. You'll have to go away and have the baby quietly. I've got it!' She clicked her fingers. 'You can go and live in my Welsh cottage. Most of the time my husband and I are here in Oxford. Your aunt could go with you, couldn't she? No one down there need know you're not respectably married. We can think of some story to explain the missing husband. As for Oxford – we can tell people you've had a nervous breakdown.' She smiled again. 'Nowadays students are constantly having nervous breakdowns – as frequently as they once used to have boils.' She was becoming increasingly excited as she elaborated a plot that struck Christine as more and more unsustainable. 'Then, when the baby has arrived, we can find someone to take it over – adopting or fostering – and you can come back here as if nothing had happened.' She slumped back in the chair opposite to Christine's and, knees wide apart, leaned forward triumphantly. 'So?'

'Well, you see …'

'Well, what? What's the matter?'

'In the first place I want to keep my baby. No fostering. Certainly no adoption. I want to look after it – bring it up – by myself.'

'But how can you? How can you possibly do that? You couldn't come back to College with a *baby*!'

'That's what I mean.'

'Are you telling me that you're prepared to throw away your career just so that you can – ?'

'Yes. I'm afraid so.'

'But that's crazy! That would be the most ghastly mistake of your life! Personally the moral side of it doesn't worry me a bit. But there's still so much prejudice around – even among the most liberal of people. You must have realised that. Is it fair to expose the poor little creature to all that?' She saw the look of anguish on Christine's face and broke off. 'I'm sorry. I'm not saying all this to upset you.'

The two gazed at each other. Then, briskly, Mrs Dunne

slapped her knees and jumped up. 'Think about it anyway. There's no need to make up your mind until the term starts. As I said, you can always have the cottage. Any time, rent-free. And if there's anything else I can do, don't hesitate to ask. I hope that you'll think of me as more than just your tutor.'

'You're very kind.'

Christine put out her hand and Mrs Dunne took it in both of hers, an intimacy rarely offered to a pupil.

As Christine was still fumbling with the door handle, Mrs Dunne sat down with a sigh of relief at the desk spread out with notes and texts.

Should she opt for 'Good Husbandry?' A terrific title for a novel but for a chapter in a work of serious scholarship? She stared out of the window and pondered.

She hoped that there would be no more interruptions.

XXI

Michael's first reaction to Christine's news was one of irritation. She had made a mess of things and, as he often would say, he hated messes. With care and forethought this particular mess could have been avoided. He decided that she had only herself to blame.

'Good God! Oh, really, Christine, what a thing to let happen! Sometimes, dear girl, I just despair of you.'

'You talk as if I'd deliberately decided to get myself pregnant.'

'Well, not *deliberately* … But has Marie Stopes really lived in vain? Not very bright of you, if I may so.'

'I didn't come here to have you tell me that.'

He laughed. 'Don't be so touchy. After all, you can hardly pretend that you haven't got a potential disaster on your hands – or, more accurately, down *there*.' He pointed. 'And it's even more of a potential disaster for poor Thomas than for you. There are pretty severe penalties for German prisoners who get English girls into what is popularly – or unpopularly – known as trouble. You realise that, don't you?'

'Of course I realise! Is it likely I'd shop him?'

'No, but someone else might. These things have a way of getting out – particularly in this busy little beehive. Poor Thomas! Have you told him yet?'

'I'm seeing him tomorrow afternoon. Somehow I'll have to break it to him. Not easy.'

'Why break it to him at all? You'll only worry the poor sod to distraction. And he has enough to worry him already.' She was about to say something but he over-rode her: 'After all, what can he do about it? He's married already. And German prisoners can't marry English girls in any case.'

'He's got to know sooner or later.'

'*Got* to know? Why? You're going to take *steps* – oh, I love that genteel euphemism – aren't you? Yes, I know, I know, an abortion sounds so horrid – and it *is* horrid when performed by some evil old Mrs Gamp in a dirty back bedroom in a slum and later reported in the *News of the Underworld*. But after all – let's face it – in our neck of the woods it can usually be done in safety and comfort. June can let you have the name of a Harley Street quack – a well-known consultant in gynaecology, no less – who has his own nursing home in, I think, salubrious and highly respectable Harrow. He *did* her – financially, I fear, as well as medically – two or three years ago, when she had briefly taken up with an American colonel from Arkansas, who subsequently disappeared to a posting at the other end of the world. Poor dear, she's such a worrier, though you wouldn't think it. She was sure that she was going to die of a haemorrhage or septicaemia. But it was really no worse than having a wisdom tooth out, she told me after it was over.'

Suddenly he noticed the look, part disgust and part horror, on Christine's face. He leaped to his feet, knelt beside her chair, and put an arm around her. 'Oh, my dear, I'm sorry, terribly sorry. I suffer from flippancy as other people suffer from halitosis. I wish I could just gargle it away. I shouldn't have talked like that. Please forgive me.'

'Oh, it's all right. By now I'm used to you. Your heart may be hard but it's in the right place. I decided that ages ago.' She sighed. 'Oh, if only I could make a decision! I haven't slept properly for nights now. And I can't face those meals that poor Margaret cooks for me and then gobbles up herself to avoid any waste.'

'Poor Christine! Don't you realise that you're supposed to be eating for *two*? Oh, I do so wish I could help you. At all events, I want you to know that if you need any money I have my chequebook at the ready. As much as you want. If you opt for that Harley Street man, then I'll settle his bill – in guineas, no doubt. In any case,' – the thought came to him only at that moment – 'why don't I settle something regular on you both? As a wedding present.'

'A *wedding* present!' She laughed.

'One of those weddings made in heaven. And not, I'm sure, one of those weddings that are made in heaven but then soon turn into absolute hell.'

'Oh, Michael, you're such a dear! But I couldn't possibly …'

'Of course, you could. For the moment I'm rolling in it – thanks to that old Armenian art-dealer friend of mine, who recently went to his maker. It's so embarrassing. Because he left me so much money, nasty people keep concluding that he and I were lovers. The mere thought of it! The poor dear suffered from psoriasis quite dreadfully.'

'And Klaus? What about Klaus?' she eventually asked. 'That's enough about myself.'

'Oh, Klaus.' He sighed. 'Poor Klaus. I went to see him yesterday. What a trek! I got back only this morning, having had to sit up all night.'

'Is he very ill?'

'Both lungs.' He sighed. 'Will he recover? Who knows? One can never tell with the white plague.'

'I'm sorry.' She put her hand over his. 'It's wretched for you. You're tired, I can see. I must be on my way, so that you can get some sleep.'

'I wish I could sleep. I'm so worried about him.'

'Oh, dear! As always, you've been such a help, and I just don't know how to reciprocate. I'll ring you tomorrow, not too early. Thank you so much.'

He had moved to his desk and pulled out a drawer, as though to take something out of it, and had then pushed it back. His chequebook? No doubt he had decided that it would be more discreet to post a cheque later. 'I've done nothing. I so much wish I could do more. But I'm a great believer in people making up their own minds. If things go wrong, then they can't blame others. Anyway, I won't forget about that cheque to tide you over for the moment – and, of course, that allowance. There at least I may be of some help.'

Since, like most people, she hated to be a recipient of charity, she almost blurted out: 'You think that every problem can be solved by throwing money at it.' But, ashamed that her immediate response to his kindness should be so ungracious, she merely walked over to him and kissed him on both cheeks.

He watched her begin to hurry down the spiral stairs until, never once looking back, she had all too soon vanished from sight. Then, with a sigh, he closed the door and wandered about the room. He envied her, how much he envied her! She was reckless, as he could never be. She grabbed what she wanted and to hell with the consequences, for her or for others. Yes, she was one of those people not afraid of getting themselves into messes – or pushing others into them. While he, with his dread of being conspicuous, talked about, ostracised ... At such moments, of introspection, he despised and hated himself.

He walked over to the sofa and sank down into its deep upholstery. He began, at first reluctantly and then with an aching longing, to think back to his visit to the bleak, bare sanatorium, perched high on a hill overlooking a small Scottish market town. Klaus's bed had been wheeled out, with a number of others, on to a terrace that faced the parsimonious sunshine of the spring afternoon. Klaus was in a woolly, grey dressing gown under a heavy tartan blanket. In contrast, Michael could feel the icy wind claw at him through his cashmere overcoat.

Except for a yellowish-brown encrustation at each side of his mouth, Klaus looked surprisingly well, his face tanned and his teeth flashing their usual smile of joyful welcome. Michael's spirits had risen; he had not yet spoken to the doctor.

'Better?' he asked in German, when Klaus had released his hand from his crushing grasp.

'Oh, yes!' He beamed back. 'Now they've operated, I'll soon be well.' Proudly he opened his pyjama jacket to display his rib resection. It was hard to believe that under that otherwise smooth skin furrowed by a long, purple scar, there lurked pain, rot, fever, and perhaps even death. Klaus smiled again. 'It's comfortable here. The grub's very good. And yet,' – he laughed – 'I often wish I was back with the lads in the camp. What do you think of that?'

'It's better to be bored than to have to work in your state of health.' Suddenly Michael noticed that Klaus's fingernails, once so short that he used to wonder if he bit them, had now become talons badly in need of cutting.

'Yesterday I had a letter from Thomas. The team has done very well. Did you know that? Perhaps he told you? I'm sorry to have missed the match against Cowley Barracks. They beat us last year but this year we beat them.'

They went on talking for the two hours that were all they would have together. Michael gave Klaus the food that he had brought and Klaus made a show of refusing to accept it. He was now sitting up in bed, cross-legged, although this was forbidden. The tartan blanket had slipped off it to the floor. He undid each package with the excited gasps and exclamations of a child unpacking a Christmas stocking. Among the gifts was a large box of chocolates brought back from the Swedish tour. Klaus held the box out to the grey-haired, grey-lipped man in the bed beside him. 'Please, please!' he urged in English. The man shook his head vigorously and then rolled away from them on to his other side, as though he could not bear having to continue to listen to their incomprehensible German or even to look at them.

'Oh, Michael, you are so good to me!' Klaus suddenly cried out. 'My best friend. And for you there's nothing, nothing I can do in return.'

Michael wanted to say, 'To sit here with you is ample return.' But he shrank from coming out with something that, if said to himself, would make him inwardly squirm at its sentimentality.

Soon, too soon, the time came for leaving. As Michael got up at the ringing of the bell, Klaus said: 'I forgot to ask you. How is your lady?'

Your lady? Oh, he must mean Christine. It was too complicated and too late, when all the visitors were saying their goodbyes, to give him the latest news about Christine and Thomas. 'Oh, she's fine. She sent her love.'

Klaus fumbled in a pocket of his dressing gown and produced a little package. 'In our workroom I made this for her. Please give it to her.' He held it out and Michael took it.

'What is it?'

'Look, please. Look.' Klaus was smiling in anticipation of Michael's reaction.

Curiously the object was wrapped in a sheet of newspaper that, because of its yellow colour, could have come only from the *Financial Times.* Michael stared down at a little wooden model of a London bobby.

'Do you think she'll like it? You remember, she liked the London bus I made for you.'

'I'm sure she'll treasure it.' Michael began to rewrap the carving.

This was what he had gone over to remove from his desk and give to Christine and had then, on an impulse, pushed back into the drawer. He now once again went over to the desk, took out the package and peeled away the friable, yellow sheet of newsprint. He turned the wooden bobby over in his hands, staring down at it. The manikin, with his shiny black hair and boots and his shiny red cheeks, seemed to grin up at him with an idiot's bonhomie. He felt an ache in his throat and a pricking of tears.

No, he would not pass it on to her. The present would mean so little to her. She would hoard it away somewhere in a cupboard or trunk. She might even throw it away when making a move from Oxford. It was highly unlikely that she and Klaus would ever meet again. He would thank Klaus from her and tell him how delighted she had been with the gift. He would keep it for himself.

He walked over to the desk and slipped it back into the drawer, with a feeling both of guilt and of joy.

XXII

Christine saw Thomas long before he saw her. He was with two other prisoners, not known to her, and they were all laughing as they passed under the railway bridge. Then one of them punched Thomas on the shoulder in play and they laughed even more uproariously. She felt a fleeting resentment that they should be so light-hearted when for the past few days she had been so anxious and depressed.

When at last he noticed her, he waved, grinned and began to race down the hill, his boots scattering gravel. Unashamedly they embraced at the corner where the main road curved up to the station, disregarding the stares, inquisitive, disapproving or amused, of the people hurrying, often laden with suitcases or bags, past them. For the first time since she had heard the news that she was pregnant, Christine felt happy.

'Oh, darling Thomas, Thomas, Thomas!' As she held him, there was an approaching rattle and then a long, melancholy whistle from an express plunging into the station overheard. Steam billowed downwards. She fancied that she could not merely taste its sulphur but also feel its heat. 'It seems such an age.'

'Years and years.'

Hands clasped, they began to walk towards the centre.

He turned his head and stared at her. He shook his head. 'Christine – you still look beautiful. But – not well.'

'Don't I? That's because I've been away from you. I feel

better already.' Her eyes shone; she put her cheek again his sleeve and hugged him closer. 'What's your news?'

'You know my news. All those long, long letters written in bad English. Or perhaps you don't read them?'

'Of course I read them. Over and over again. I think I must know them by heart.'

'And yet your letters become shorter and shorter.'

'That was because nothing ever happened. Home was worse, far worse than I'd ever expected. My father so difficult, everything so *boring*. I don't think I'll ever live there again.'

'What are you saying? I'm sure your father needs you.'

Hurriedly she changed the subject. Later she would tell him about her father's death – and everything else. 'Everything else' was chiefly her shameful absence from the funeral.

Aunt Eva had been clearly disbelieving when Christine had produced her excuse of a bout of flu. 'If you're seedy, perhaps Michael might drive you over? After all, he's a cousin by marriage of your father – even if they never got on.'

'But I've told you – I've got flu. I have a temperature. Well over a hundred. In a draughty church and at a graveside in this weather, I might easily get pneumonia.'

'I do think that you should forget all about that little showdown. Unkind and silly things were said. But now is not the time to – '

'The "little showdown", as you call it, has absolutely nothing to do with my not being able to come. Can't you get it? I've got flu. I'm ill. *Ill!*' It was with the desperation of someone whose lie has failed to be convincing that she shouted the last word.

'What an odd girl you are! Well, if that's the case – we'll just have to manage without you, I suppose. Though how I'll explain to everyone … Fortunately all his British Legion friends have been quite marvellous in rallying round. And so has everyone at the church.'

Yes, she would confess her mean-spirited behaviour to Thomas in due course – but not now, when she and he were both so overjoyed at being re-united. 'Oh, Thomas, you haven't shaved properly. Look!' She ran the back of her hand under his chin and over a cheek. 'It's dreadful.'

He laughed. 'I can't help it. For five, six days now I've had to use the same blade.'

'And I promised to send you some! I'm sorry, I'm so sorry.'

When they arrived at Michael's room, it was to find a note, large Italian italic letters in red ink, on the hall table: 'Sorry. Last minute change of plan. Have had to go to London to see June's dress rehearsal. Clothes in bedroom. Love and kisses, M.'

Christine looked up from it, smiling. 'I don't know if I'll shed many tears over that.' She handed the note to Thomas. 'I'm glad we're going to be alone. Aren't you?' At once she felt a twinge of guilt for her disloyalty.

Thomas frowned down at the note as he read it. Then, as if shrugging off some disagreeable reminder, he screwed it into a ball and neatly lobbed it into the wastepaper basket. He smiled at her. 'Yes, that's good news.'

She followed him into the bedroom and watched him as he changed. She had always found both a pathos and an attraction in the rough khaki vests and pants issued to him and she did so now. She crossed over and put her arms around his neck. But on this occasion, mysteriously, the touch of his flesh and her pressure against his body filled her with nothing but desolation.

'Christine.' He ran a hand down her neck and repeated: 'Christine.'

'Yes.'

'There's something I must tell you. Bad news.'

'Bad news?'

'I didn't wish to write and tell you. I don't wish to tell you now because I'm so happy to see you again.'

'What is it?'

'I've been posted.'

'Posted?'

He nodded, 'To Norfolk.' He pronounced the last syllable as in 'folk'. 'I must leave next week.'

'Oh, Christ!' She put her hands to her cheeks. Then she sank on to the bed.

Puzzled he sat down beside her, the shirt that he had just put on unbuttoned and his feet in only the borrowed socks. 'What is it? Don't be so upset. Come on.' He pulled her towards him but she jerked away. 'We knew such a thing can happen. We can write. You can come to visit. Christine!' Suddenly there was a scolding note in this voice. 'What's the matter with you?'

She sat up. 'Well, I'm afraid I've also got some bad news. Even worse news than yours.' She stared fixedly at him. He stared back, waiting for what she might reveal. 'I'm going to have a baby.'

'Oh, Christine!' She did not know whether it was with horror or joy that he grasped both her hands in his. 'Is this true? Are you sure?'

She nodded.

'No mistake?'

'Not unless the doctor has made a mistake.'

There was a silence. Then he said: 'What do we do?'

'Well, that's what we have to decide. Now, if possible – this evening. Oh, I've been so worried.'

Listlessly he began to button up Michael's monogrammed shirt. Then with a sigh, he got to his feet, to look for the shoes that Michael had put out for him. 'It is you. We must think of you, Christine, you only, what's best for *you*.' He reached for the tie, crossed to the glass and, peering into it, fastened the knot and then tugged it tight.

'Oh, your tie! Can't you ever get it straight?' She went over and pulled the knot leftwards. As she did so, he slid an arm round her waist. She looked up and saw only despair.

Together they once more sank on to the bed. A hand on his knee, she began to explain to him the possible alternatives that they must face. But he seemed barely to listen. From time to time he would nod, shake his head or ask some question in a flat, almost peevish voice. It was only when she spoke of the possibility of brazening the whole thing out that she aroused him.

'No, no. Impossible. We can't do that.'

'Why not?'

'It'll be terrible for you. We can't do that. I forbid you to do it. Forbid you, you understand?' He got up off the bed and stared down at her. 'It's a mad idea.'

'Mad? What's mad about it? For me that's the best – the only – solution.'

'Yes, yes, now. Now it's easy to say – this is the solution. Such solutions seem very brave, very romantic. But later …' He bent over and grabbed her hands. 'You can't do it. You must have adoption. Or someone to look after baby. Anything. You cannot keep baby. Anything better than disgrace for you.' His English was becoming increasingly incoherent, as always under the pressure of some uncontrollable emotion. 'Yes, you're a strong, a brave woman. But that's not enough, not enough. Everything is against us. Everything, everyone. We're alone. Understand? *Alone.*'

'Oh, all that doesn't frighten me.' But already his fatalistic acceptance of defeat had unnerved her. She had looked to him for support, believing that with it she was capable of anything. But without it her determination drifted and blurred, even as she argued with him.

'Always what we were trying to do was impossible. Why didn't we understand that before? We were fools. I was a fool. Now see what I've done to you. I'm terribly to blame. I've spoiled your life.'

'Of course you're not to blame. You're no more to blame than I am. I went into this with eyes wide open – and arms outstretched.'

So they continued to argue, he confusedly stumbling over words and snatching at phrases, she urgent and precise. In all that he said there was reason, logic, commonsense; while her own arguments – yes, he was right – betrayed her feeble, self-deluding romanticism. Now it seemed a heroic thing to defy the world; but next year, and the year after that, and in all the years to come …? She rested her head against the bedpost, overcome by a shattering weariness. Never before had she felt so destitute of hope, self-confidence, even the desire to go on living. Meanwhile Thomas's unhappy voice went on and on, on and on, eager to persuade her of all the things that, in her heart, she knew to be true.

Finally she said: 'Yes, you're right. You're quite right.'

'What will you do then?'

She wished that he had said: 'What will *we* do then?' As it was, he seemed to be making the decision solely hers. She shrugged. 'Oh, I could go and stay in the Dunnes' cottage. Or I might even go to June's doctor.'

He gripped her arm. 'No. No doctor! Never! Promise me. Promise me!'

'You're hurting me. Let me go!' She shook herself free. At that moment she hated him.

They went out and had a morose tea at Fuller's. As they both fell silent, the thought came to her: she had still said not a word to Thomas of her father's death. She had thought nothing about her father since his funeral less than a week before. She had not even telephoned Aunt Eva to ask how it had gone off and if all was well with her. She was now horrified that she had been so self-centred.

As though by mutual consent, they went back to Balliol as soon as their tea was over. Thomas changed back into his uniform in silence while she leafed through a copy of *The New Statesman*. Not a word flickered between them. Then, still in silence, they began to walk slowly back to the camp. Thomas whistled under his breath the first notes of his setting of the psalm 137, over and over again, until it so much got on her nerves that eventually she burst out: 'Oh, can't you either whistle the whole thing or drop it altogether?' He looked at her in hurt astonishment and fell silent.

From the strip of waste ground just before the intersection where the slushy path veered first right and then upwards towards the camp, the blare of over-amplified music assaulted them. Through the barely fledged trees, they could see the caravans, tents and booths of a fair. People began to pass them, coming and going. Nearer the entrance some prisoners, clearly without any money, slouched, hands deep in pockets, before a coconut shy. A girl of ten or eleven in a pink rayon dress and black patent-leather shoes, a pink ribbon in her hair, raised a hooter to her lips and, as she ran behind these prisoners, blew it repeatedly into the backs of their necks. She skipped on, giggling wildly, while her victims slowly turned, scowled after her, and then resumed their apathetic stance.

'We're very early. Shall we go in?'

'Go in?'

'Why not?'

A pause, a shrug. 'If you wish.'

They pushed their way through a mass of laughing, sweating people in their best weekend clothes, and emerged on to an open space surrounded by sideshows. While a small boy was noisily vomiting into the grass, his mother stood unconcerned beside him, his half-finished ice-cream cone held in her hand. From the nearby swings there came the piercing screams of girls clutching at their billowing skirts. An old drunk in a cloth cap, with an almost bridgeless nose, lurched against Thomas and then demanded: 'Who d'you think you're shoving? Fucking Kraut,' he muttered as he staggered off. A few drops of rain fell out of the clear sky. It was unusually hot and humid for March.

Christine found herself taking a perverse, self-taunting pleasure in the ugliness of the scene. She had always loved fairs, with their din, their milling crowds, and their smells of cheap scent, sweat and frying foods. But now the garishness and crudity filled her with arrogant distaste. Perched on some railings, a boy with an acne-scarred face let out a piercing whistle as she passed him, hands pulling at the corners of his mouth, so that he looked like a malevolent gargoyle. Her contempt and loathing intensified.

'Mind out, Fritz!' Two workmen in overalls thrust their way past, hefting a roundabout horse between them. One of them looked down at Christine's legs and shouted at Thomas: 'You're in luck today, aren't you?'

A few more drops of rain spattered down out of the clear sky. The amplifier of the giant Ferris wheel at the centre of the fair was blaring out 'I want to be happy'. A baby in an apparently unattended pram began to wail. No one paid any attention to it.

'Let's go,' Thomas said in a low, miserable voice. 'Why do we stay here?'

At that moment a group of youths overtook them. One of them elbowed Thomas and another put a hand on his shoulders and pushed him aside. Then another turned and, with an attempt at playfulness, flipped off his cap. Wearily, lips compressed, Thomas picked up the cap and dusted it off on his sleeve. His mouth sagged like a child's on the verge of tears. 'Fuck you!' he muttered. He clutched Christine's arm, 'Why do we not leave?'

'No, it's all rather fun. Enjoy yourself, let yourself go.' She was now hating the whole scene even more than ever. But she felt the desire not merely to hurt and humiliate him but, by descending deeper and deeper into the revulsion and horror with which the crowds now filled her, to batter her sensibilities until she lost all feeling. She found herself obsessively searching out more and more sordid details of the scene. Even the condoms abandoned by couples, many of them no doubt prisoners and their girlfriends, who had used the area as their place of assignation before the arrival of the fair, compelled her fastidious, fascinated gaze.

'Let's go on the wheel.'

He stared at her, bewildered and stricken. 'But it's so noisy. And maybe dangerous.'

'*Dangerous*! Don't be silly. They have all sorts of safety regulations. Come on!'

Reluctantly he trailed after her, to wait in a jostling crowd for the wheel to descend and halt for its next load. Not far ahead of them a large woman in a man's black overcoat turned to survey the queue and then began to cackle with laughter, her mouth so wide open that Christine could see her uvula wriggling up and down like a baby's finger. Thomas turned away, imagining that her boisterous mirth was directed at him and Christine, rather than at some of her friends immediately behind them.

At last their turn came, and they squeezed themselves into a tiny, swaying gondola. They were so tightly packed that Thomas had to slip an arm round Christine's waist. The two youths in the gondola ahead were attempting to spit down on to the ancient, elongated greyhound asleep below the wheel on a bed of straw. From time to time the dog grunted, looked up at the ascending wheel and scratched an ear.

Yet again the amplifier began to blare out 'I want to be happy.' The gondola creaked, jerked forward, jerked backwards and then juddered off. A strand of Christine's hair blew across Thomas's mouth. Impatiently he brushed it away, even though in the past he had always taken so much pleasure in stroking it or kissing it. As they rose higher, his arm tightened round her waist. Far away, they could now glimpse the winding river, the squat station, the soaring towers of Christ Church and All Souls, and the entrance to the camp. Immediately below, the crowds milled, shouted, laughed, sweated, embraced, won and lost money, sucked their ice creams, smoked their cigarettes. But she would not look below. However briefly, they had escaped from all that, as on to a mountain peak. *Oh, Thomas, I love you, how much I love you!* She had forgotten that during their argument earlier she had called him 'Doubting Thomas'. She felt towards him none of the previous exasperation and despair, only tenderness. She rested her head on his chest, feeling the pressure of his collarbone through his rough battledress tunic.

Suddenly the gondola jolted and tipped first forward and then, more violently, back, while the music briefly became a discordantly amplified screech before grating into silence. Almost at the summit of their ascent, they were now motionless, dangling over a void. One of the two boys ahead let out an anguished wail. The amplifier began to crackle. Then over the crackling a North County voice boomed: 'Nothing to worry about, ladies and gents. We'll have this fixed in a moment now. Just keep calm, ladies and gents, and enjoy the view. That's the way, just keep calm.'

All the couples in their gondolas remained eerily still and silent. Slumped, many of them with their arms round each other, they might have been dummies. Christine stared down at the moon faces staring up. Strangely she felt no fear. Then she looked at Thomas. Their gazes interlocked for a second, until he turned his head aside and downwards. His eyes were now fixed on the faces below. His own face, clammy and white, lips drawn back in an extraordinary rictus, expressed only terror. She grasped his hand and squeezed it tighter and tighter. 'It's all right. Perfectly all right. They'll have it mended any moment now. Don't worry.'

Again the North Country voice reverberated over the crackling static. 'Be patient, ladies and gents. No problem. No problem at all. You'll soon be travelling down.'

'Look at Tom Tower!' Christine pointed. 'Doesn't it look wonderful in the setting sun? What a view!' She was not merely trying to distract him from his panic; the beauty of it all genuinely overwhelmed her. She wriggled in the narrow seat in an attempt to look behind her. As the gondola shuddered at her sudden movement, his hand shot out to clutch the strut beside him. 'And one can see all the camp. I'd never realised how huge it is. Look!' But he did not look. His eyes were squeezed shut.

When he opened his eyes, he asked in the voice of a fretful, frightened child: 'Why are we not moving?'

'We will. Soon.'

Minutes passed and gradually she sensed the panic ebbing from him. His body, previously so taut against hers, began to relax. His face was no longer ashen and glistening.

'Okay, ladies and gents! That seems to be fixed. Hold on tight!'

Thomas let out a small groan as the gondola shuddered, swayed from side to side, and began to jerk upwards, as though with tremendous effort. He again gripped Christine's hand. At last it reached the summit and then, slowly and smoothly, began its descent. He gave a delighted laugh. 'Everything is all right.'

'It always was. Silly!'

Arm in arm, they trudged in silence up Harcourt Hill. Then suddenly he said: 'Like swimming.'

'What do you mean?'

'We're like two swimmers – one strong, one weak. The sea is dangerous. The weak swimmer will drown. But the strong swimmer is always there to rescue him and bring him back to shore. You're the strong swimmer. I am the weak one.'

'Anyone can have a bad head for heights.'

'Those boys ahead of us – after the first shock they were calm.'

'So what? Perhaps heights don't bother them.'

He pulled her closer to him. 'You're a strong swimmer, very strong. You will never drown.'

'And neither will you.'

'Only if you are with me.'

Without their realising it, they had reached a decision.

1950

XXIII

As Michael rapped on the door of the cottage, a fine shower
of snow, detaching itself from the overhanging thatch, stung
his face. Had another winter similar to that ghastly one of
three years back gripped this remote area, while in Oxford
there was sunshine? All at once, having so much looked
forward to the visit, he now felt tired and dispirited. From
inside he could hear the baby beginning to cry. That only
intensified his gloom.

'Michael! Come in!' Her joy at seeing him was clearly
genuine. 'That walk across the fields is hell in this weather.
You must have got soaked.'

'Do you remember how during that last winter of yours
at Oxford everyone was constantly asking everyone else "Is
this winter never going to end?" It certainly looks as if it still
hasn't done so here.'

'It's awful for poor Thomas, working outdoors. As it was
awful for him then.'

'Well, at least you now have a warm house – and are living
with each other.'

The door opened into what once had been the con-
stricted, overcrowded parlour, rarely used except for chris-
tenings, birthdays, marriages and funerals; but now, with
its honey-coloured utility furniture, its two Dürer prints
in passepartout frames and the plain beige carpet that he
himself had bought them, it seemed unfamiliar and bare.
A cot stood in one corner, from which the baby bawled in
furious desolation. Christine hurried across to it.

'Do sit down. Oh, throw your things anywhere for the moment. The important thing is that you should get dry.'

But Michael knew that at that moment the only really important thing for her was the child. In that realisation he experienced what he acknowledged to be a ludicrous sense of exclusion.

'Thomas says that I oughtn't to pick the poor darling up when he cries. But I can't bear listening to him … Oh, he's wet himself again. Did mother's little darling wet himself then? Did he? Did he?' She went off into baby talk of a kind that usually filled him with exasperation and embarrassment; but on this occasion, the pang of jealousy having turned out to be no more than a momentary acid reflux, he only thought how loveable she looked, as she gazed down at the baby. Fuller, plainer, its skin shiny for lack of make-up, her face expressed a tenderness that in the past he had rarely seen there. As she rolled up her sleeves, he noticed how robust her once delicate arms had become.

'I see you've settled in very comfortably.'

'Thanks to you. I don't have to say how grateful we are. You know that already.'

'If you're so grateful, why didn't you cash my last cheque?'

'It was sweet of you to send it. But really – we can't accept so much. The allowance is all we need. Honestly.'

'Oh, I think that sort of pride so silly. I hoped you both would have more sense.'

'I was afraid you would be cross.'

'Yes, I am cross. I can so easily spare the money. I don't know what to do with all that I have. It seems wrong – when I did nothing to earn it. And if it helps you to have a few things that otherwise you couldn't afford, well, what's wrong in that? In any case,' – he smiled – 'you forget that I have a special interest in that little blighter. After all, he is my godson.'

'You can hold him for a moment.'

Gingerly, Michael took the baby and, frowning with concentration, rocked him in his arms. Christine burst into laughter.

'What's the matter?'

'You look so funny.'

'Thank you.'

'Nervous. Somehow embarrassed.'

'Do you think I've never held a baby before?'

'Here – give him back to me.'

'Oh, very well. You mothers are always so possessive. If I can handle a valuable Meissen vase – as I was doing in the Ashmolean this morning – then I can certainly handle a baby.' He placed the burden in Christine's arms, with a sigh. 'How's Thomas?'

'Working awfully hard. He still feels whacked at the end of the day.'

'But he likes it here?'

'Oh, of course. Better than the camp, far better. It was sweet of you to fix it up. I hope – I hope we shan't let you down.'

'Why should you?'

'Oh, I don't know.' As she bent over the baby, a safety pin in one corner of her mouth, she all at once look harassed and sad; but Michael, who had suddenly thought of Klaus, as he so often did at totally unexpected moments, did not notice the change. 'Thomas doesn't get in till after five. We have a high tea then. Do you mind that?'

'What? A high tea?' He turned an abstracted gaze on her, then once more peered into the heart of the bright, sizzling logs.

'Do you mind?' she repeated.

'No. No, of course not. One must always obey the customs of the country – and of one's host and hostess.'

Perversely, she continued to needle him. 'I don't imagine that you often find yourself eating high tea.'

'Oh, during the war I ate far worse things than that.'

'There!' She put the baby back in his cot. 'I suppose I'd better see about it. Thomas hates to wait.'

'Can I lend a hand?'

She laughed. 'Oh, no! Really. Thank you.' She was thinking: potatoes to be peeled, carrots to be sliced, meat to be minced, biscuits to be mixed, bottle to be scalded. Worse, she was once again in pain. Ever since the birth of the baby, she had had an intermittent backache, for which the doctor had prescribed one course of pills and then another, and rest, rest, rest, She could swallow the pills but how could she rest? She tapped Michael on the shoulder. 'Can you look after yourself?' He merely nodded. Then he crossed to the upright piano and raised its lid.

'Out of tune, I'm, afraid. This cottage is so damp.'

'Has Thomas written anything since you got here?'

'Only settings of two poems by Stefan George, when he had some sick leave. He has so little time. He gets so tired by the end of the day.'

Michael had now seated himself at the piano. He hasn't listened to a word, she thought. The most generous people were often the most self-centred. She went across to him and leant over, a hand on his shoulder. He played a fumbled arpeggio, then another, firmer one.

'Can you keep an eye on the fire? That wood burns quickly. Which explains why we have to spend so much time sawing it. Can you do that? Can I trust you?'

Having now embarked on 'Onward Christian Soldiers', from a copy of *Hymns Ancient and Modern* left by the previous tenants, Michael merely nodded vigorously.

'And see that Tim doesn't get up to any mischief.'

'Yes, madam. Certainly, madam.'

Some forty minutes later, long since bored with his playing of once familiar hymns, he ambled into the kitchen to find her at the shallow, long stone sink, washing up some plates.

'Can't I help you with that?'

She shook her head. 'I wish you hadn't found me washing up the breakfast things. I'm an awful slut, I'm afraid. No method, no efficiency.' She sighed. 'No energy. Oxford taught me how to make only one thing. Coffee. And not all that well, at that. Thomas is always patient with me. But I think the poor dear must often wonder what sort of wife he has married. Or not married – if we must be truthful.'

'Nonsense. Any man would be proud of you.'

'You don't mean that.'

'Certainly I mean it. Here, let me dry.' He pulled a cloth off a chair in front of the Essen.

'Not that! That's one of Tim's nappies.'

'Is it? Oh, lord!'

They both laughed.

When Christine had finished the washing, there was still a large pile of crockery and cutlery that, finicky and clumsy from lack of practice, he had not yet dried. She began to scrub the sink. 'This soda makes my hands sting. It gets into all the cracks.' She held out a hand.

For the first time he noticed the red, roughened skin. 'Poor Christine!'

'Oh, please don't keep calling me *poor*! It makes me feel myself to be an object of pity.' She sighed. 'I'm afraid I'm totally incompetent as a housewife. I've no natural gift for servitude, that's the problem.'

A door slammed and Thomas came in, cap and the shoulders of his greatcoat white with snow. He had grown a beard, black prematurely threaded with grey, on which the flakes soon began to melt in the warmth of the kitchen. 'Hello, Michael!' He pulled off a khaki mitten to shake hands and then walked across to Christine and kissed her on the lips with a fervour that made Michael jerk his head away in embarrassment.

'Sorry I'm so late. More of this bloody snow. And that cow is still on her side. I'll have to go out again.'

'Thomas! Your English is now almost the real thing.'

'Do you really think so? Well, I never talk German here. And I've promised Christine I'm not going to talk German to you now. Some people even tell me that I've acquired a Shropshire accent.'

'I haven't noticed that. But if you have, you must get rid of it.'

'Yes, I'm now almost an Englishman. Soon I hope to be Thomas Holliday, if I can cut through all the red tape. Deed poll. That way no one will guess our dreadful secret. Christine doesn't care. But I want to be respectable.' He laughed. 'What do you think of Tim?'

'I can only say what I always say on these occasions when that sort of question is put to me – "Now that's what I *really* call a baby!" By the way, I've brought him a delayed Christmas present.'

'We have far too many presents from you.' Thomas laid an affectionate hand on Michael's shoulder; then he looked down and exclaimed: 'Look what you've done. You have splashed water on to your beautiful forty-guinea suit.'

'Fifty guineas. Prices have gone up.'

'Christine should have given you an apron – or you should have asked for one.' He reached for a cloth and began to wipe down the suit. As he knelt at the task, Michael realised that he, no less than Christine, had undergone a physical transformation. His fingers had become wider, blunter, almost coarse. Under the constriction of his check shirt the muscles of his now broad back shifted visibly at each move. For the first time Michael found him sexually attractive. 'There you are! Now I'll just take a glance at our little Tim.' Yes, Michael thought ruefully, there was certainly the trace of a Shropshire accent.

Almost at once Thomas returned, angrily kicking the door open. 'Really, Christine! You've let that fire go out. How many times have I told you that wood burns quickly? Any kindling?' He peered into a basket in a corner. 'No, there wouldn't be. Now I'll have to go out to the shed. Bloody hell!' He began to pull on his boots.

'I'm sorry, darling. I was thinking of other things.' Loyalty prevented Christine from putting the blame on to Michael; but she was indignant that he did not himself own up to his neglect. 'I'll go. You've had a busy day. Let me go. You sit down.'

'No. You get on with the tea.' He wrenched the door open and slammed it behind him as he disappeared into the dark and falling snow.

'That was your fault,' Christine could not restrain herself from saying.

'My fault? How my fault?'

His surprised protest of innocence intensified her annoyance. But she merely said: 'Oh, it doesn't matter.'

Tea over, it was still snowing, large flakes drifting past the window from which Michael had raised the old blackout blind in order to peer out. 'I'll have to leave soon.' Michael was staying with friends up at the big house.

'I'd better take you on the back of my motorbike,' Thomas volunteered.

'No, no! Certainly not! It's no distance across the fields.'

'Why don't you stay?' Christine suggested.

'Stay?'

'The night. Here. Why not? Thomas can walk up to the farmhouse and phone from there to tell them. Stay in comfort and you can walk back to the manor in the morning. Much better.'

'Oh, it'll be far too much bother for you.' Michael was thinking of his guestroom at the manor, with its four-poster bed, central heating and large bathroom.

'Bother? What bother? No bother at all. Is it, Thomas?'

'No, of course not.'

'Very well then,' he agreed, trying not to betray his reluctance. 'That's very kind of you.'

Thomas followed Christine out into the kitchen, when she went there to fetch a glass of water for which Michael, thirsty from her over-salted shepherd's pie, had asked. 'What did you want to do that for?'

'We couldn't let him walk across the fields in this weather. Haven't you noticed his shoes?'

'Now you'll have all the trouble of airing sheets and making up the bed. You've got enough to do without all that sort of thing.'

'Sh! He'll hear you.'

'Well, let him hear me. It's so inconsiderate. Can't he see you're worked to the bone, as it is? I must say I liked the calm way he accepted –'

'That's not fair. At first he made a protest. Anyway he'd have done the same for us in the same circumstances. You know that.'

'Yes, but he would have been able to ask a college servant to make up a bed and put out some towels.'

'Oh, do leave it! I don't mind. He's helped us so much. It's the least we can do.'

'I hate all his help! I'm sorry, it's wrong of me, but I have to say it.' He was now tipping coal from the hod into the Essen. In his vehemence he sent a surplus cascading to the floor. 'Damn, damn, damn!' He picked up the loose pieces in his fingers and flung them into the stove.

'I'd better get back to him. He'll be wondering what we're up to.'

As Christine returned, the glass of water in her hand, Michael held out an envelope to her. 'Tim's belated Christmas present. I keep forgetting about it.'

'Oh, thank you so much. But really …'

Even before she had torn open the envelope and found the three newly minted ten-pound notes, her expression was one of dismay, however hard she tried to control it.

XXIV

They had gone to bed but still Michael could not sleep. Turning from side to side in sheets that were still damp despite a hanging above the Essen, he felt an area of cold extending slowly, tremor by tremor, from the pit of his stomach to his chest, from his chest to his jaws, and then, in remorseless sequence, downwards and outwards to each of his limbs. He got up, pulled on his vest and shirt over the flannel pyjamas lent to him by Thomas, and laid his overcoat across the bed. But it was useless. His teeth continued to chatter; he was shaking in every joint. How extraordinary that the room should have no means of heating at all. Perhaps they never used it except as a repository for the junk now scattered about it.

Hours later, as it seemed, he looked at the illuminated hands of his watch. Only 12.45. Oh, he must sleep, he must sleep! His craving for sleep now resembled the thirst that he had quenched only by the drinking of three glasses of water. By a conscious effort of will he tried to master the tremors. But they were like some external force, no more to be controlled than an earthquake or a rough sea. Eventually he made a decision. He would go and sit by the fire in the living room and try somehow to warm himself. Pulling the blanket off the bed and draping it over his shoulders, he tiptoed down. But, once there, he found that the grate now contained only ashes and a few embers smouldering to extinction. In dejected incredulity he stared downwards, until a sound made him swing round to face the other door, at the far end of the room. Two voices came from it, attenuated yet clear to his overwrought hearing. He tiptoed to it, soundless footstep by footstep, and stood beside it. Then he bent forward, and pressed an ear against it. For a long time he stayed there, an unseen, unsuspected partner in all that was happening. Strangely, he felt none of the shame that he knew he ought to be feeling.

The sounds became less frequent and less easy to distinguish; then they ceased altogether. He straightened, aware all at once of the ache in his back, the scraping tick of the clock on the mantelpiece, the sudden revolver-shot of a last fragment of green laurel at the edge of the grate, and the incessant shudder of the loose window against the wind and snow. He went back to his room and stood looking out of its single window, one hand raising the tattered, dusty blind, while with the friction of the other against the diamond panes he slowly thawed out the frost-flowers on them. He could make out little. Square and dense, a holly bush gleamed; the wire netting that shut in the small, extinguished garden sagged as if beneath the weight of some vast, grey blanket; and always out of the stiflingly close sky the snow fluttered down and down.

Suddenly, in this desolation, he felt wholly at peace. *I could be happy here, at least here I could be happy*, he thought in self-deluding amazement. At that, he returned to the hard, icy bed, drew the covers up to this chin, and fell into a dreamless sleep from which not even the screaming of the baby an hour later could jerk him back to consciousness.

XXV

'I can find my own way. Please don't bother.'

'No, I'd like the walk. Mrs Avon can keep an eye on Tim. Fortunately they get on well together. He always enjoys her weekly visit. I've a bit of a headache and the fresh air will do me good. Since I came to live in the country I've had not one of those awful migraines.' Christine yawned with no attempt at concealment, as she pulled on a rubber boot. 'Oh, by the way, Thomas asked me to say goodbye to you from him. He forgot that he wouldn't be seeing you before he left for work.'

Michael was frowning down at a crack in her boot. 'Won't the water get into that boot?'

'Yes, it will.' She straightened up, brushing the loose strands of hair away from her flushed, shiny face. 'I keep meaning to have it mended. I've put in a permit to the Min of Ag for a new pair. Being on a farm, I'm apparently entitled.'

'Ludicrous,' Michael muttered. 'So much red tape.'

'Oh, the fire!' Kneeling now to make it up, she revealed a ladder that stretched up the back of her woollen stocking. Unlike many beautiful women, she had never worried about her appearance, Michael thought. If she were not careful, she would soon be a slut.

He went across to the ancient piano and touched the warped keys, running up the pentatonic scale again and yet again. Those five notes always induced in him a mood of sadness. 'I *have* enjoyed being here.'

She staggered to her feet. 'Have you? I'm glad. I wasn't sure.' She had begun to prowl the room, as though looking for something. 'It's been lovely having you. But too short.'

'I love this little cottage. You know, when I was a boy and we used to come to stay at the manor – '

'Damn!' She had come to an abrupt halt in the middle of the room. 'I know what I've forgotten. What an idiot I am! I meant to ask Thomas to pick up a loaf from the store. Oh, well, I suppose I can make a detour on my way back … What were you saying?'

'Oh, nothing important. I've forgotten.'

Emerging from the cottage, they both momentarily screwed up their eyes against the glare that bounced up to greet them. They felt breathless, as at a sudden change of altitude; the blood thumped in their ears. Slowly they began to trudge up the slope until, after several long, silent minutes, Michael stopped and Christine stopped beside him. They both gazed back. One of the windows of the cottage flashed a semaphore at them as Mrs Avon opened it. Michael clutched his umbrella horizontally in both gloved hands, as though he were about to attempt to snap it in two. 'Yes, I feel sad at going. Tomorrow I'll be back at Oxford. I've come to hate the place.'

'Yes, I'm glad to have got away. And, as I've so often said before, I'm awfully grateful to you for having arranged things for us. It's marvellous that Thomas is allowed to work like this – away from a camp.'

'He looks so different, healthier and happier. And I'm so pleased that his English has improved so much. Thanks to you, I should guess. Oh, but do try to rid him of that Shropshire accent.'

She laughed. 'I like it.'

He turned to her. 'I do envy you both. I feel so strongly, it's *the* life, isn't it?'

'*The* life? What do you mean?'

'Well, the sort of life that everyone should be living.'

She stared at him for a moment, eyes narrowed. Then she laughed derisively. 'Don't be so silly. You know you'd loathe it.'

'Would I?'

'Of course you would. I can't imagine you stoking up the boiler – or doing the sort of jobs that Thomas has to do in this freezing weather. No, it's not "*the* life"' – she put the two words into mocking inverted commas – 'as you so romantically call it. It's far, far from being that. It's the sort of life we have to lead for want of a better one.'

'Then – then aren't you happy here?'

'Oh, I don't know.' She got out the words between breathless gasps from the effort of their ascent. 'I suppose I am in a way. But, frankly, it's so silly for people like you to romanticise country life. Margaret's the same. She was here the weekend before last and she went on saying how much she envied me. *Envied* me – I ask you! What on earth for? It's all right living in the country if you're up at the manor. There, if you want anything done, someone does it for you. Whereas all that we can afford is three hours each week of Mrs Avon's time for the rough. You just try running an isolated cottage with a baby – and no main drainage, only a cesspit – and wiring so antiquated that the power keeps fusing if one uses the Hoover or the iron. And of course that long trudge to the village and a boiler that … Oh, you've no idea, Michael. Being a visitor for a night or a weekend is hardly the same thing.'

Michael stopped to stare at her in astonishment. Her

cheeks were flushed and there were tears – whether of cold or anger, he could not be sure – in her eyes. 'I'm sorry. It's not that I … Oh, I merely meant …' He swung his umbrella, handle downwards, like a golf club, so that it scattered snow in the wind. 'Well, all I thought was that surely all those material inconveniences don't really matter all that much. Do they? You both seem to be wonderfully – enviably – happy together, still so much in love.' Again he scattered snow with the inverted umbrella, but this time the veering wind blew it back, in minute, stinging granules, into his face. 'Damn!'

'You're talking as I talked after we first came here for the interview. Thomas knew better. It's not as easy as all that, you know.' She began to walk on, without looking back at him. Slowly, effortfully he trudged after her. She swung round. 'Sometimes I wonder if I'd have gone through with it if I'd realised all that it would mean.'

Panting, he hastened his pace to catch up with her. 'Then – you're not happy?' His voice was forlorn.

'Oh, I don't know.'

'Have you stopped loving him?'

The question seemed to amuse her. She gave a small laugh, her eyes always on him. 'No – no, I don't think I've done that. But this idea that you've only got to be with someone you love in order to be happy – it's rubbish, absolute rubbish.'

'I'd have thought that to love and be loved is the most important thing of all in life. I've never had that myself. I've longed for it. Are your outside circumstances really so awful? Isn't there anything I could do? We could start with the cottage …'

'Oh, you're very kind, dear Michael – as I'm constantly telling you.' Then she softened, slipping an arm through his and linking their gloved fingers. 'When Thomas is allowed to do something other than farm work, I think life should be easier. You see, he has to work such long hours up at the farm, and then there are all the jobs at the cottage when he gets back. And Tim disturbs him, so that he's more or less given up on the music. And of course that makes him feel frustrated and irritable – one can't blame him.' A few seconds later she went on: 'There's another problem. The head cowman. If it weren't for him, the work might not be so bad. The man's a bastard. He and Thomas are constantly at loggerheads. Thomas wants to introduce more modern methods, milking machines, that sort of thing. But the man wants things to go on just as they've always gone on, for generations and generations. And since Thomas is a Jerry that makes things only worse.'

'Perhaps if I spoke to Jack or Lucy … I know they have little interest in the farm and leave it all to that lazy slug of a bailiff. But I could put in a word. Who knows, they might even have Thomas moved to a different job.'

'No, no, please don't do that!' She laughed. 'We'd become even less popular than we are now. As it is, the other labourers grumble about our having been given the cottage. They seem to regard it as a prize. And though – thanks to you – Jack and Lucy go out of their way to be kind to us, I think that for them we're really little more than a nuisance.'

'Oh, I don't honestly believe that.'

'Yes, Michael. They've given Thomas the job and us the cottage for only one reason. Jack was once your student and they're fond of you. But socially we're an embarrassment to them. They know that I'm your cousin and that our family is – let's not be modest about it – quite as distinguished as theirs. But Thomas is one of their labourers and he and I are not even married. In a country village these things take on an exaggerated importance.'

'I thought you were not going to say anything about not being married.'

'That was the plan. But like so many plans … Secrets have a disconcerting way of getting out.'

'How did this particular secret –?'

'How?' She laughed. 'Oh, Jack and Lucy told that silly old vicar – and the vicar told his wife – and his wife told old Miss Pendlebury, who runs that tea room – The Muffin Man – with her simple-minded brother. Something like that. We'd always planned that Jack and Lucy should never learn the dreadful truth …'

Michael halted, hand to mouth as though he were about to chew on its glove. 'Oh, lord! That was my fault. I told them – and you'd asked me not to. I told them, didn't I? Oh, I *am* sorry. Will you ever forgive me?'

'Oh, forget it! It doesn't really matter. Someone would have found out anyway. You're not to blame.'

'I am, I am!'

A silence followed, as they trudged on.

'Any news of Klaus?'

'Nothing for months and months. After they sent him back, we wrote to each other for a while. But his letters were barely literate. An effort for him to write, I'm certain. I sent him parcels of food and clothes. Sometimes I also sent him money. Then silence. I went on sending things. Still silence. So – eventually – I gave up. I've thought of somehow getting to Germany on a lecture tour or something like that. But then I decided – what was the point? Perhaps he no longer wants the contact. Perhaps – one has to face it – he has died. When I last spoke to that fierce woman doctor at the sanatorium, she told me that it was likely that – as she put it – he was "on the way out". He grimaced, his eyes staring fixedly ahead of him.

They were nearing the top of the hill, where the path joined the drive to the manor. 'We're all but there,' Christine said.

'Yes, all but there. Would you like to come in for a moment to say hello?'

She shook her head. 'I must get back to Tim. And in any case I don't imagine they …' She broke off.

'Before we say goodbye – I want to get this straight. Has it – has it all really been a mistake? Is that what you feel – what you've been trying to tell me?'

She pondered for a moment. 'Oh, I don't know, I just don't know. I suppose I'd do it all again, in spite of everything. I just don't know.'

The words were not reassuring. He stared into her face. Then he turned his head and looked back down the hill to the far-off cottage.

'Goodbye, Michael.' His head remained averted, so that she had to stand on tiptoe to kiss his cold cheek. 'Don't take what I've said too seriously. It's been a bad day. I'm really very happy.'

'I'd like to think you were. Well … That's it then. That's it. Thank you again.'

'Give Jack and Lucy my greetings. I'm so sorry about Klaus. I hope that some day you'll get some good news of him.'

He shrugged, pulling the collar of his raincoat up over his chin. He said nothing more.

She watched him as he set off down the drive at first slowly and then at a brisker and brisker pace. Eventually she turned and began to retrace her steps.

At the bottom of the first field, suddenly overcome by an unaccountable weariness, she halted and leaned against the stile. The ice-coated bar froze her through her woollen jacket and frayed woollen gloves. In the late sunlight the snow was pink as flesh, bruised here and there by the long, purple shadows of the trees. Globes of melted water slipped from time to time from the hedge by which the stile stood and, in doing so, bored holes into the otherwise smooth surface of the snow. She wanted to cry but could not, as if the ice had frozen the tears at their source. Far away, above her, she could see the manor house, three of its chimneys wreathed in smoke. There was always malicious gossip in the village about the amount of fuel used there. Eventually she clambered over the stile and walked on, her shadow, as rigid as the shadows of the trees, stalking across the snow ahead of her.

When she neared the cottage, she could hear the sound of sawing from their small shed. Thomas must be back early. She hesitated whether to go to him or to Tim and Mrs Avon indoors. In the end she walked across to the open door of the shed and stood there, watching him in silence, as he severed one aromatic and mildewed branch after another, to be thrown on to a heap. His greatcoat and sweater festooned a vast limb of oak on which the dead leaves still rustled with each gust of wind. There was sawdust in his hair, and drops of sweat glistened along his eyebrows and among the hairs at the opening of his khaki shirt. For a long time he remained unaware of her scrutiny. Then at last he glanced up.

'How long have you been there?'

She shrugged,

'Michael gone?'

'Yes.'

'Good.' He grinned at her.

'You don't like him anymore, do you?'

He threw another log on to the heap. 'You know how I hate being so much in his debt. It's unreasonable of me, I suppose.'

'Why aren't you working?'

'The old man said I could go when I'd finished with the cowsheds.'

'Why bother with this? Why not get on with your music?'

'We have to have wood.'

'I'll help you.' Now, for the first time during this conversation, she entered the shed. Pulling off her gloves and jacket, she reached for the double saw.

'You're tired. I can manage alone.'

'No. I'll help you.'

'But it's not –'

'I'll help you.'

At each stroke she dragged the saw towards her with a ferocious, yet always precise, movement. Log after log she threw on the heap; nothing could tire her. When she glanced up, she saw that Thomas's face, bare arms and throat were all shiny with sweat and that his breath came in rapid gulps. She herself showed no such signs of fatigue; nor did she feel any.

'You're sawing as if for your life.' In the brief interval between one log and another, he took out his handkerchief and began to mop his forehead. He was staring at her. Then he asked: 'What's the matter? What's happened?'

'Oh, Thomas!' As she went to him, she attempted to balance the saw across the block; but she performed this action so clumsily that it at once slid to the floor with a clatter, followed by a high, metallic ping. 'I feel so ashamed. I've been so mean and disloyal.'

'What on earth about?'

'Michael – he was asking about our life here … And I said things – oh, horrible things – that were not really true.'

'If Michael's been upsetting you – '

'Oh, don't be silly! It wasn't Michael.'

He came over to her and put an arm round her waist. 'Well, tell me about it.'

'There's really nothing to tell. It's just that I – I made him think that our life here together had been some kind of failure. As if we were making the best of a bad job, because that was all that we could do … But it's not really like that? It isn't, is it?'

'Of course not.' He put his lips to her temple. 'I've never had regrets. None. None at all.'

'It's just that things are difficult. And sometimes I think it might be better if you were free, without having to think of Tim and me. We're such a burden and a tie.'

'You mustn't say such things.'

'But aren't they true?'

'No.' His voice was emphatic. He released her. 'We must get a move on if we're to finish this before the light fails.'

In silence they pulled the saw back and forth between them for several minutes on end. Then, as though by mutual consent, they both stopped, released the saw, still embedded in a branch, and looked across at each other at first with a surprised satisfaction and then with a no less surprised joy.

1983

XXVI

Michael's hands are gripping the lectern for support. He has spread his address out on it, but he never looks at its pages. Before they set off, he told Christine: 'I always used to be able to talk impromptu about almost anything – as you may remember. But now I so often find that I have absolutely no idea what's to come next. So as a precautionary measure …'

Age and illness have made his voice hoarse. It would be inaudible except to the people in the front three or four rows were it not for the microphone ('How I loathe these gadgets!' he muttered earlier to the chaplain) that relays it, exaggerating its sibilance and its breathiness, to the farthest corners of what is generally regarded as one of the finest of Gilbert Scott's smaller churches.

He begins by speaking of the suitability of holding this memorial concert not in the assembly hall but in this chapel, since for so many years Thomas played its organ and trained its choir. Thomas and Christine, he says, found happiness at the school, he as music master and she as head of the classical side, after some difficult years. Their son, Tim, is now himself music master, he adds. He peers down at Tim over the tops of his reading glasses and gives him a gentle, loving smile. Tim, always ill at ease with Michael's devotion, nods and smiles back uncertainly.

Soon after that, Michael has lost his way. In panic, he looks first down at Christine and Tim, and then up at the rose window at the far end of the nave, while the frail twigs of his hands, twisted from rheumatoid arthritis, shuffle the papers. Everyone in the audience experiences an identical embarrassment and dread. But eventually, after many seconds, his voice becomes stronger and clearer, and he resumes.

'Sadly, he never had enough time for his own composition. When he was a young man – a prisoner of war in Oxford, where I, like his future wife Christine, first met him – I felt sure that he would eventually become as famous as, well, Hans Werner Henze and, oh dear, yes,' – he gives a wintry smile – 'Karlheinz Stockhausen. But sadly – such were the circumstances – that was not to be. *Dis aliter visum.*' He again grips the lectern, leaning across it, so that the thick lenses of his glasses momentarily flash. 'However ... however ... It would be wrong to conclude that his life was a disappointment, much less a failure. As I have said, he and Christine found happiness, great happiness, here. And they brought happiness, great happiness, to the pupils not merely of their own house but of the whole school. Isn't that the most important thing in life – to be happy, to make others happy?' He looks round at the mostly young faces of the audience, as though expecting an answer.

Christine feels Tim's hand closing over hers. She turns her head to give him a questioning glance. He pats her hand twice, then pulls a small face, more to himself than to her.

'... To begin this concert, the choir is going to sing one of the first pieces of music that he wrote. I well remember a wintry afternoon in Oxford, so many years ago now, when he played it over to Christine – then a brilliant student at Oxford – and myself on her piano. I knew then that he had a gift wholly out of the ordinary – one to be cherished and encouraged. What you're going to hear is a setting of the 137th psalm. You will all know the one, I'm sure. The one,'

– he clears his throat – 'the one that begins "By the rivers of Babylon, there we sat down, yes, we wept, when we remembered Sion." A beautiful psalm. And a beautiful setting – made at the time for four singers but later rescored for full choir.' He pauses. 'What more is there to say? Nothing.' He smiles. 'The music says it all – far better than I could or anyone could. That is the way of good music. And this *is* good music, I can promise you that. So … here endeth the first – and from me, perhaps fortunately, last – lesson. I hope it has not been too long. Or too boring. The young have a better capacity for getting bored than ancients such as myself have.' At that last remark, one or two students titter. He gives a little bow and begins unsteadily to edge round the lectern, preparatory to descending to his seat in the front row, next to Christine. He totters, all but falls. Tim leaps up and grips his arm, frowning with concentration, and then supports him down the three steps.

The chapel is overheated because of the installation of a new system over the Christmas vacation. But nonetheless Christine shivers as the vinegary, ethereal voices of the boys' choir flutter around her.

How shall we sing the Lord's song in a strange land?

The voices grow louder and more and more insistent. They seem to beat at her with invisible wings. She turns, in incipient terror, to Michael, who sits slouched forward, head bowed and eyes closed, as though, his address over, he had at once fallen asleep.

How shall we sing the Lord's song in a strange land?

The wings crowd around her, their beating deafening her.

She wants to ask Michael: 'How, how, how?' She wills him to open his eyes, to look at her, and to tell her.

At last he does so, turning his head and gazing into her

face with a rapturous vagueness. Soundlessly he mouths a single word: 'Beautiful.'

Then he shuts his eyes again, totally absorbed in the clamorous, yearning, inconsolable sound of the youthful voices echoing down to them both not merely from the high, Victorian Gothic ceiling, but from a time that they had thought to be lost forever.